continued . . .

HOW TO CATCH A CAT

REBECCA M. HALE

BERKLEY PRIME CRIME, NEW YORK

THE BERKLEY PUBLISHING GROUP
Published by the Penguin Group
Penguin Group (USA) LLC
375 Hudson Street, New York, New York 10014

USA • Canada • UK • Ireland • Australia • New Zealand • India • South Africa • China

penguin.com

A Penguin Random House Company

HOW TO CATCH A CAT

A Berkley Prime Crime Book / published by arrangement with the author

Berkley Prime Crime Books are published by The Berkley Publishing Group.
BERKLEY® PRIME CRIME and the PRIME CRIME logo are trademarks of
Penguin Group (USA) LLC.

For information, address: The Berkley Publishing Group,
a division of Penguin Group (USA) LLC,
375 Hudson Street, New York, New York 10014.

ISBN: 978-0-425-25888-0

PUBLISHING HISTORY
Berkley Prime Crime mass-market edition / March 2015

PRINTED IN THE UNITED STATES OF AMERICA

10 9 8 7 6 5 4 3 2 1

Cover illustration by Mary Ann Lasher.
Cover design by Diana Kolsky.
Interior text design by Kristin del Rosario.

This book is dedicated to our readers:
It's been a pleasure to share our adventures with you.
—Rupert, Isabella, and Rebecca

On Board the *San Carlos*

Off the California Coast

August 1775

Introduction

A SPANISH SUPPLY ship bobbed in the Pacific swells off the California coast. Dual masts of square-shaped sails billowed in the wind, powering the ship forward as its rigging creaked and groaned under the strain.

The *San Carlos* had recently departed the Mexican port of San Blas on a mission to find the ocean entrance to a protected bay that a Spanish land exploration had stumbled upon a few years earlier.

The reported dimensions of the enormous cove didn't match any of the geographic formations depicted on available maps. The *San Carlos* was searching for an opening that had been missed by several experienced explorers—a passage to a fabled bay many still doubted existed.

It was a journey into uncharted and frequently mischarted territory, undertaken at a time when the full breadth of the Pacific had yet to be appreciated. Most navigators thought East Asia lay almost adjacent to the North American continent and that only a narrow straight separated the two landmasses.

The path ahead lay fraught with danger and uncertainty—
for both the boat's human and feline passengers—but the
San Carlos was destined to change the course of history.

The discovery of the Golden Gate entrance to the San
Francisco Bay would forever alter the settlement and colo-
nization of America's West Coast.

FAR BELOW THE ship's whipping sails, a pudgy white
cat with orange-tipped ears and tail skidded across the
wooden deck. Claws scrambling on the wet floorboards,
Rupert chased after his prey, a green parrot with a bright
red head and a yellow beak.

The boat dipped behind a swell, causing it to rock into a
steep tilt, but Rupert continued his pursuit, smashing into
buckets and crates as he barreled down the length of the deck.

He reached the bow and spun around, his fluffy tail swishing through the air. The bird pulled up into a holding pattern,
and Rupert sensed he was about to be mocked with a flyby.

Not this time, Rupert thought with determination. Tens-
ing his muscles, he crouched for an epic leap.

Sure enough, the bird dipped his wings and feinted
toward the deck. Rupert launched into the air, his front feet
wildly swatting, to no avail.

The parrot swooped upward, easily evading the cat's
swiping paws.

Rupert landed with a wheezing *thump* on the deck.

Cackling with delight, the parrot soared into the sky, his
red head bobbing in and out of the sails. He landed on the
rim of the crow's nest and looked down toward the deck,
smirking in triumph at another successful ruse.

Rupert regrouped for a second attempt. He hoisted himself onto the rigging of the ship's forward sail and quickly
climbed twenty feet up the main mast.

Intrigued, the bird fluttered off his perch. He flew a tight
circle around the pole, taunting his adversary.

Wretched creature, Rupert thought as he wrapped one paw around the mast and clawed the air with the other.

After a few more dizzying circles, the parrot landed just out of reach, on a webbed netting that stretched beneath the nearest sail.

His frustration mounting, Rupert released the pole and wobbled onto the net.

This was exactly the response the parrot had hoped to elicit. He gripped his toes into the webbing and swung beneath it. For a few short seconds, he eyed the cat's pudgy belly through the holes in the knotted ropes.

The target was too tempting to resist.

With a loud *squawk*, he bumped his head up through the netting and into the pillow of white fur.

Rupert jumped, startled and offended. He tumbled across the net, swatting at the feathered fiend who had so rudely poked him in the stomach. But in his zeal to catch the bird, he lost his footing and rolled off the webbing.

Luckily, the next lower sail broke his fall.

He bounced onto the top end of the canvas sheet and slid down its length. Flailing wildly, his chunky feet caught the sail's hem as he slipped off the edge.

He dangled in this undignified position, swinging back and forth, until his person climbed a rope ladder and brought him down to safety.

"Oh, Rupert," she said with a sigh, cuddling him in her arms. "What am I going to do with you?"

Twittering triumphantly, the parrot landed on the captain's shoulder.

Chalk up another win for the bird.

A SECOND CAT with similar coloring but far sleeker physique sat on the deck near the captain's feet. She watched Rupert's antics with minimal interest. The game had played out countless times before.

Her brother never caught the bird. He wouldn't know what to do with it if he did.

Cheeky parrot, Isabella thought.

But she resisted the urge to assist in her brother's hunt.

Occasionally a stray pigeon or a passing gull made the mistake of roosting on her boat. Those feathered intruders met a quick end. Petey the Parrot, however, wasn't meant for meals. The captain had made that quite clear.

Isabella sniffed derisively. The bird didn't have enough meat on his bones to make him worth her effort—even if he hadn't been declared off-limits.

She returned her attention to the boat's helm and the watery path ahead. She couldn't be distracted by such nonsense; there were far more important tasks on her agenda that afternoon.

It was her job to guide the *San Carlos* safely through the camouflaged entrance to the largest—and still unknown—bay on the Pacific's West Coast.

The Embarcadero

Modern-Day San Francisco

Chapter 1

THE KNITTING NEEDLE NINJA

AN ELDERLY MAN with short rounded shoulders hobbled along San Francisco's waterfront Embarcadero. His pace was stilted and slow, every other step paired with the *thump* of a wooden cane.

Red and white banners lined the route, part of an advertising campaign plastered across the city that promoted the America's Cup sailboat regatta. The prestigious competition had reached its final day. After months of hoopla and weeks of racing, the two teams representing the United States and New Zealand were tied eight to eight. Whoever took the next race would secure enough points in the "best of seventeen" format to be crowned the champion.

San Franciscans filled the Embarcadero's wide sidewalk, a stream of newly minted racing enthusiasts anticipating the day's matchup. Even those who had been blasé about sailing at the start of the event now eagerly joined in the fun.

It was a typical summer morning on the bay—which meant the weather could be anything from sunny and bright to soupy and overcast. Often, a single day would showcase both extremes.

For the moment, the city's shoreline enjoyed a clear sky, but the wind blowing in from the Pacific carried the sharp edge of a cooling front. The red peaks of the Golden Gate Bridge had begun to feather with fog.

Oscar looked out across the water and cracked a weary smile.

These were perfect conditions for the regatta's finale—and, he thought as the smile disappeared—for tracking down a serial killer.

Unlike the rest of the pedestrians flocking to the America's Cup pavilion, Oscar had little interest in the outcome of the pivotal last race.

He was on the trail of a cunning criminal, a woman known throughout the Bay Area as the Knitting Needle Ninja.

THE COLORFUL CROWDS on the Embarcadero walked at a much faster clip than the determined old man. Oscar's weary eyes scanned each individual and group that strolled by, all the while knowing that the Ninja might pass within inches without his detection.

He gummed his dentures back and forth, reflecting on the Ninja's bloody history—and her proficiency with disguise.

The Ninja's crimes had first come to light earlier that year. Revelations that a mayoral intern had been murdered by the former mayor's long-serving administrative assistant had rocked San Francisco's City Hall.

The story had quickly captured the morbid fascination of the local news media, and it wasn't long before an enterprising reporter came up with the alliterative nickname, the Knitting Needle Ninja. The moniker was a reference to the Ninja's unique method of attack: a pair of knitting needles that had once been used as a weapon of self-defense on the rowdy streets of San Francisco's Barbary Coast.

The curved metal rods contained a hollow compartment

fitted with razor-sharp blades. Unsheathed, the handy implements became a deadly means of stabbing, slicing, or viciously goring an unsuspecting victim.

They were also quite useful for knitting and crochet.

Despite her lengthy killing spree and unusual MO, the Knitting Needle Ninja operated undetected for almost a decade. No one had suspected Mabel, a demure woman in her late sixties, of harboring violent tendencies.

She had arrived for work each day at City Hall, a model of propriety and efficiency. Invariably, she was clad in a heather-gray skirt, soft cotton sweater, and sensible heeled shoes. Her wardrobe rarely varied from these staples.

She was a diligent employee, rigorously professional and deeply loyal to her boss. Never once had she showed up tardy or unprepared. She occasionally mingled with the administrative staff for the board of supervisors, but she shared few personal details with her colleagues.

No one knew much about her private life—other than, of course, her penchant for knitting.

The homicidal aspect of her favorite hobby had slipped under everyone's radar.

Up until her last kill, Mabel had been careful to select prey who were unlikely to be missed. Her targets were generally low-level interns that she hired specifically for the job of becoming her next victim. The deceased bodies were neatly dismembered and disposed of in out-of-the-way locations, the remains often left to decompose in secluded tracts of public forest.

Any concerned friends or loved ones of the victims had concluded that the missing person had voluntarily left town.

City Hall's myriad employees and elected officials had merely shrugged off the disappearances and continued on about their business. Political interns were a transient group. Mabel seemed to go through a lot of them, but no one ever guessed the reason why.

Until she hired Spider Jones.

JUST OUT OF high school, Spider was an inquisitive young man, killing time, so to speak, while retaking his college admissions exams. With his skinny jeans and high-top canvas sneakers, Mabel might have initially pegged him as a wayward youth.

If so, she had greatly misjudged his character. Raised by a single mother, he was firmly grounded, committed to his family, and looking forward to his academic future.

Innately curious about the world, Spider had pedaled his bike up and down San Francisco's steep streets. A daredevil on wheels, he had explored almost every corner of the city. He had also nosed through City Hall's basement archives—and the files secured in Mabel's desk. Sadly, it was the last activity that had proved most dangerous to his well-being.

Late one night, Mabel overheard Spider planning to share a secret he'd uncovered in his file snooping. She erroneously concluded that Spider was about to divulge her connection to the missing interns. Panicked, she lured Spider to City Hall's ceremonial rotunda, a decorative cove on the building's second floor.

The poor lad never knew what hit him. The Ninja attacked him from behind, reaching around his torso to stab him in the chest with her curved needle knife.

OSCAR DISCOVERED THE gruesome scene seconds too late to help the hapless intern. Spider's spirit had already left his blood-soaked body.

But the former antique dealer had recognized the killer's handiwork and quickly connected the weapon to its owner.

Not wanting to draw police attention to himself—as he had been declared legally dead a few years earlier—Oscar revealed the identity of Spider's murderer through a painting. In a replica of one of Coit Tower's famous WPA murals depicting scenes from early nineteenth-century San

Francisco, Oscar inserted an image of Mabel, wielding her unique weapons against the slain intern.

That, combined with the discovery of a pair of bloody knitting needles taped beneath the center drawer of the mayor's office desk, had blown open the case.

ONCE THE SECRET was revealed, the Knitting Needle Ninja became an overnight sensation. Instantly infamous, her grandmotherly face was plastered across every available news outlet, along with the grisly details of her crimes.

With the verified body count still rising, Mabel was now listed as one of San Francisco's most prolific serial killers—in a town that had some competition for the title. The number of kills attributed to her handiwork had topped two dozen and was expected to climb as more missing interns were identified.

While citizens initially expressed shock and horror at the hideous nature of the crimes, over the course of the ensuing months, the Ninja had become a macabre celebrity.

T-shirts, sweatshirts, and mugs appeared in the tourist shops at Fisherman's Wharf. Ninja jewelry was displayed across the fold-out tables of the vendors who set up daily outside the Ferry Building.

In May, a number of runners had dressed up as Nanny Ninjas for the annual Bay to Breakers footrace (and citywide street party). She'd been spoofed on late-night television and mocked in countless newspaper columns and online blogs.

But despite the humorous publicity, the Ninja was still a dangerous—and deranged—criminal.

Oscar would forever feel responsible for her slayings.

He had sold the woman her first set of dagger-fitted needles.

Chapter 2

WEST COAST DIVA

OSCAR CONTINUED HIS labored walk along the Embarcadero, stopping every couple of blocks to catch his breath until he reached the flagged entrance to the America's Cup pavilion.

Located about a mile from the Ferry Building, the event staging area had taken over piers Twenty-seven and Twenty-nine on the city's north shore. It was a massive enterprise, one that had transformed the abandoned platforms into a festive sports venue.

The pavilion piers stretched several hundred meters out into the bay. Spectators could enjoy jaw-dropping views of the Bay and Golden Gate bridges, Alcatraz, Angel Island, and a gorgeous backdrop of the city.

Inland from the event entrance, San Francisco's steep hills rose up like bleacher seating. Directly south of the pavilion, Telegraph Hill hoisted Coit Tower's concrete nozzle up onto its shoulders, as if giving the landmark a boost to look out over the venue piers.

Oscar squinted up at the tower as a swarm of green

parrots circled it, chattered at the activity on the shoreline below, and then settled back into the surrounding trees.

Given the distance, he couldn't be sure, but he thought he recognized one of the redheaded birds in the flock.

With a grunt, Oscar turned toward the entrance and joined the queue of spectators waiting to be admitted to the event piers.

Security personnel in matching red shirts inspected everyone who entered the pavilion. Most visitors received a diligent screening, but they gave the old man in the navy blue shirt stained with cooking grease just a quick glance before waving him through the gates. He had no bags to search, no bulky pockets to pat down. All he carried was the wooden cane that he clearly needed to keep himself upright.

The nearest attendant called out cheerfully, "Enjoy the race, sir."

Oscar nodded weakly, trying to ignore the constricting pain in his chest. The walk had depleted him and drained his meager energy reserves.

He had but one concern—and it wasn't watching the race.

He only hoped he could hang on long enough to catch the Ninja.

PAST THE SECURITY station, Oscar hobbled down the pavilion's main walkway lining the pier's east edge. Most of the regatta infrastructure was located at the far end of the platform, where it jutted out over the water to offer the best racing views.

Oscar soon paused for another break. Propping his cane against the walkway's side railing, he reached up to adjust his cap. His thinning white hair covered less and less of the bald spot on his crown, and he needed the cap's extra coverage to prevent sunburn.

Pulling the rim down over his eyes, he stared at the high-end boats docked along the pier and shook his head in amazement.

San Francisco was accustomed to glamour and glitz. She had hosted the world's finest royalty, fêted the grandest moguls of business. She proudly claimed some of the country's most elite hotels and restaurants. The West Coast diva was no stranger to ostentatious display. She knew how to show off while still maintaining a sense of elegant refinement.

As for maritime interests, the city had plenty of experience as a global hub. Starting with the swarm of boats that swamped the bay during the Gold Rush and continuing to modern day where massive container ships routinely bellowed through the fog, her waters had rarely been vacant.

But San Francisco had never seen anything quite like this.

Oscar gazed at the lineup of flashy multimillion-dollar yachts tethered next to the walkway. The ships varied in size, but even the smallest was large enough to comfortably house several dozen people. They were luxurious homes on water, lavishly designed to entertain their wealthy owners and any number of lucky invited guests. One ship even had a helipad—complete with the requisite helicopter. The collection of vessels lined up along this once-abandoned pier would have fit right in at Monte Carlo, St. Barths, or any other exclusive yachting location around the globe.

A formal placard affixed to the security railing listed each boat's name, point of origin, size, and unique features. Oscar skimmed the nearest summary and then tilted his head to watch the onboard activity.

It took a lot of manpower to keep these vanity vessels in showroom shape. Workers scurried about on deck and inside the living quarters, cleaning and polishing every square inch of wood, chrome, and Plexiglas.

San Francisco's inaugural hosting of the age-old regatta had attracted a sizeable crowd, he mused, rubbing the gray stubble on his chin.

Millionaires, sailing enthusiasts, countless support staff, hordes of casual spectators—and, he feared, the Ninja.

GRIMLY, OSCAR RESUMED his walk, shifting his attention from the docked ships to the various structures spread across the pier's wide platform.

Several gourmet food stalls were set up around the grounds, some inside large tented structures that had been constructed to provide shelter from the elements, be it sun, wind, or rain. Oscar let his nose sift through the decadent smells wafting up from the eating areas.

Here, the yachting crowd and San Francisco's regular citizens shared a common interest, he thought as he spied several patrons sipping wine and champagne. No matter how casual the venue, only the finest food would do.

He detected roasted, barbecued, and curried meat dishes—but, he noted with disappointment, no fried chicken.

He amended his last comment: the finest food—with one notable omission.

With a dismissive *snort*, Oscar turned his attention to the main stage. Spectators had filled in around the raised platform, blocking his view. Using the cane for leverage, he straightened his posture, but there were too many taller heads blocking his line of sight.

Giving up on the stage, he pivoted toward a video screen positioned on the far side of the commons. The screen broadcast footage from a live feed of the prerace ceremonies, offering additional viewing for those not able to get close enough to the stage to watch the events directly.

Oscar peeled off from the crowd and headed for the seating area in front of the screen. By the time he had crossed the commons, the screen had shifted to a stunt plane swirling through the air above the pavilion. The pilot performed a number of daredevil maneuvers that caused the crowd to gasp and applaud.

Oscar gripped his cane, frowning at the close-up image of the smiling man hanging upside down in the cockpit. In Oscar's view, the pilot was a darn fool.

After tracking the plane's last white plume across the sky, the video returned its focus to the center stage. The figure standing on the podium was instantly recognizable to almost everyone who lived in the Bay Area.

It was the wealthy entrepreneur responsible for bringing the regatta to San Francisco.

The Baron of Silicon Valley.

Chapter 3

THE BARON

THE BARON GAZED out at the crowd of spectators and beamed with satisfaction. The late-morning sun shone on his peppered mustache and beard. Both had been cropped in an eccentric style that gave him the appearance of an eighteenth-century nobleman.

It had been a long and gritty ride to reach this critical last race, but he couldn't have asked for a more dramatic story line.

He was either on the verge of a prize greater than all of his entrepreneurial triumphs combined—or he was about to suffer a crippling loss that would wound him far deeper than the sharpest blow from his strongest business competitor.

He felt his pulse quicken with the thrill of competition. After years of preparation, training, and investment, this was the moment for which he had been waiting.

"Welcome to the grand finale of San Francisco's America's Cup!"

AN ICON OF the computer world and one of the top-earning CEOs of Silicon Valley, the Baron had dedicated a sizeable portion of his vast wealth to the sport of competitive sailing. It was his sponsorship of the sailing team from the local yacht club that had brought the America's Cup to San Francisco. Winner of the last competition in Valencia, Spain, the Baron's team was the official defender of the cup and, consequently, the host of the current event.

The Baron had applied the same relentless mind-set to sailing as he had to his business empire. He took a hands-on approach to his sponsorship. He was actively involved in the team's race strategy, directly participating in the optimization of the boat's streamlined design as well as specific gear choices and personnel decisions.

The Baron's ambitious agenda extended far beyond defending the cup title. He had his sights set on modernizing the age-old regatta and making sailing a spectator-friendly sport.

As the reigning champions, the Baron and his team had the privilege of setting the rules for this year's race. He had taken a number of measures to ensure the competition would be more accessible—and exciting—to lay viewers with no nautical expertise.

First off, the San Francisco race format was dramatically different than any America's Cup that had come before. Instead of traditional long-haul segments, the Baron had devised a short sprint course that took advantage of the bay's natural amphitheater.

Each race started with a high-speed launch on the bay's west end heading toward the Golden Gate, followed by a blitz back along the San Francisco shoreline toward the Bay Bridge. Sharp tacking skills were required to flip the boats around at the east side of the course, just south of Alcatraz. The teams then charged once more across the length of the course, before taking a last leg along the waterfront and a final tacking pivot at the eastern boundary. From there, it was a short sprint into the finish, near the event pavilion off the Embarcadero.

From start to finish, no race could exceed a preset forty-minute time limit. In the sixteen successful heats that had been completed over the course of the last two weeks, most of the races had taken less than twenty-five minutes.

The head-to-head battles had included several heart-stopping down-to-the-wire finishes, leaving fans breathless and clamoring for more.

The racing boats, too, had been souped up for mass appeal. The craft designed for this year's regatta were much faster than any that had ever faced off in the competition.

The sailboats were specially built catamarans with forty-meter-high sails that balanced on a pair of streamlined canoe-shaped hulls. The lightweight contraptions were built for speed, flashing across the bay at previously unheard-of velocities. On tight turns or in heavy gusts, one or even both of the hulls lifted completely out of the water. In this elevated hydrofoiling posture, the pronged rudders and lone daggerboard that extended from the bottom of the craft were all that kept it stabilized on the water.

The distinctive boats could be spotted from almost every viewing angle in and around the bay. From Coit Tower to the Marina Green, the enormous triangular-shaped sails moved like chess pieces as they circled the buoys that demarcated the race route. Of course, the swooping helicopters hovering in the air just above the craft were also hard to miss.

Sailing purists had railed against the Baron's changes, decrying the speedy course, the flashy merchandizing, and the dangerously unstable new boats.

But as each day of racing progressed, the event drew increasing numbers of spectators. Now, with the competition tied up and everything riding on the results of the final segment, the whole city was mesmerized.

While the Baron desperately wanted to win, the regatta was already a phenomenal success.

He could hardly contain his excitement.

"Let's introduce the two teams and get them out there on the water!"

Chapter 4

THERE, AMONG THE SPECTATORS

OSCAR GRIMACED AT the scene on the stage.

He didn't have anything against the Baron—or rather, that wasn't the primary reason for his negative reaction. Oscar could think of several worthy causes that would have been a better use of the Baron's money than some snooty sailboating competition.

Nor was his objection directed to the event's nautical theme. He liked boats well enough—just not these flashy, flimsy contraptions that were zooming around the bay. He preferred a far more solid craft, one that could brave the waves of the Pacific on a long-haul voyage.

It was the brazen politicization of the event that had drawn Oscar's scorn.

The Baron had just introduced San Francisco's interim mayor. After an overzealous handshake with the Baron, Mayor Montgomery Carmichael had taken control of the podium and was now in the midst of lengthy self-promoting remarks (to which no one was listening).

Perhaps noting the widespread yawns and overall

boredom in the crowd, the Baron cut in and, with difficulty, ushered Monty to the rear of the stage.

"For that act of mercy, Baron, I've upped your standing," Oscar muttered under his breath.

While the mayor was being (somewhat forcibly) repositioned, the camera widened its lens and turned its focus to the crowd.

Near the far right side of the stage, Oscar spied his niece standing next to a green nylon carriage. While not visible from the video feed, Oscar knew that inside the carriage's mesh-covered passenger compartment, a plump orange and white cat had curled himself up into a tight ball. Rupert had likely snoozed through the performance of the daredevil pilot, the thirty-piece military band that played before the Baron's speech, and the rest of the prerace ceremony.

Oscar smiled. Rupert was a champion sleeper.

The wind whipped the woman's long brown hair as she watched the proceedings on stage. In her arms, she held Rupert's sister, a sleeker, more slender Siamese mix. Isabella trained her focus on the crowd. Her ice blue eyes scanned the assembled spectators.

The niece winced as Isabella extended her claws.

Oscar sucked in his breath, startled by the expression on the cat's face. The feline had detected an ominous presence.

His hunch had been right.

The Ninja was lurking somewhere in the audience.

GRIPPING HIS CANE, Oscar leaned toward the Jumbo-tron. He stared intensely at the screen as the camera panned the crowd.

A number of colorful characters had gathered near the pavilion stage. There were racing fans from New Zealand, easily identified by their painted faces, fuzzy stovepipe hats, and the emblems of their country's flag. Still new to the sport, the American counterparts were somewhat more muted in dress, but just as vocal in shouting for their team.

Beyond the partisan supporters, the crowd also included the regular handful of bizarrely dressed individuals that one frequently saw on the streets of San Francisco, including a woman dressed up in a Marilyn Monroe costume.

The Jumbotron feed flashed briefly back to the stage. Mayor Carmichael had apparently forgotten to mention a critical point in his remarks, and he was attempting to return to the podium's microphone. The camera caught a glimpse of the Baron and his security team tackling the mayor, before swinging once more to the crowd.

Oscar groaned at Monty's antics, but he kept his eyes focused on the video screen.

He recognized more faces in the audience.

Reporter Hoxton Finn scribbled on the pocket-sized note-pad that he carried everywhere he went. As the commotion at the podium continued, Hox glanced up from his notes and scowled at the spectacle of the mayor being dragged from the front of the stage.

The camera slid a few feet over, capturing an image of Humphrey, the news station's stylist and the reporter's ever-present sidekick. Humphrey appeared more concerned with Hox's hair, which had been ruffled by the wind blowing across the pier, than the scuffle involving the mayor.

Keep moving, Oscar urged the cameraman.

He stared intensely at the television screen, seeking confirmation of the warning he'd read in Isabella's expression.

The video passed over the contingent from City Hall, capturing the president of the board of supervisors, who looked bemused at the mayor's antics, and several members of his administrative staff . . .

And there, in a passing frame, Oscar spotted her. It was just a fleeting glimpse, but he knew her in an instant.

It was the woman he'd been tracking for the last six months.

In that brief moment, he saw through the disguise that had hidden her identity.

Mabel.

Aka, the Knitting Needle Ninja.

Chapter 5

HIKE AND SEEK

THE CANE'S RUBBER tip squeaked against the concrete as Oscar pivoted toward the pavilion's main stage. He pulled down the brim of his cap, shielding his eyes so that he could squint into the sunlight.

The stage was at least a hundred feet away from the wide screen that had been set up for the overflow audience. The crowd stood with their backs turned to him, but after several minutes' scrutiny, Oscar identified Hoxton Finn's ruffled head and, beside him, the shorter noggin of the news station's stylist.

Mabel was nowhere to be found.

The camera had captured the Ninja somewhere in the reporter's vicinity, but the woman had been on the move. Surprisingly nimble for her age and physique, at this point, she could be anywhere in the crowd—or on her way out the front gates.

Frustrated, Oscar hobbled toward the stage. In six months of searching, he'd never been this close to catching her. He couldn't give up now.

He coughed out a short wheeze, and his chest constricted. His heart was giving out on him; he knew his long life was nearing its end.

He didn't have much time left.

This might be his last chance to stop Mabel's killing spree.

PANTING FOR BREATH, Oscar reached the rear of the audience, just as the mass of people turned to face him.

The onlookers had shifted their attention to a roped-off corridor that would be used to bring the America's Cup trophy onto the stage.

Forged in 1851 to commemorate the first regatta, the silver chalice was carried on a gilded platter held at shoulder level by a pair of tuxedo-clad ushers, who were in turn flanked by armed security guards.

The crowd migrated toward the corridor, and Oscar was soon caught in a crush of spectators angling for a view of the famous trophy. Heads bobbed up and down, bodies weaved from side to side, and arms stretched high, holding camera phones up in the air.

The frenzy intensified as the sailing crews joined the cup in the corridor, preparing to escort it onstage.

The sailors would be boarding their boats immediately following the cup presentation ceremony, so they were already dressed for the day's crucial race. Each man was covered from head to toe in a specially constructed wetsuit made of a reinforced material that looked like high-tech chain mail.

In yet another change over the cup's earlier competitions, the crew members were professional athletes, brawny men who had trained for over a year to handle the physical demands of the flighty new boats—and who were difficult for an aging old codger with a cane to see over.

Stymied, Oscar glanced back at the television screen. The shot homed in on the silver cup as the ushers lifted it onto the stage. But in the background at the corner of the frame, he caught a glimpse of moving clothing.

Mabel was headed toward a hangar at the far end of the pavilion grounds.

With everyone's attention focused on the stage, the hangar's technical display would likely be unoccupied.

Clutching the cane, Oscar lumbered toward the hangar's wide entrance, determined to nab the Ninja and end her killing ways for good.

He didn't stop to consider that his own image might have been flashed across the event camera's wide screen—or that he and his clunky cane had been spotted, an easily discernible discrepancy among the face-painted, flag-waving racing fans.

The Ninja had waited six long months for the opportunity to finish off the man who had exposed her crimes.

She'd spent endless hours contemplating how to exact her revenge on the meddler who had upended her murderous routine.

As Oscar approached the hangar entrance, the question had to be asked.

Who was hunting whom?

OSCAR STEPPED INTO the hangar and cautiously looked around.

It was a cavernous building, capable of accommodating several hundred spectators.

But at this moment, Oscar appeared to be the only person inside its exhibit area.

The applause from the pavilion stage echoed dully through the open rafters, amplifying the emptiness of the space.

Monty had attempted to reinsert himself into the proceedings. There was a sound of shuffling followed by the Baron's crisp voice as he regained control of the microphone.

"Thank you, Monty. Let's have another round of applause for Mayor Carmichael . . ."

Oscar shook his head. Monty would not be kept silent for long.

He dismissed the noise from the stage and concentrated on the hangar.

The main display featured several practice boats. These were prototypes that had been used by the competing teams early on in their training. The finely tuned details of the versions being used in the championship were guarded secrets, despite the fact that the boats were visible to the public during the actual races.

At this high level of competition, seconds of advantage could make all the difference, and each team claimed to have developed numerous improvements to the initial designs.

It was impossible to know whether there was any truth to these assertions. If nothing else, the claims alone had the effect of psyching out the opponent.

With so much of their fate left up to the fickle nature of the wind, sailors—particularly those involved in racing—tended to be both paranoid and highly superstitious.

Oscar edged toward the nearest boat, his senses on high alert. The Ninja had proven her elusive skills time and again. Even with her face plastered across the local news media, she had circulated freely in San Francisco, evading capture without a single reported sighting.

If she could hide so easily in plain sight, she could find plenty of ways to mask her presence in a near-empty hangar.

The catamaran's shiny surface gleamed in the dim light. Leaning on his cane, Oscar peeked beneath the boat's polished hulls.

The space was empty, save for the sharp rudders that extended down from the hulls' curved surface.

He lifted his gaze to the upper portion of the craft. The boat had been staged without its extended sails—even the hangar's high roof was unable to accommodate the sky-high sheets.

Sturdy bracing welded to the metal sides held the two hulls together. A canvas of thick webbing stretched between the hulls, a support feature that allowed crew members to move from one side of the boat to the other.

The narrow hulls provided the boat's only interior space. Most of the crew members spent the race balancing on top of the craft, leaping across the support netting, and manning the rigging, a complicated network of ropes and pulleys that controlled the sails.

As Oscar examined the craft's sophisticated structure, he detected a small flicker of light inside the nearest hull. He leaned over to look down the interior length—and gasped at a sharp pain in his chest.

The cane fell clattering to the ground, quickly followed by the heavy *thump* of his body.

Chapter 6

SEMICONSCIOUS

"SAN FRANCISCO IS a young city."

The Baron's words echoed into the hangar from the stage outside. After the introduction of the two competing teams and the exhibition of the America's Cup trophy, the business mogul had reserved a few minutes in the program for his concluding remarks.

Lying on the hangar's concrete floor, Oscar winced at the stabbing ache that raked through his chest, but the voice continued, overlaying the pain.

"Compared to its older East Coast cousins and the gray-haired dowagers of Europe and South America, our beloved city is just a frisky green upstart. I think that's what first drew me to her. She offers a clean slate for anyone who's bold enough to write upon. There's a sense of newness, that anything is possible—and nothing is forbidden."

Oscar felt his weakened body drift toward a semiconscious state.

"Even among California settlements, San Francisco has a surprisingly late birth date. The remoteness of the location is partly responsible. Throughout much of the last millennium, the Northern California coast was seen as the end of the world. On maps, this faraway region was drawn as a sketchy, ill-defined mass positioned at the edge of the page, if it was shown at all. Before the development of commercial airlines, automobiles, and transcontinental trains, the area was almost impossible to reach. Only the bravest—or most foolhardy—souls dared to attempt the seaborne journey."

The Baron paused for a sip of water. The microphone picked up a light slurp before he continued.

"But the city's tender age is also the result of a geographic fluke. For over two hundred years, European explorers repeatedly missed the Pacific Ocean entrance to the San Francisco Bay. A couple of ships even landed on the Farralones, that cluster of rocks just thirty miles to the west, but their captains somehow didn't see the opening. That all of these mariners were specifically looking for protected ports suitable for settlement makes the failure that much more remarkable. Each one sailed right past the Golden Gate, the passage to the largest estuary on the Pacific side of both North and South America."

The Baron tapped his fingers against the podium.

"How is that possible?" he asked the silent audience. No one volunteered a response.

"The anomaly can't be explained by the fog that frequents our coast. Look around you, my friends. We get a number of clear, sunny days. Surely a ship sailing past on a day like this would have seen the opening."

The crowd murmured in puzzled agreement. Taking another sip of water, the Baron let his listeners ponder this curious circumstance for several seconds before he provided the answer.

"I'll tell you why they missed it, because I've been out there myself. In good weather, an optical illusion masks the bay's mile-wide channel. If it weren't for the city now built up on the shoreline and the boats that constantly populate these waters, I might even sail past it myself.

"When you look in through the Golden Gate from the Pacific Ocean side, the inner islands of Angel and Alcatraz fill in the space above the water, making the opening look like uninterrupted coastline. The Berkeley Hills fill in the distant horizon, enhancing the effect."

The crowd shuffled, as many stared across the bay, trying to envision the illusion the Baron had described.

"It wasn't until 1769—nearly two hundred years after the first European ships began sailing these waters—that a land expedition led by Governor Portola overshot Monterey and stumbled across what would later become one of the busiest ports in North America. Even then, it took another six years before a small Spanish packet ship found the ocean opening.

"As we prepare to embark on the regatta's last race and the end of what has been an historic America's Cup, I thought I'd take a moment to share with you the story of the *San Carlos*, the first sailboat to enter the San Francisco Bay. The first ever to cross through the Golden Gate."

He coughed an aside.

"And, of course, let's hope that team New Zealand doesn't get distracted on the far west turn of the racecourse trying to make out the optical illusion."

OSCAR'S EYES FLUTTERED. The voice from the loudspeaker blurred as images flitted through his brain.

A few details were missing from the Baron's recap of that signature voyage.

He knew this from his research—and from firsthand experience.

In addition to its Spanish captain, the unique crew of the *San Carlos* had included a portly chef with short rounded shoulders, the man's niece, and her two cats, a pair of Siamese flame point mixes with white coats and orange-tipped ears and tails.

On Board the *San Carlos*

Off the California Coast

August 1775

Chapter 7

SEA LEGS

CAPTAIN JUAN DE Ayala stood at the helm of the *San Carlos*, surveying the rocky shoreline. The Spanish seaman gripped the ship's steering wheel, bracing himself against the buffeting wind and the deck's constant roll. A seasoned mariner, he hardly noticed the disturbance.

The *San Carlos* was a tiny ship, especially compared to the rest of the fleet, but he'd take her any day over the Commodore's finicky galleon. His vessel had daring and pluck, along with a dogged determination that he couldn't help but admire.

Ayala looked up at the complicated network of heavy canvas cloth and roped rigging. The *San Carlos* featured two masts, with the forward pole being slightly taller than the one in the rear. Each mast bore three trapezoid-shaped sails, arranged so that the sheets decreased in size as they rose in height. A second set of triangular sails or jibs were strung semihorizontally from the mast poles to the ship's pointed front bow.

It was a masterful design, optimized to harness the wind, capture the current, and wrangle the ever-changing pull of the tide.

Ayala beamed with pride, a captain in love with his ship.

AYALA HAD PICKED up his assignment on the *San Carlos* just a few weeks earlier. It was his first opportunity to perform as a ship's top-ranking officer. The position would give him far more visibility within the fleet hierarchy—for better or worse. Any number of Spanish sailors had seen their once-promising careers plummet while attempting to make this type of transition.

Undaunted by the risk of failure, the captain had eagerly accepted the new post. He was ready for the challenge—and for the change of scenery.

Ayala had been serving as second in command to a testy commodore on the fleet's largest vessel when the opening on the *San Carlos* came up. After months of chafing under the commodore's niggling constraints, Ayala had leapt at the chance to jump ship.

He wasn't the least bit bothered by the odd circumstances that had led to his promotion.

The previous captain of the *San Carlos* had fallen ill while the ship was docked at San Blas, a port on Mexico's west coast.

According to the whispers circulating throughout the Spanish fleet, the man had gone mad and been committed to a sanatorium. The previous crew members had all fled or demanded transfer. Ayala was sailing with a completely new staff, quickly culled, like himself, from nearby ships.

It was a strange way to receive a commission, he thought blithely, but it was a substantial step up over his last position. He had simply ignored the rumors that the ship was haunted.

He was a practical man, and he didn't believe in such nonsense.

He glanced down at the delicate white cat who sat perched

on an upturned bucket by the ship's steering wheel. She had also transferred over from the commodore's ship—along with the chef, his niece, and a second feline named Rupert.

"What do you think, Isabella?"

As a rule, Ayala generally didn't like cats. He certainly didn't spend a lot of time talking to them.

He was more of a bird person.

The previous captain of the *San Carlos* had left behind a parrot in his stateroom. Ayala had been happy to let the bird stay on board. He named him Petey and warned the chef's niece that her felines would be evicted from the ship if they harmed his parrot.

The feline propensity for parrot-eating wasn't Ayala's only complaint about the furry creatures. He also blamed cats for his constant allergies.

Squinting toward the bow, he scowled at Rupert's fluffy orange and white lump, snoozing in the sun.

"Flea-bitten freeloader."

But despite all this feline animosity, the captain made an exception for Isabella.

After checking to make sure no one was looking, he reached over and stroked her orange-tipped ears. "Don't you agree, Issy? There's no such thing as ghosts."

Isabella tilted her head, purring at the gentle rub.

"Mrao."

AYALA RETURNED HIS attention to the ocean and the rocky shoreline off the ship's starboard side.

He did have one concern about his new command: finding their intended destination.

The captain wasn't altogether convinced of the accuracy of the intel he'd received for the current mission. Gaspar Portola and his men had been in pretty bad shape by the time they arrived in Monterey after their disastrous land expedition. The enormous bay Portola had described sounded like the delusions of a madman.

"Crazy fool," Ayala muttered. If a bay that large existed off this coast, it would have been sighted long before now.

He'd scoured every map he could get his hands on. The closest landmark was Drakes Bay by Point Reyes. Likely, that's what Portola's men had seen.

"I think Gaspar has sent us on a wild-goose chase."

Isabella stared up at Ayala, her eyes the clear blue of the ocean. The expression on her tiny pixie face conveyed a level of confidence that far surpassed that of the captain.

"Mrao."

IF THIS RUN up the coast was a fool's errand, Ayala didn't much mind.

It had been a good time to get away from Mexico City, he thought as Petey landed on his shoulder and began preening his feathers.

Due to the nature of his employment, Ayala was often away from home for months at a time. During one of his recent extended absences, his wife, a glamorous opera singer, had started an affair with a young actor.

The revelation was hardly a surprise to Ayala. He and his wife had been growing apart for several years.

She had met up with him in San Blas right before the *San Carlos* departed. It was a last (but unenthusiastic) attempt at reconciliation. The unhappy couple had taken a walk in a local park to discuss the state of their relationship.

The tense situation went from bad to worse when they happened upon an exotic lizard. Ayala plucked a berry from a nearby tree and offered it to the sharp-toothed creature. Instead of eating the fruit, the beast took off a chunk of the captain's left big toe.

After the blood, the screaming, and the partial amputation, Ayala and the opera singer decided to formally end their marriage.

Being Catholic, divorce wasn't an option, but he had

readily agreed to an annulment. He had no desire to keep her tied to him—or to compete with the actor.

With the marriage officially over, all Ayala wanted to do was escape it, to match a physical distance to the emotional one he'd already achieved.

He stomped his foot in agitation, startling the parrot, who flew off chattering in affront.

Ayala scowled. The foot injury was affecting his sea legs. He planted his left foot and, despite the pain, pressed down against the deck.

That blasted woman had brought him nothing but bad luck.

Chapter 8

IN THE KITCHEN

ONE LEVEL BELOW the main deck, the ship's chef looked up at the ceiling, and frowned at an odd grinding sound that he'd been hearing ever since they left San Blas.

Oscar, his niece, and her two cats had followed Captain Ayala over from his previous boat just days before the new one's departure. It had been an abrupt and hastily planned transfer.

He was still getting used to the cooking facilities in the galley of the *San Carlos*. The previous chef had left the place in complete disarray. Pots and pans had been strewn haphazardly across the floor. Many of the glasses and plates had been broken beyond use. The provisions were completely depleted.

Oscar and his niece had spent every waking hour trying to restock the pantries and put things in order before the ship started its trip up the coast.

It had been a scramble, but the work had paid off. The long narrow kitchen was now fully functional, a warm inviting room, comfortably dusted with flour and spatters of chicken grease.

The same could be said for the chef working at the counter.

Oscar wore a dingy gray apron strapped over his short rounded shoulders and tied across his plump middle. He bent over a wooden counter in front of a skinned and partially dismembered chicken, slicing off pieces and parts and tossing them into a round metal bowl.

The ship's captain had requested a special dinner that evening. Ayala anticipated that they would dock that night at their trip's northern terminus, most likely Point Reyes. Instead of the staple of soupy gruel that was served for most onboard meals, the captain had asked the chef to prepare his signature dish, fried chicken.

Oscar had picked up a dozen hens during a brief stop in Monterey the day before. Most of the birds would remain—alive—in the ship's chicken coop as an ongoing source of eggs, but he had culled a few from the herd to sacrifice for the evening's celebratory dinner.

Glancing once more up at the ceiling, Oscar wiped his hands on a dish towel.

"Where did we put the cleaver?" He pulled open a drawer and squinted inside. "Bah, I can't find anything in this kitchen."

Oscar's gruff exterior didn't fool his niece, who sat on a nearby stool, reading a book. Without looking up from the page, she pointed at a cupboard halfway down the galley's length.

"You hung it on a rack, inside the third door down."

Grumbling, Oscar hobbled to the indicated cupboard and pulled it open.

"Should never have agreed to leave the old ship," he said, waving the cleaver in the air.

The niece smiled to herself. Her uncle's last kitchen had been meticulously organized—but in a cryptic categorization scheme known only to him. She had never been able to understand his bizarre sorting system.

At least now she could locate all of the basic cooking tools. That is, until he started moving things around.

THE NIECE RESUMED her reading as Rupert wandered into the kitchen, the orange tip of his tail poked inquisitively into the air.

He rubbed his head and shoulders against the niece's shin, his stomach rumbling an inquiry about the night's dinner.

At the sight of the chicken operation laid out on the counter, he licked his lips with anticipation.

Question answered.

If fried chicken was on the menu, this cat was staying in the kitchen to supervise.

Rupert gazed up at the heavy iron pots mounted to the wall behind the stove. These would be called into service later that evening when the ship reached its destination. Fried chicken needed calm waters for the final step of its preparation—Rupert knew this as an expert on the matter.

Point Reyes or the protected bay, if in fact it existed, would be far more amenable to cooking than the open ocean.

In the meantime, Oscar struggled to maintain his balance against the ship's constant rolling while using the meat cleaver on the chicken remains. Every so often, a splash of salt water sprayed against the kitchen's half-open window, evidence of the rocking waves. To further complicate matters, the chef's hands were slick from the various juices that had oozed out of the meat.

Sniffing loudly, Rupert left the niece's stool and crept toward the kitchen counter. He might just need to take a peek at the carcass . . .

Whack. The cleaver slammed down on the wooden surface.

Thump. Another piece of meat landed in the bowl.

Whiskers twitching, Rupert crouched on the floor beside Oscar's feet. His back haunches tensed, preparing to jump up onto the counter for a closer inspection.

The cat's movements went unnoticed by the niece, who had reached a particularly gripping plot twist in her book.

Out of the corner of one eye, Oscar spied the cat about to leap.

"Scat!"

The chef shifted his weight to block Rupert from invading his workspace, but the quick movement, combined with another steep roll from a passing wave, caused him to lose his grip on the knife.

Rupert froze in place as the cleaver slipped out of Oscar's fingers, flew up into the air, and tumbled to the ground—its blade landing inches away from the cat's furry white paws.

The niece gasped in horror. Oscar pursed his lips.

"Out," he commanded tersely. He pulled the cleaver from the floorboard and turned to the sink.

"I don't have any recipes for diced cat."

LEAVING HER BOOK on the stool, the niece scooped up Rupert and carried him toward the kitchen's exit.

"That's the second fright you've given me today," she scolded, gently rubbing the soft crown on the top of his head.

Rupert didn't struggle to break from her grasp, but his gaze remained fixed on the kitchen counter.

"One-track mind," the niece said with a sigh. "Let's go find Isabella."

The niece headed out of the galley and turned left on the main corridor that ran down the center of the ship's interior. She'd last seen her other cat on deck, assisting Captain Ayala.

As she walked toward the steps at the far end of the hallway, a voice called out from an open room opposite the kitchen.

"Howdy ho, there, neighbor!"

Rupert peeped out a protest at the niece's instinctive squeeze of his stomach.

She closed her eyes and muttered darkly, "Hello, Father Monty."

Chapter 9

FROM THE CHAPEL

FATHER VINCENT SANTA Maria Montgomery Carmichael strode briskly into the corridor and flagged down the niece.

"Hello, there. Hello!"

The curly haired priest had been yet another last-minute appointment in the scramble to fill the abandoned ship's positions at San Blas.

The last religious counselor to serve the *San Carlos* had reportedly left the church altogether following his departure from the ship.

No one was quite sure where the Spanish navy had found Father Carmichael. His religious résumé was a bit of a mystery. Some thought he'd been pulled from one of the smaller vessels in the South Atlantic fleet. Others speculated that he'd been brought in from the Mexican countryside.

On the following two points, however, everyone agreed: he didn't appear to have much religious experience—and the five-word moniker was far too much of a mouthful for regular conversation.

His name had quickly been shortened to Father Monty.

THE NEW PRIEST'S first order of business had been to set up a temporary chapel.

The room that had originally been designed for that purpose had suffered extensive damage during the changeover in captain and crew. Repairs were scheduled to begin when the *San Carlos* returned to San Blas.

Until then, Father Monty was headquartered in an unused space located directly across from the kitchen—a fact that the niece had momentarily forgotten.

She'd been so shaken by Rupert's near miss with the meat cleaver that she'd hurried out of the kitchen and turned left on the main corridor without first checking the chapel for signs of the pesky priest.

She would have taken the long way around to the stairs leading up to the deck if she'd been on the lookout.

The niece smoothed Rupert's fur, giving him an apologetic look for her earlier squeeze.

Father Monty was the most unorthodox religious official the niece had ever met. Among the passengers and crew, she was the most skeptical of his credentials.

He seemed far too young to be such a senior member of the clergy. There wasn't a touch of gray in his curly brown hair, and she thought it was fashioned in an odd style, particularly for a priest.

Monty's hair was cut short on the sides and long on the top, exaggerating the already pointed shape of his face. The tight curls bounced off his forehead when he walked.

The hairstyle wasn't his only eccentricity. Beneath his vestments, Father Monty wore a strange collection of cuff links. He was constantly pulling back the sleeves of his robe to show off the day's selection.

This afternoon was no exception.

The niece picked up her pace, but Monty quickly matched it.

"What do you think of the frogs?" he asked, holding up his wrist to flash the latest gold piece. "Picked these up at a market in Caracas. I got a great deal. The jeweler was practically giving them away."

"They're very . . . nice," she replied, stopping only so she could avoid being beamed by the priest's bobbing wrist.

This was the problem with ships, she thought with an irritated sigh. There was no way to escape your fellow passengers, other than pushing them overboard—something she had considered doing to Father Monty on more than one occasion during the days since he'd arrived.

"Hello, Rupert."

Monty bent to the cat's face and tickled his furry chin.

"I heard your favorite dish is on the menu tonight—fried chicken!"

The niece shook her head. How had Father Monty found out about the captain's dinner request or, for that matter, her cat's food preferences?

She could hazard a guess.

Within hours of his arrival, Father Monty had fixed up the new chapel room to hear confessions. He then began encouraging, soliciting, and out-and-out badgering his fellow passengers to schedule penitence appointments.

Sailors had been traipsing in and out of the curtained confession box for the last couple of days.

While the niece conceded that this was a legitimate part of Monty's job, she found his eagerness to listen to the deepest secrets of his new acquaintances off-putting, if not downright suspicious.

She had refused to participate, but Father Monty wasn't one to accept no for an answer.

"I have an opening this afternoon at two," he said, pumping his thin eyebrows. "In case there's anything you—or Rupert—need to confess." He wagged a finger at Rupert's wobbly blue eyes. "Gluttony is a deadly sin, my furry friend."

The niece frowned, puzzling on who would have shared Rupert's love of fried chicken with the priest during a confession session. She couldn't imagine her uncle volunteering any information to this nosy man. And as far as she knew, Rupert was incapable of human speech.

With difficulty, she stepped around Monty and headed toward the stairwell at the end of the corridor. "We're headed up to the deck. Nice to see you, Father . . ."

"What a wonderful idea. I think I'll join you. You know, I've never seen this part of the Pacific coast before."

His flat-soled shoes slapped against the floorboards as he trotted after her.

"I hear we're on a special mission to find the opening to an undiscovered bay. What do you think about that?"

• • •

AS THE WOMAN carried her cat down the hallway, chased by the persistent priest, a knot in the wood paneling to one of the chapel walls opened up, revealing a small hole.

There was a shuffling sound.

Then a yellowed eye peered out into the room, blinked, and disappeared.

Chapter 10

THE BARON

THE NIECE REACHED the top of the stairs and scurried across the deck. Rupert rode in her arms, startled by his person's fast pace.

Father Monty followed closely behind, chattering about the benefits of confession.

"I've had many parishioners tell me that it brightens their day. The mere act of sharing one's sins helps heal a person's soul. It lifts the spirit, warms the heart . . ."

But about five steps across the deck, Monty cut off the sales pitch and gave up his pursuit of the niece—at least temporarily. He'd just caught sight of another sought-after confession target.

"Baron, how nice to see you." He sidled up to the nobleman standing near the ship's helm. "Enjoying the view?"

A silver-haired man with a closely cropped beard and mustache turned to look at the priest.

"Father Monty. What a surprise," he said in a tone that conveyed just the opposite.

THE BARON WAS a special guest on the *San Carlos*. His passage and VIP status had been directly arranged by the head of the Spanish fleet.

The Baron was a self-made man. With nothing more than his natural talents for industry and finance—along with a little luck—he'd built a powerful business empire. His vast personal fortune had enabled him to purchase his nobility status, a move that had rankled many who had inherited their titles.

As crafty as he was competitive, the Baron had read the reports from the earlier land expedition that first sighted the protected bay. He had personally interviewed Governor Portola and several of his men, in an attempt to extract all available details.

Unlike Captain Ayala, the Baron had no doubt of the bay's existence.

He had contributed a hefty sum to the Spanish crown in order to ensure his seat on the *San Carlos*.

Now, he was positioned to get his own firsthand look at the rumored harbor—and to assess its potential in person.

He'd been warned that the ship wouldn't be able to provide the many luxuries to which he was accustomed. This did not deter him in the least. He had packed extra gear and supplies. He was prepared for whatever challenges he might face.

So far, it turned out the greatest onboard hardship had been enduring obligatory conversations with the vessel's priest.

But today, even the presence of Father Monty couldn't sour the Baron's mood.

As the priest yammered away about the success of the confessional booth he'd set up in the makeshift chapel, the dearth of reliable maps for this part of the world, and the main course on the night's dinner menu, the Baron simply tuned him out.

The businessman returned his gaze to the rocky shoreline.

If everything went according to plan, by late afternoon, the ship would have found the elusive entrance to the bay.

Chapter 11

A STYLISH MATE

THE *SAN CARLOS* continued up the California coast, bobbing like a tiny cork in the bathtub of the Pacific. It was a blustery, unforgiving day. Bullying waves pummeled the boat's sides and washed over the deck.

Captain Ayala muscled his weight against the steering wheel, struggling to keep the ship on course, while Isabella manned her stool, chirping advice. Ayala hated to admit it, but he was relying far more on Isabella's instincts and guidance than that of his first mate Humphretto.

It wasn't that the first mate wasn't trying to be helpful; he was just ill equipped to do so.

Humphretto was a petite man, with delicate hands and a slight build. Prone to worried hovering, he lacked the most basic of nautical skills. He had yet to master even a limited understanding of the *San Carlos*'s complicated network of pulleys and ropes. He was utterly confounded by how to adjust the new ship's sails to adapt to changing wind conditions.

Luckily, Humphretto was useful in other ways. He was a wiz with a pair of scissors; his haircutting expertise easily matched that of the finest fashion designers in Paris. Particularly during extended voyages, Humphretto stayed busy in his off-hours maintaining the many coifs of the crew. For this reason alone, he was a sought-after member of any sailing team. The commodore on Ayala's previous ship had petitioned for Humphretto to stay on his galleon—to no avail.

Likely, it was the Baron's anticipated presence on the *San Carlos* that had caused the commodore's request to be denied. The man's face had turned purple with frustration, but he had been powerless to stop the transfer. Indignant, he had insisted on one last haircut before Humphretto left for the *San Carlos*.

Ayala allowed himself a short smirk of triumph. Then he grimaced at the memory of a recent conversation with his first mate.

Humphretto was greatly concerned about the captain's image, particularly his hair. He was convinced that Ayala could become a world-renowned sailor and explorer, as famous as Sir Francis Drake—if only he took a little more care to his physical appearance.

Frowning up at the captain's head, Humphretto had posed the following question.

"You know what Sir Drake had, Captain? The thing that put him over the top?"

"No, but I'm sure you'll tell me."

"Style, panache . . . and a traveling barber."

IN ADDITION TO his hairstyling expertise, Humphretto was also an amateur tailor, a skill that came in handy on long deployments. He carried onboard a portable sewing machine capable of performing a wide range of stitches. He could mend the most severely rendered garment so that no one could determine where the hole had been.

The first mate designed his own clothes from scratch. His most recent creation was a horsehair coat whose thick waterproof fabric he hoped would shut out the cold wet weather that was anticipated for their northern excursion.

The verdict was still out on the coat's effectiveness. With a shiver, Humphretto pulled up his collar as yet another wave splashed onto the deck.

Then there was the matter of aesthetics. Ayala thought the coat made his first mate look like a beaver—an opinion that hadn't been well received by the coat's wearer.

"I'm telling you, Captain, this is the latest rage in Madrid."

Ayala had grunted his response.

"All you need is some oversized teeth."

AND SO, AS Humphretto called out a warning for the treacherous rocks of Farallones, Ayala didn't immediately veer away from the hazard.

"Better steer clear, Captain! We'll run aground for sure!"

Isabella issued a correcting chirp, raising a front paw in the air.

Ayala whipped out his binoculars and scanned the shoreline beyond the rocks. His lips pursed together in consternation. There was no discernible disruption in the transition between water and land.

"I don't see it, Issy," he said, dropping the glasses.

He began to spin the wheel away from the impediment, but Isabella insisted.

"Wrao."

With a grunt, Ayala returned his binoculars to his face. A cloud passed over the afternoon sun, shifting the shadows on the land below.

"I can't believe it."

He pulled his face away from the magnification, rubbed his eyes, and then returned his focus to the lenses. The brief shift in lighting had created just enough differential to reveal the anomaly in the shoreline. What had appeared to be a solid stretch of land was instead a narrow passage masked

by a pair of islands—located much farther inside a protected bay.

Once he had seen through the illusion, the opening was
as clear as day.

He handed the binoculars to Humphretto.

"Crikey, Captain. It was there all along. We would have
sailed right past if not for . . ."

The first mate looked down at the slender cat sitting on
the overturned bucket, her sleek head proudly tilted upward.

"How did she . . . ?"

Isabella provided a pert explanation.

"Mrao."

Ayala reclaimed the binoculars and focused on the possible paths around the Farallones.

"Worry about that later. First we've got to get the ship
through without sinking on the rocks."

Chapter 12

THROUGH THE GOLDEN GATE

THE PASSENGERS AND crew of the *San Carlos* thought they were alone during their windblown journey up the Northern California coast, but throughout the day, the ship's progress had been monitored from above—far, far above.

The moon's glowing orb spent her daytime hours sleepily tucked into the blanket folds of the deep blue sky. But even as she snoozed, she kept a close watch on her beloved bay and the turbulent waters surrounding its entrance.

From her lofty perch, the moon watched with at first casual interest and then increasing concern as the *San Carlos* neared the Farallones and, just beyond, the Golden Gate.

She held her breath, waiting for the vessel to continue up the shoreline—and then gasped with alarm when the boat turned inland toward the opening that had been missed by all of the mariners who had come before.

"No," she cried, swooping down through the atmosphere. "It can't be."

For hundreds of years, she had successfully kept the Europeans out of the enormous estuary. She wasn't yet ready to share her pristine playground with such heathens. Hadn't those pale-faced polluters fouled enough of the earth already?

"No," she repeated. "I won't allow it." She eyed the tiny craft. She had sunk far bigger ships in her day. This one, she could easily wreck on the rocks, delaying the discovery a little bit longer.

Mankind had created sails to harness the wind—a crafty invention, she had to admit, but she controlled the tide. And that, she knew from previous experience, gave her the upper hand.

The moon surged at the thought, pulling the current like a loose tablecloth beneath the ship's hull, yanking it backward.

Captain Ayala hollered to his crew, sending men scurrying about the deck and up the masts.

Sails were hoisted, turned, and lowered in rapid succession, an attempt to break free of the tide's viselike grip.

But every forward motion was matched by a slip of equal or greater length, dragging the boat farther and farther west, dangerously close to the rocky Farallones.

The captain wrapped his hands around the ship's steering wheel, tensely gripping its rim. Never in his life had he encountered conditions this challenging. He fixed his gaze on the horizon, determined to see the ship through the distant passage.

The moon leered down at the captain. The steely expression on his face only riled her temper.

If this mortal man intended to breach the bay's liquid barrier, he would have to summon his sharpest sailing skills.

With every uptick in lunar rage, the tide's strength increased. Ayala grumbled in frustration, finally conceding to the insurmountable force. They would have to turn back and try again tomorrow.

Silly little captain, the moon beamed triumphantly, sensing she had him beat. She had no intention of letting him escape.

But just as she was about to inflict a final swamping blow, she detected a presence on the boat that caused her to reconsider.

A slender white cat stood defiantly on the deck, her claws digging into the slick wooden floorboards. Her blue eyes sparkled up at the moon, issuing a mental command.

You will let this ship through.

The moon rolled back on her hips, taken aback by the cat's brazen demand. She was unaccustomed to direct communications with the beings that lived on the ground below. Certainly, it was the first time she'd been so boldly addressed by a cat.

The globe flickered in the darkening sky as she considered the request.

Why?

Isabella transmitted her reply, her expression stern and unflinching.

It is time.

The moon stroked her round chin, puzzled by the audacity of this tiny creature. The cat possessed a bewitching presence almost as powerful as her own.

While still hesitant to share her precious jewel with the rest of the world, the moon's wrath began to dissipate. With a last look down at the persistent cat, she decided to bless the ship's passing.

The moon released the ship, and the *San Carlos* popped through the Golden Gate as if attached to a rubber band that had been tethered to the opposite shore.

A sudden *whoosh* of wind propelled the ship into the bay's wide middle.

The moon gazed down at the tired little vessel, with its

human, feline, and avian occupants—and then drew in her breath, aghast.

Her glowing tendrils reached out, trying to claw the boat back, but it had traveled beyond her grasp.

Too late, the moon had glimpsed the evil that lurked beneath the deck.

Chapter 13

ANGEL ISLAND

CAPTAIN AYALA STOOD at the helm of the *San Carlos*, warily surveying the bay's dark water. The moonlight provided a dim outline of the surrounding shore, but he was wary of getting too close.

After the grueling fight to gain entrance to the bay, it would be a shame to wreck the boat now. Better to wait until morning, when he could devise a safe approach to land.

An eerie quiet settled in around the ship. The encircling hills blocked the Pacific's fierce winds. The water glistened with a deceptive calm.

The captain nodded to his second in command.

"Humphretto, let's see if we can drop anchor here."

As the first mate supervised the lowering of a heavy metal hook, the passengers who had taken shelter belowdecks slowly began to emerge.

Father Monty staggered up the stairs from the second level looking green around the gills.

A crew member dipped a bucket of water from the bay and set it beside the priest.

Monty splashed a handful onto his face. "No offense, Captain, but for a while there, I didn't think we were going to make it."

Just then the ship lurched.

The priest fell face-forward into the bucket.

The bay was much deeper than Ayala had anticipated, and the anchor had failed to hit bottom. The current had snagged the hull and jerked the boat back toward the opening it had fought so hard to clear.

They had reached their destination, but the voyage wasn't quite finished.

IT TOOK ANOTHER two hours for the captain to find a location shallow enough to anchor that was safely beyond the direct pull of the tide.

Ayala tried several lodgings in the open water, but each time, the vessel failed to hold in place. He finally circled to the far side of the bay's largest island and edged the ship into a small cove.

There was a collective sigh of relief as the anchor hit bottom—none issued more vehemently than by Father Monty, who collapsed into a deck chair and dramatically flung his arms up over his head.

"Sweet heavens to Betsy! Thank the Lord that's over!"

Noting the stares from his fellow shipmates, he switched to a more reverent tone.

"I mean, thank you, our heavenly father. I never doubted your wisdom and providence throughout that entire turbulent episode."

Isabella's pert comment reflected the sentiments of the surrounding humans.

"Mrao."

CAPTAIN AYALA FOCUSED his attention on the shadowed island lying just off the ship's bow.

Touching a hand to the gold cross that hung around his neck, he called out solemnly, "I hereby christen thee Isla Santa Maria de Los Angelos."

Translated, the title read, roughly, St. Mary Island of the Angels. The title followed the Spanish tradition of naming newly discovered landmarks in honor of the nearest religious holiday, in this case, the Catholic festival in August celebrating the Assumption of Mary.

In any event, Angel Island seemed like a suitable nickname for the safe harbor that had allowed the passengers and crew aboard the *San Carlos* to sit down for their long-delayed dinner.

Even seasick Father Monty felt a rumbling in his stomach as he performed the ritual blessing the new island.

With the formalities completed, Captain Ayala made the much-anticipated announcement:

"Tell Oscar to get a move on. I'm ready to eat!"

Chapter 14

STOWAWAY

AS SOON AS the *San Carlos* dropped anchor off Angel Island and the ship was at last truly stabilized, Oscar swung into high gear finishing up the night's dinner.

While the christening ceremony commenced on deck, the kitchen below was transformed into a blur of sizzling pans, boiling pots, and flour-coated cutting boards.

The menu included lumpy mashed potatoes loaded with butter and cream, fresh green beans picked up during the stop at Monterey, and thick gravy simmered to golden brown perfection. The headliner, of course, was Oscar's signature dish: crispy fried chicken, Captain Ayala's favorite meal and a much-anticipated treat for the crew.

The niece maneuvered deftly around her uncle, stacking plates and silverware and carrying them up to the long table on the top deck, where the dinner would be served.

The pair had worked together through several of Oscar's naval cooking assignments. Even in the kitchen's narrow galley, they generally avoided running into each other.

Isabella sat on a stool, supervising the action, chirping out a warning if it looked like the two were about to collide.

Rupert sat on the floor beneath the stool, huffing and puffing as his pink nose sucked in the scents of the sizzling fried chicken. He could hardly wait for dinner to begin and—most important—for the cats to be served. Given the nearness of the meal, he didn't dare risk hopping on the counter (for fear he might get into trouble and be banished from the feast), but he wasn't letting the chicken serving bowl out of his sight.

As the niece sped out of the galley with yet another load of dishes, Oscar stepped back from the stove. Surveying the spread, he ran through his mental meal checklist.

"I think we've got everything covered . . ." he said, glancing down at Isabella. She tilted her head, as if conducting her own review, and then confirmed his assumption.

"Mrao."

"Well, that settles it, then."

Oscar picked up the tongs and lifted the last piece of chicken out of the skillet. As he placed the crispy leg into the bowl, he felt the slightest twinge of unease.

He was alone in the kitchen with the two cats—or so he thought.

Turning toward the hallway, he spied a shadow in the space just beyond the door.

There was a strange scent in the air. It took him a moment to separate the foreign smell from that of the cooking food.

It was a sweet, lemony perfume.

He held the tongs out like a weapon, a defensive posture that had nothing to do with the ship being docked near an unknown land.

Isabella's growling hiss confirmed his suspicions. Rupert's sniffing terminated in a startled *snork*, and he flattened his body against the floor.

Somewhere along the way, they had picked up a stowaway.

Or perhaps, Oscar thought with a start, she had been with them since San Blas.

Chapter 15

THE CONFESSION

ACROSS THE HALLWAY from the ship's kitchen, Father Monty sat behind the confessional curtain, waiting for a last-minute appointment that had been penciled into his schedule book during the perilous passage into the bay.

The priest had been incapacitated throughout much of the ordeal, lying on a cot on the side of the room with a blanket pulled over his head, wishing he'd never left the firm comfort of land.

Given his distraught condition, he hadn't noticed the person who had inscribed the entry in the logbook. Of course, the process was intended to be anonymous, but Father Monty frequently found himself challenged to uphold that ethical standard.

He peered down at the writing, scrutinizing the script. Whoever his stealthy confessor was, he or she had impeccable handwriting. The appointment had been scrawled in near-perfect penmanship, despite the ship's violent rolling.

Who could it be? he wondered with increasing interest. Oscar's niece was the only female on board. Had she finally decided to divulge her secrets? He tapped the toe of his shoe, anticipating the information that might be revealed. He could hardly contain his excitement.

Per protocol, Monty's view of the door was blocked by the confession booth's dark curtain, but every few seconds, he edged his chair a little closer to the fabric's edge.

Once his guest arrived, he might have to take a peek around to the opposite side—and then make his own quick confession before dinner.

DESPITE MONTY'S VIGILANT surveillance, the confessor slipped in without his notice. He was admiring the craftsmanship on his frog-shaped cuff links when the chair on the other side of the curtain scraped against the floor.

He jumped, startled by the sound, and nearly fell off his seat. Scrambling to regain his balance, he managed to sputter out a jumbled version of the standard mantra.

The mishmashed liturgy appeared not to matter to the person behind the curtain.

"Father, forgive me, for I have sinned."

The voice was scratchy and high-pitched but with a strained tone, as if the speaker was making an effort at disguise.

It could be anyone, Monty thought, more intrigued than ever.

And then a distinctive scent floated through the chapel room, overriding the aroma of the fried chicken being cooked across the hall.

Monty took a sniff—and he sensed that his confessor was not the niece.

They'd only met a few days earlier, but she was not the type of woman to wear perfume, definitely not one with this lemony-sweet scent.

Just then, the ship's dinner bell rang.

The bell was a deafening device that Oscar operated from the far end of the kitchen, its ringer designed to efficiently send its alert throughout the entire vessel.

When the noise stopped, Monty waited for his guest to continue, but the curtain beside him remained silent.

After a few minutes, Monty eased up in his chair and cautiously poked his nose over the top of the fabric.

The chair on the other side was empty.

Chapter 16

DINNER INTERRUPTED

WITH THE CELEBRATORY dinner ready, the passengers and crew of the *San Carlos* assembled around a long wooden table on the ship's top deck.

Most of the ship's meals were casual affairs, but the discovery of a previously unknown portal to a protected bay of vast commercial potential warranted a more elaborate feast.

Of course, Captain Ayala needed little excuse to call for a full course of Oscar's fried chicken. He would have requested it even if they hadn't found the bay.

Water lapped against the hull, and a breeze rustled the sails. A row of candles illuminated the place settings.

Captain Ayala presided at the head of the table. Humphretto took his appointed chair at the opposite end. The rest of the seats filled in with hungry passengers and crew members.

The gathered eaters let out appreciative sighs as Oscar and his niece carried up the last trays of food. The chef allowed himself a rare beam of pride as he placed the fried chicken in front of the captain's plate.

Petey the parrot was the only one who disapproved of the meal's main ingredient. With a loud squawk, he fluttered off Ayala's shoulder and swooped up to the top of the main mast.

WHEN THE LAST steaming dish had been delivered, the niece slid into her chair. She glanced beneath the table, checking for her feline companions.

Rupert and Isabella sat on the floor at her feet, eagerly waiting for their person to hand down special saucers filled with their cat-sized portions of the meal. Squirming, Rupert smacked his lips.

Father Monty stood from his seat at the table's middle and prepared to bless the meal. As he raised his hands, the sleeves of his robe slipped down. The candlelight flickered on the gold hilts of the jumping frog cuff links pinned into the shirt he wore underneath as he began a ritual incantation—and then stopped.

He pointed at an empty seat on the table's opposite side.

"Are we missing someone?"

Humphretto held up his index finger, counting the gathered heads.

"One of the crew," he said, frowning as he tried to remember the name. "Alberto, I think."

Ayala shrugged. "Let's eat."

Monty gestured for patience. "I'll check down below to see if he's coming."

THE NIECE WATCHED the priest disappear down the stairs, her brow furrowed with concern. Her uncle's meal was going to get cold if they waited much longer.

Three quick footsteps echoed up from the lower level—followed by a gasp of disbelief.

The subsequent high-pitched scream was unlike any the niece had ever heard uttered from the throat of a man.

Afraid the captain's parrot had met an untimely end, she peeked under the table and confirmed that both cats were still at her feet and visibly hungry. Glancing up, she spied the green-feathered bird perched on the mast above the deck.

Thank goodness, it's not the parrot, she couldn't help thinking.

It was a death of both more and less significance.

The scrub hand missing for dinner had met a gruesome and untimely end.

•   •   •

DEATH WAS NOT uncommon aboard the vessels of the Spanish fleet. All manner of sickness besieged the brave mariners. Mysterious illnesses were often contracted in the faraway lands to which they visited. Pirate attacks felled other unfortunate souls with either cannon fire or bayonets. Occasional mutinies resulted in ship-wide carnage.

But none of the passengers and crew of the *San Carlos* had ever experienced a death quite like this.

A secretive stabbing was somewhat unique.

The murder weapon used in the crime drew even more interest.

There in the pool of blood surrounding the victim lay a curved knitting needle whose tip end had been fitted with a sharp attacking blade.

Modern-Day San Francisco

Six Months Prior to the America's Cup Regatta

Chapter 17

THE INTERIM MAYOR

IT WAS THE beginning of March, just six weeks into interim mayor Montgomery Carmichael's shortened term at San Francisco's City Hall.

He had been appointed to fill a vacancy created when the elected mayor was promoted to the office of the state's lieutenant governor.

The mayoral selection process had been controversial—if not downright puzzling. Mr. Carmichael's name had been proposed, seemingly out of nowhere, several hours into a lengthy board of supervisors meeting dedicated to filling the opening. Despite the complete lack of consensus on all of the candidates that had previously been considered, Monty's nomination had sailed through with unanimous approval.

The city was still adjusting to the idea of Mayor Monty.

He was an odd choice for the caretaker position. With no previous governing experience and very little practical business knowledge to fall back on, he was ill prepared for the task of running such a large metropolis.

Beyond that, everyone thought him a bit weird.

But then, San Franciscans had grown accustomed to eccentricity from their mayors. The last man to hold the position had famously admitted to a lifelong frog phobia (following an inexplicable amphibian invasion of City Hall). Part of his psychological recovery had involved hiring a personal life coach, a slot that had been filled by the then-unknown Jackson Square art dealer Montgomery Carmichael.

It was one of the most bizarre stepping-stones into elected office that anyone could remember, even in the unorthodox history of Northern California.

Mere moments after the board of supervisors confirmed his appointment, Monty had been filmed in a wet suit and flippers, being chased out of San Francisco's Mountain Lake by an albino alligator who had escaped from the Academy of Sciences.

With that introduction, no one knew what to expect from Monty's brief tenure.

Even though the last two months had passed without incident, few expected the status quo to last.

But whatever shenanigans ensued, most viewed Mayor Carmichael as nothing more than a paperweight meant to hold down the position until the next round of formal voting could be held in the fall.

The Bay Area's political pundits gave him no chance of winning that election.

Of course, this was no deterrent to Monty.

• • •

MAYOR MONTY APPROACHED each spring day with the same zeal that he had applied from the start of his mayoral term. He was a blind optimist, one of those unique individuals who managed to view every stumble and fall as a success.

There was no fence he couldn't hurdle, no mountain he couldn't summit. Obstacles were simply ignored or imagined away.

In Monty's mind, he was the most popular mayor in San Francisco's recent history and the unquestioned front-runner in the upcoming election.

He stood in front of a mirror inside the second-floor apartment above his Jackson Square art studio and gazed at his reflection with smiling approval. He held up a wrist, admiring the frog-shaped cuff link attached to his dress shirt. Then he hooked a finger around the collar of his suit jacket and casually threw it over his shoulder.

"Who's that handsome guy?" he asked, striking a last pose.

With a tight pivot, he bounded down the stairs. The flat soles of his dress shoes slapped against the steps as he answered the question.

"Me!"

DESPITE HIS OVERWHELMING confidence, Monty wasn't taking November's upcoming election lightly. He had eight months left in office, and he planned to devote every waking moment to his campaign.

Monty had devised a number of slogans and strategies that he was fine-tuning for imminent release, but his primary election scheme was to gain public support and approval by affiliating himself with San Francisco's upcoming sailboat regatta. It sounded like a harebrained idea, but, to be fair, in the city's colorful history, mayors had been swept into office using far more absurd propaganda.

Later that summer, the America's Cup would be staged in the San Francisco Bay for the first time in the championship's history. Monty intended to plant himself front and center in every photo, video, and other publicity-related opportunity that arose.

Preparations for the event were well under way, thanks to the efforts of the last mayor, who had drummed up financial support for the necessary infrastructure along the city's shoreline and strong-armed supervisors to ensure the venue received the requisite permits to allow construction of the related pavilions.

In other words, the political heavy lifting had already been done. All that was left was for the interim mayor to take credit for the success.

The Monty train—or boat, as the case may be—was paddling full steam ahead.

It was his race to lose.

No one could convince him otherwise.

He wasn't the least bit worried that a serial killer might be circling his office, her needles at the ready for another kill.

Chapter 18

THE ADMINISTRATIVE ASSISTANT

ACROSS THE STREET from Monty's art studio, the occupants of the redbrick building that housed the Green Vase antique shop bustled about their regular morning activities.

Oscar's niece trudged sleepily down the stairs from the second-floor kitchen carrying a plastic mug filled with fresh-brewed coffee. Halfway down, she waved the cup beneath her nose, sniffing the caffeinated steam wafting out the vents in the lid.

Isabella looked up from the bottom of the stairwell and issued a series of sharp chirps. Her tail poked authoritatively into the air like the baton of a traffic guard leading a child through a crosswalk.

The cat took seriously her role in getting her person out of bed each morning and to their day job at City Hall.

The niece had reluctantly agreed to serve as the interim mayor's administrative assistant for the first few months of his term.

She had no real interest in the field of secretarial services.

Truth be told, she had no idea what running the mayor's office entailed—but then again, neither did Monty.

The niece had only taken the position as a means of conducting surveillance on the workspace that had previously been occupied by the woman now known as the Knitting Needle Ninja.

SO FAR, THE police had had little luck in tracking down City Hall's serial killer.

Mabel was last seen leaving the Capitol Building in Sacramento, where she had been working for her old boss in his new lieutenant governor's office. Luckily, news of her San Francisco crimes broke before any Sacramento interns could fall victim to her deadly slaying needles.

However, despite widespread media coverage and the Bay Area's entire population being on the lookout for the gray-haired administrative assistant, there had been no reported sightings.

The Ninja had vanished.

Or had she?

Uncle Oscar felt certain that Mabel would return to her regular hunting grounds. He'd organized a team to watch for her at City Hall.

The niece couldn't imagine Mabel would risk showing her face anywhere in San Francisco, much less City Hall, but she had grudgingly signed on for a short stint in the mayor's office.

She had to admit that, at first, it was a little creepy sitting for hours at the desk where Mabel had plotted so many murders.

That discomfort was minimal, she soon discovered, compared to the hassle of working with Mayor Monty on a daily basis.

THE NIECE PEERED out the antique shop's front glass windows across the street to where Monty stood waiting for his city-issued town car.

There was no escaping the man, she thought with a sigh.

She winced as Monty cupped a hand over his brow and tried to see through the showroom's front glass. He must have spied her shadow at the back of the room, because he suddenly lifted his hand and waved it in the air over his head.

Grimacing, the niece wiggled a few fingers in return.

If they ever did track down the elusive Knitting Needle Ninja, she would have to ask the woman how she'd pulled off such an effective disappearing act.

THE NIECE SET her coffee on a display table, turned away from the window, and bent to slip on her tennis shoes.

She wore a practical skirt and blouse, the uniform she had grudgingly chosen for her duties at City Hall. She'd acceded to the necessity of wearing business attire, but she'd drawn the line at panty hose. A pair of running tights would keep her otherwise bare legs warm until she reached the office.

One of the many benefits of living in casual California, she thought as she stood and adjusted the leggings. And then there was the bonus, she added wryly, of not caring if you were fired.

That would solve a lot of my problems, she mused as she picked up the coffee cup and took a tentative sip of the hot liquid.

The lid wasn't securely fastened, and a few drops spilled onto the floor, narrowly missing Isabella's head.

At the cat's scolding chatter, the niece noticed a spot of coffee on her blouse.

"That's not too bad, is it?" she asked, wiping the smudge with her hand.

Isabella gave her person a disapproving stare.

"I mean, really. No one will see it."

The cat's orange ears turned sideways in disagreement.

"Oh, all right, I'll go change."

Warbling her concurrence, Isabella followed her person back upstairs to the third-floor bedroom.

The tip end of her tail snapped the air with importance. The niece would need feline guidance to pick out a suitable replacement shirt.

A FEW MINUTES later, Isabella and her person—clad in a clean blouse—returned to the showroom.

Isabella padded circles around the niece as she opened a closet and removed a large green stroller. After wrangling with the various levers and latches, the niece unfolded the contraption to its operational configuration.

Sturdy nylon fabric had been wrapped around a light-weight metal frame to create a stroller that was specifically adapted for pet transport. The passenger compartment had a mesh cover that could be zipped over the stroller's furry occupants, safely securing them inside.

While initially skeptical of the device, Isabella now enjoyed her stroller outings. She lifted herself up on her haunches and inspected the interior before issuing her formal approval.

"Mrao."

"Where's Rupert?" the niece asked, looking around the shop.

She was unable to interpret Isabella's muttered response from inside the stroller.

"Hmm . . ."

The niece conducted a quick search of the showroom.

Antiques from San Francisco's Gold Rush era took up much of the space. During his time running the Green Vase, her uncle had amassed a wide array of historic relics.

There were mining tools, gambling paraphernalia, and a number of gold-related fashion items. Most notable was Oscar's collection of gold teeth, which Barbary Coast dentists had been commissioned to insert into the Forty-Niners' mouths. In the fashion of the day, nothing conveyed success more effectively than a gold-toothed smile.

Next to a collection of rudimentary tooth extraction devices stood a leather dental recliner that had been used during the gruesome procedures.

The niece often sat in the recliner to relax, read a book, or ponder her uncle's latest schemes. It was a surprisingly comfortable place to think—despite the immeasurable pain that had been endured by the chair's previous occupants.

THE SOUND OF scrambling claws and pounding cat feet echoed down from the third-floor bathroom, growing louder as the noisemaker charged down the steps to the building's midlevel and romped across the kitchen.

Hands on her hips, the niece glanced up at the ceiling, anticipating the cause of the commotion.

Moments later, Rupert rounded the corner at the bottom of the stairs and bounced into the showroom.

He'd just completed his morning routine in the red igloo litter box, including the ever-important spastic litter box dance.

Stopping in front of the niece, he threw his body into a head-to-toe vibration, shaking loose the last pieces of litter still clinging to his fuzzy coat.

"*Wrao-wao*," he called out when he was finished, announcing his arrival.

Isabella peeked out of the stroller to give her brother a disparaging look. Rupert happily allowed himself to be scooped up by the niece and set inside the passenger compartment. Undeterred by Isabella's frosty demeanor, he leaned over and gave his sister an adoring lick across the face.

Smiling at Rupert's antics, the niece zipped up the carriage netting and spun the stroller toward the door.

Pausing by the entrance, she stuffed her raincoat into the

stroller's side pocket, a precaution against San Francisco's unpredictable spring weather.

As the niece nudged the stroller through the iron-framed doorway, the town car assigned to drive Monty to City Hall stopped in front of his art studio.

He had offered several times to give the niece and her cats a ride to the office, but she had steadfastly refused. She shuddered to think of the gossip that would ensue if she arrived at City Hall in the same vehicle as her boss. She received enough attention for bringing the cats into work with her, but that had been one of the many conditions she'd negotiated for her short-term employment.

As she set off down the street, Isabella's guiding chirp floated up from the stroller. They had walked the route numerous times, but the cat never failed to issue her navigational commands. It was her duty to make sure the stroller didn't veer off course.

Rupert, meanwhile, snuggled into the carriage blankets, ready for his morning stroller snooze.

The town car pulled up beside the niece at the first corner. The rear passenger window rolled down, and Monty stuck out his head.

"Sure you don't want a lift?" he asked brightly.

Before the niece could answer, Isabella called out a negative reply.

Even the cat was concerned about the damage that might be done to her reputation if she was seen riding in a car with Mayor Monty.

"Mrao."

Chapter 19

FRIED CHICKEN DONUTS

AFTER A TWO-MILE walk, Isabella announced their arrival at City Hall.

"Wrao."

"Yes, I know," the niece replied as she lifted the stroller up the building's front steps. "We're here."

Isabella pushed her head against the netting that covered the passenger compartment, trying to see out over the front of the carriage. A constant string of feline chatter warbled up from the stroller. So far, the niece had yet to tip over the contraption while the cats were inside it, but Isabella wasn't taking any chances.

A security guard pulled open the door and held it for the niece while she steered the carriage through. The green nylon cat stroller—and its feline occupants—were by now well known to the security staff.

"Good morning, Rupert and Isabella," the guard said as he swallowed a bite from his morning donut. He wiped powdered sugar from his lips and nodded to his colleague standing behind the security scanner inside.

"Hardest-working cats I know."

The niece smiled her greeting and guided the stroller up to the security counter. The second guard waved the stroller through with only a quick glance at the interior.

As the niece reached the opposite side of the scanner's walk-through portal, the first guard bent toward the zipped netting and held out a small chunk of donut.

"Hey, there, Rupert. You want to give this a try?"

Hearing the cat's lips smack with anticipation, the niece quickly intervened.

"Sorry," she said, rolling the stroller sideways to block the transfer. "That's not on his diet."

The guard peered through the mesh cover and gave Rupert a conspiring wink.

"That's right, I forgot. I'll have to get a *fried chicken* donut for you, won't I, little buddy?"

"How did you know about . . ." the niece began, but then stopped.

With a sigh, she moved the stroller toward the main foyer.

"Monty."

MUTTERING ABOUT HER gossipy neighbor and the donut-pushing guard, the niece braked in front of the building's first-floor elevator bank and pushed the call button for an upward-traveling cart.

With a *ding*, the closest set of heavy metal doors slid open. The niece rolled the cats over the threshold and turned to wait for the unit to close.

Before the panels could shut, a second woman strode briskly inside.

"Morning, Wanda," the niece said, suppressing a groan.

Every morning, it seemed, she shared the elevator with the administrative assistant for the president of the board of supervisors.

Wanda Williams greeted her with a cold accusing stare, and the niece wondered, not for the first time, why she'd ever agreed to this stint at City Hall. The place was a thicket of unexploded land mines, and the niece felt as if she stepped on one each time she entered the building.

Wanda's bruised ego was an easy fault wire to trip.

She had applied for the position of Monty's admin after he was appointed to the interim mayor's slot, and she was still bitter that the niece had been awarded the job.

Wanda had thick black hair, which she wore in a short bouffant style that lifted several inches off her forehead. Silver streaks streamed out from each temple, the gray highlighted by the pearl drop earrings hanging from her earlobes.

The woman clearly disapproved of everything the niece did, starting, of course, with the fact that she brought her cats into work each day. But there was little Wanda could do about that since Mayor Carmichael had officially sanctioned the felines' presence.

She glared down at the stroller and sniffed derisively at the occupants.

Curled up in the blankets dreaming about the mythical concoction of fried chicken donuts, Rupert was unaware of the snub. Isabella, however, sat stiffly in her seat, the hair on the back of her neck spiked with distrust.

Their eyes met, Isabella's and those of the woman with the wounded pride.

Wanda was the first to look away.

The elevator *ding*ed again, signifying they'd reached the second floor.

The niece smiled to herself. She would happily yield her position as soon as she was relieved of Knitting Needle Ninja duty.

Until then, Wanda was destined to lose her daily staring contests with Isabella.

Chapter 20

THE SOUP CART VENDOR

THE NIECE ROLLED the cat stroller into the second-floor mayor's office suite, unaware that another member of the Ninja surveillance team had just arrived through City Hall's subterranean service entrance.

A vendor cart laden with several gallon-sized metal vats squeaked along a dark basement hallway. Barely visible behind the heavy load, an elderly cook slowly pushed the cart down the corridor.

The cart carried eight different soups, each one prepared from scratch the previous evening. This being San Francisco, there needed to be at least three vegetarian options. Each serving came with a piece of fresh bread that was sliced to order on a wooden cutting board mounted to the cart's front end.

Once the chef reached City Hall's main floor, he would plug the cart's electrical cord into a designated wall socket. Heating elements attached to the vats would then simmer the contents under low heat for the next several hours. By late morning, a tempting smell would filter up through the rotunda to the second-floor offices.

The Soup Vendor, as he was known throughout the Civic Center Plaza, had only serviced City Hall for a couple of months, but his hearty meals had quickly become a staple for the building's office workers and the multitudes of tourists who stopped in to marvel at the ornate interior.

No one knew much about the grumpy old man behind the soup cart. He wore a cap pulled down over his eyes, and he rarely spoke to his hungry patrons. Each vat was clearly labeled; the price for a generous serving of soup was displayed on the cart's front panels. There was little need for extraneous communication, and the vendor typically didn't respond to casual chitchat.

For Uncle Oscar, the soup cart was the perfect cover for keeping a close watch over his niece—and the rest of City Hall.

He was convinced that this is where the Ninja would resurface.

It was only a matter of time.

He only hoped that he lived long enough to capture the killer.

OSCAR HAD LIVED a long eventful life, full of fond memories of meals shared with his eclectic group of friends, his niece, and her two cats. The years he'd spent puttering around in his beloved antique shop had been some of his happiest. Overall, he was pleased with the way his life had turned out, tickled by its many twists and turns, satisfied with the end result.

But he knew he had reached his last days.

The cumulative effect of several illnesses had deteriorated his health, and his ailing heart struggled to perform its pumping duties. He'd only recently regained the strength to walk after the latest bout of illness in January. The soup cart was often a prop to aid in his balance. He kept a wooden cane tucked into the metal side railing to use when he needed to step away from the cart's support.

Oscar had lived a shadowy existence for years. The time would soon come for him to fade into a permanent retirement. He was almost ready.

He had one last mission to complete. Then he would let his weary body rest.

WITH A GRUNT, Oscar heaved the soup cart out of a service elevator and onto City Hall's main level. Breathing heavily, he guided it across the marble floor to the edge of the rotunda. The soup vendor's reserved electrical plug was located on a side wall, next to a street lamp–style light fixture.

Gripping the cart with one hand, an ache in his back with the other, he stared up at the dome. The soaring structure was shaped like the interior of an eggshell, studded with circular tiers of decorative detailing that culminated in a faux ceiling. A tiny round orifice in the roof led to a gilded cupola at the very top of the building.

After craning to squint up at the rotunda ceiling, Oscar's gaze slowly drifted downward. His eyes paused on the windows that framed the upper walls beneath the dome. A section of stained glass had been mounted in the center of each wide pane. The decorative glass featured the outline of a dual-masted packet ship, the first European vessel to enter the San Francisco Bay.

He lingered only a moment on the image of the *San Carlos* before his line of sight dropped from the window to the second-floor platform at the upper end of the building's central marble staircase.

The pained expression on Oscar's face had nothing to do with his aching back. It was caused by the memory of the gory scene he had stumbled across a few months earlier.

As he focused on the spot where the Ninja's last intern victim had been murdered, he recalled the moment he recognized the signature wound marks on the body—and realized that Mabel had become a serial killer.

THE SOUP CONTAINERS began to warm, and the various mixtures of vegetables, broth, and meat started to release their flavors.

Oscar checked the cart's heat settings. Lifting the metal lids, he gave the contents of each vat a thorough stirring. Then he stepped back and wiped his hands on the apron he had tied over his navy blue collared shirt and matching pants.

The cart and its cookers were safe to leave for a few minutes. He would make a quick pass through the building, his regular morning search for any sign of Mabel.

The cane's rubber tip squeaked against the marble floor as he lumbered toward the central staircase. The climb required strenuous effort, but the view from the elevated center provided a unique perspective and, in his opinion, was well worth the work.

Halfway up the steps, he noticed a man walking briskly toward the mayor's office suite on the rotunda's upper south side. The distinctive left-limp gait of reporter Hoxton Finn was easy to pick out. The hobble was the result of an injury Hox had incurred several years earlier during a visit to the Los Angeles Zoo. He and his estranged spouse had received a behind-the-scenes tour of a Komodo dragon exhibit. The session was abruptly terminated when the ungracious lizard nipped off the end of Hox's left toe. The marriage followed a similar course, culminating in divorce shortly thereafter.

Hox didn't let the amputated toe slow him down. If anything, the impairment only made him walk faster, as a means of compensation. The residual pain he dulled by smacking his notebook against his left leg, a popping sound that could routinely be heard throughout City Hall's marble-filled interior.

The reporter's relentless energy was more than a reflection of his professional work ethic. He had made the Ninja case his personal cause, devoting numerous columns to the ongoing investigation, the lingering questions, and the societal threat.

Hox, too, was on the hunt for the psychopathic secretary.

Oscar rubbed the scruff on his chin as Hox passed the elevator bank and turned for the reception entrance to the mayor's suite. With so many watchful eyes focused on City Hall, surely Mabel would be identified the moment she ventured inside.

But then, he reflected with a disconcerted grunt, it had been far too easy for him to slip into the building using his soup vendor disguise.

There was nothing left to do but wait for the next clue.

He feared it would be a bloody one.

• • •

AS OSCAR STOOD at the midpoint of the central staircase, pondering the possible ways Mabel might infiltrate City Hall, he was unaware of how accurate he'd been in his intuitions.

The Ninja had indeed returned to the building where she'd started her killing spree.

And she had made the connection between the surly soup vendor and the former antique dealer who had publicly connected her to the knifed knitting needles.

She hoped to find a few more interns on which to practice, but Oscar was now her main target.

Chapter 21

THE DESK

THE NIECE PARKED the cat-filled stroller inside the reception area for the mayor's office suite, pulled shut the main door, and began to unpack for the day's work session.

The first order of business was to immediately unzip the stroller to release the cats—or, at least, the female half of the pair.

Isabella was very particular about the proper order of the morning activities. Once they'd reached their destination, the cat's patience with being cooped up inside the stroller came to an end. Any delay in her being freed from the passenger compartment was met with a low growl that could quickly escalate to an offended hiss.

"Here you go, Issy."

The niece flipped open the cover and stepped out of the way.

A white blur leapt through the opening and landed delicately on the red carpet. Nose sniffing, ears and tail erect, Isabella set off on her daily tour of the office suite. She completed a brief inspection of the front reception and then slipped through the open door to Monty's inner quarters.

The niece followed Isabella into the room, which was missing its mayor.

Monty had arrived earlier, having covered the distance from Jackson Square much quicker in the town car. The niece saw his raincoat hanging on a rack in the corner.

"He's probably bopping around the building," the niece mused. She turned to follow Isabella back to the reception area. "And talking to security guards about fried chicken donuts."

The phrase elicited a sleepy grunt from the stroller. Rupert still snoozed in the carriage blankets, but certain words could penetrate his sleep.

Isabella assumed a watchful stance on a filing cabinet beside the niece's desk. Looking down from her perch, she issued a confirming opinion as to Monty's likely whereabouts.

"Mrao."

THE NIECE KICKED off her tennis shoes and socks, slipped off the running tights from beneath her skirt, and slid on a pair of flats she kept stored in a desk drawer. She pulled out her ponytail, smoothed her hair with her fingers, and retied it in a neater knot.

There, she thought with a shrug, *I guess I look somewhat presentable*. That was the extent of her effort to clean herself up for the office—or anywhere else, for that matter. She took a natural, low-maintenance approach to her physical appearance. She'd never developed the hair and makeup skills that seemed to come so easily to other women.

What you see is what you get, she added ruefully.

Returning to the stroller, she bent to scoop up Rupert. One furry eyelid cracked open as the niece carried the snoring lump to a wire cage set up in a corner of the room. The inside was outfitted with a cat bed and a travel-sized igloo-shaped litter box.

Most of the time, the cage was propped open so that Rupert and Isabella could lounge as they liked in the reception area or Monty's office. Monty didn't receive many visitors, and the suite's main door generally remained shut. Plus, having spent several years hanging out in the Jackson Square antique shop, the cats were accustomed to occasional foot traffic.

Leaning into the cage, the niece rolled Rupert onto the cat bed. He stretched his body into a long arc and yawned contentedly.

She shook her head at the cat's dreamy lip smack.

"I don't have the heart to tell him there's no such thing as fried chicken donuts."

From the stroller's various side pockets, the niece removed a small bag of cat food, a few cat toys, and the day's reading material: a dog-eared text on the Europeans' first foray into the San Francisco Bay that her uncle had mailed to her.

So far, her work duties had been pretty minimal. She fielded the occasional phone call, organized Monty's few appointments, and reviewed his official mail.

The last category provided a regular source of humor. Monty was the type of public figure to attract bizarre constituent correspondence.

The letters included all manner of off-the-wall suggestions for improving the city, various critiques on Monty's well-known cuff link collection, and, perhaps most disturbing, a number of elaborately drafted marriage proposals.

The last category, the niece flagged for City Hall security.

Even on a heavy mail day, the niece could generally complete her secretarial duties within the first hour. That left plenty of time for reading.

So far, she'd perused several chapters in the history book dedicated to the *San Carlos*, the first European vessel to pass through the Golden Gate, but it was slow going. Her uncle had marked up many of the pages, and she'd spent hours trying to decipher his cramped handwriting.

She was still puzzling over the comments he'd left in the margins, but she gathered he thought the writer had missed several important elements in the recounting.

AS FOR HER primary purpose for taking the admin position—that is, keeping an eye out for Mabel or any valuable information she might have left behind—the niece had little to report.

She had explored every inch of the mayor's office suite, but she'd found nothing of use. No evidence remained of the woman who had staffed the reception area for the last six years.

Mabel's desk had been wiped clean, the filing cabinets purged of all but the most routine documentation. There were no trinkets or mementos, not even a stray bobby pin wedged into the corner of a drawer or a seam in the carpet.

The woman who had left her last murder weapon strapped beneath the center planking of the mayor's desk had wiped the rest of the office space completely clean.

The niece had all but given up on her assigned mission. She was on the verge of suggesting that she return to the Green Vase and cede her position to the wretched Wanda— until she took her seat in the reception area that morning.

THE MOMENT THE niece settled into her chair, her nose began to tickle. At first, there was just a faint trace of odor, difficult to identify.

But the scent quickly intensified, increasing in potency.

Soon, an aromatic cloud of lemony-sweet perfume swirled around the niece, clogging her sinuses.

"What is that smell?" she demanded, fighting off a sneeze. "And where is it coming from?" She pulled open each of the desk drawers and dug through the contents, to no avail. She was soon on her hands and knees, crawling beneath the center console, searching for the source.

Isabella glanced down from the filing cabinet. She blinked knowingly and then meted out a cryptic reply.

"*Mrao.*"

UNABLE TO FIND any scent-emitting object within the desk or its immediate radius, the niece switched tactics. She dug into a sack of cleaning supplies from an office closet and began attacking the invading smell with a can of air freshener.

She sprayed the desk's top surface and inside each of its drawers, but the aerosol's application had no effect.

She was puzzling at the product description written on the canister when Hoxton Finn walked through the reception's main door.

The reporter was one of the few regular visitors to the mayor's office suite—despite being allergic to cats.

Hox looked sternly down at the wire cage as Rupert strutted out of the igloo-shaped litter box. He took a step back as the cat shook loose litter from his fur, sending a few sandy particles out onto the floor.

Isabella called out a warning to the niece, who was still fixated on the label for the apparently ineffective air cleaner.

Stifling a sneeze, the niece looked up.

Hox nodded to Isabella with a grudging half smile and then wrinkled his nose.

"She's back, isn't she?" he said dourly.

Frowning, the niece set the canister on her desk. "Who?"

With a grunt, Hox popped his notebook against his left leg. "I've only known one woman to wear that particular perfume."

The niece cringed as he sniffed the air and scowled.

"Mabel."

Chapter 22

THE WEDDING PLANNER

DIRECTLY BELOW THE mayor's office suite, in a foyer outside the City Hall office that issued marriage licenses, a small group gathered for a morning wedding ceremony.

The bride wore a sleeveless white silk dress whose length fell just below her knees. Kid gloves covered her hands, and a short mesh veil had been stretched over her face. She fiddled nervously with her matching white purse, opening and closing the clasp.

Standing beside her, the groom started to sweat in his rented tuxedo. He shoved his hand into his pocket, thumbing the velvet cover of a tiny ring box, checking and rechecking that the box and its contents were secure.

The rest of the wedding party milled about nearby as the group waited patiently—or in some cases impatiently—for the wedding planner to arrive.

AFTER THE GRUESOME murder of the mayoral intern last November, there had been a temporary lull in City Hall weddings. The previous flood of daily nuptials had slowed to a trickle. The ceremonial rotunda at the top of the central marble staircase, which had held up to fifty ceremonies over the course of a busy Friday afternoon, had been left vacant.

No couple wanted to risk jinxing their marital future with such a macabre association.

But once the Knitting Needle Ninja was identified as the intern's murderer and the bizarre nature of the crime propelled it into nationwide celebrity status, City Hall regained its popularity with the wedding crowds. The notoriety tipped the scales and, if anything, the ceremonial rotunda was now a more popular location for tying the knot than before.

The building's elaborate interior and the low cost of getting hitched beneath the public dome, combined with the infamous setting, made for an irresistible locale.

The reasoning had apparently shifted: if the marriage was destined for acrimony and divorce, at least let the union ceremony be memorable.

THE BRIDE'S FATHER checked his watch. Their fifteen-minute time slot was rapidly approaching, but the wedding planner was still nowhere to be seen. The woman had come highly recommended, particularly for City Hall weddings, but he was starting to worry. If today's ceremony fell through, he feared he would be on the hook for a formal church service and a much more expensive reception.

He grinned reassuringly at his daughter, and then stepped around a corner to make a phone call.

At precisely ten A.M. on the dot, not a second before, the wedding coordinator emerged from a side hallway and purposefully but politely approached the soon-to-be-betrothed couple.

"There she is." The father sighed with relief, sliding his phone into his coat pocket.

The bride and groom registered a somewhat more startled response.

The wedding planner looked like a human cartoon. She wore an oversized blond wig, styled with retro curly waves, and a tight-fitting knit sweater stretched over a fake inflated chest. The woman's lips were painted with bright red lipstick, and her face was covered with enough makeup to make her age impossible to determine—other than that she was middle-aged.

Her neck bore a light, barely discernible spritz of perfume, a lemony-sweet scent that lingered in the air.

"Good morning, ladies and gentlemen. Welcome to City Hall."

She smiled through a set of gleaming false teeth that gave her mouth an eerie symmetry.

"My name is Marilyn Monroe."

THE COSTUME (AND related shtick) was a not-so-subtle reference to Marilyn Monroe's 1954 marriage to Joe DiMaggio, which took place inside San Francisco's City Hall. Theirs was a brief union. The celebrity pair wed in January; by October, the couple had filed for divorce. But the ceremony was one of the most famous in the rotunda's long history.

If the current bride and groom were surprised by the wedding planner's attire, she was exactly what the bride's father had expected.

"Miss Monroe, so glad to see you." He pointed at the watch strapped to his wrist. "We're anxious to get started."

"Of course," she replied, in a voice that sounded oddly altered. "Let's head up to the ceremonial rotunda. The judge will meet us there to officiate. The photographer is already in position."

MOMENTS LATER, MARILYN'S sensible soled dress shoes—the only sensible piece of clothing on her body—clicked across the smooth marble floor as she led the wedding party through the rotunda and up the central marble staircase.

Her outrageous outfit drew only a few curious glances and the occasional shrug. Such was the nature of San Francisco and, indeed, City Hall during wedding hours. The Marilyn Monroe impersonator was far from the most unusual character traipsing through the building that morning.

As the group reached the top of the stairs, the bride's father called out, "Is this where they found the murdered intern?"

The others fell silent. The bride clutched her purse like a security blanket, and the groom's face paled. But the father pressed on with his inquiry, undeterred by the other's obvious discomfort.

"Is this where the Knitting Needle Ninja got him?"

The wedding planner turned, so that the light streaming through the rotunda's upper windows cast its rays across the pancake coating on her face. Her eyes flickered with a strange mix of bemusement and intensity.

"That's what they say."

• • •

BELOW THE WEDDING party, on the rotunda's first floor, the soup vendor looked up from his cart. A strange lemony scent had just floated past, the smell almost masked by those of the simmering soups.

Oscar hobbled toward the staircase and stared curiously up at the bride, the groom, the officiating judge, and their assorted family members. He studied the group standing in the ceremonial rotunda for several minutes, scratching the stubble beneath his chin, before returning to his station.

The wedding organizer, positioned at the rear of the second-floor platform, near the Harvey Milk bust and a pair of stone columns, had been blocked from his view.

Chapter 23

AN IMPROMPTU TÊTE-À-TÊTE

THE NIECE SHOOK her head as Hoxton Finn scowled at the perfume-scented air above the reception desk.

"I don't see how Mabel could be responsible for this, this . . ." She stopped for a high-pitched sneeze. "This *smell*. I can assure you, she hasn't been in here today."

She wrinkled up her nose, fighting, unsuccessfully, to tamp down a second sneeze.

"Ah-*choo*!"

Grabbing a tissue, she blew her nose. Eyes watering, she announced, "That's it."

The niece picked up the air freshener canister and resumed her efforts to eradicate the lemony perfume. She pressed down on the nozzle and expanded the spray zone out from her desk, gradually encompassing the entire reception area.

Isabella glared down from the filing cabinet, conveying her disapproval of this tactic. Rupert scuttled inside the igloo litter box to hide.

Even Hox dove behind the desk to avoid being hit by the aerosol's thick mist.

Monty opened the main door and took a direct spray to the face.

The niece dropped the canister. Her mouth fell open in surprise.

"Oops."

The mayor blinked, shook his head like a dog who'd been given a bath, and smiled.

"Smells like a fresh spring day," he said brightly, wiping a handkerchief across his cheeks.

The niece frowned, puzzling. The lemony perfume had departed, but she had the sneaking suspicion that its removal wasn't due to her overapplication of air cleaner.

"Yeah, it does." She craned her neck toward the ceiling, trying to figure out what had generated the smell—and what had caused it to suddenly disappear.

Monty was too excited by other matters to be distracted by the near-blinding aerosol attack.

"Hold on to your socks, folks. I just got out of a fantastic meeting. *This* is going to change everything!"

Brow furrowed, the niece set the canister on the desk and squinted at Monty's blank calendar. "You had a meeting?"

"Well, more like an impromptu tête-à-tête," he replied with an impish grin. "I ran into the Baron at his favorite breakfast spot."

Hox muttered a correction. "You mean you stalked him to the diner and set up an ambush." The reporter leaned against the niece's desk, whipped out his notepad, and began scribbling. "I bet the Baron has a new favorite breakfast joint picked out by tomorrow morning."

Before the niece could comment, Monty propped open the reception door, stepped back outside, and retrieved a three-by-five-foot framed poster.

"Tadah!" With a flourish, he turned the poster toward the niece and Hox. "Look, I got the Baron to autograph the glass on the bottom corner."

The poster was an advert for the upcoming America's Cup regatta race. The majority of the frame was taken up by an image of the high-tech sailboat for the US team, its supertall sail pillowed with wind, its hulls tilted out of the water, and its wet-suited crew members clinging to the top netting for dear life.

Monty set the poster on the floor across from the niece's desk. Then he stepped back to admire his handiwork.

"What do you think, eh?" He skipped to the side of the desk and gave Hox a gleeful slap across the back. "I told the Baron I was a huge sailing fan. When I showed him this poster, he couldn't help but bring me on board. I've just been named an official honorary member of the America's Cup publicity committee."

RUPERT EMERGED TENTATIVELY from the igloo, curious to see what all the commotion was about. Crouched to the ground in case there was a second aerosol bombardment, he sneaked out the cage opening and across the floor to the poster. His fluffy orange and white tail whirled through the air as he sniffed the frame's bottom corner. His snorkeling picked up the scents from the diner where Monty had lain in wait, hoping to spring his poster on the Baron.

After sifting through an assortment of bacon, egg, and coffee odors, Rupert gazed up at the mayor in disappointment. No fried chicken donuts. With a yawn, he turned back toward the cat bed.

He would speak with Monty about tracking down this delicacy—once he'd completed his late-morning nap.

"THIS IS GOING to be huge. Epic. Enormous."

Monty paced back and forth in front of his audience, nodding as if they were reciprocating his comments with enthusiastic support. "This fall, we'll print new business cards. No more Interim Mayor Monty." He tapped the poster with confidence. "I'm going to be elected in a landslide."

Hox cocked an eyebrow. The niece pursed her lips.

The mayor scampered into his office and quickly returned with a hammer, nail, and hanger hook. He pressed his ear against the wall and thumped its surface, searching for a stud on which to hang the poster.

"Wait—why are you putting that in here?" the niece asked as he selected a mounting location across from her desk.

Monty tapped the nail into the wall with his hammer. With the hook secured, he looked over his shoulder at the niece.

"So that everyone who enters will know that San Francisco—and its charming mayor—are sailing fans."

The niece drummed her fingers against the desk. "It's kind of an elitist sport, isn't it?"

Monty wagged his index finger in the air. "No, no, no. We're bringing sailing to the masses. There will be world-wide television coverage for the event, journalists reporting from every major news organization, and spectators from across the globe. This is now my most important initiative: showcasing our city during the regatta."

Pausing to stick out his chest, Monty added, "I'm even going to take sailing lessons."

"That sounds dangerous," the niece said, only partially in jest.

Isabella had been skeptically observing the proceedings from her filing cabinet perch. She voiced her first opinion of the session.

"Mrao."

Ignoring them both, Monty lifted the poster onto the wall.

"Oh, and I forgot to tell you. We're organizing an event for the local sponsors." Stepping back from the poster, he reached into his pocket, pulled out a cocktail napkin covered in blurry ink, and tossed it onto the niece's desk.

The niece frowned suspiciously. "By *we*, you mean . . ."

"You!" Monty slapped his hands together. "Come on, let's get busy. Chop, chop!"

Hox closed his notepad and moved toward the door. "That's a winning idea you've got there, Mayor."

Monty failed to notice the sarcasm in the reporter's voice.

"We'll send you an invite, Hox!"

As Hox disappeared through the exit, the niece grimaced at Monty's ubiquitous—and misleading—use of the pronoun *we*.

Then she read the instructions Monty had written on the cocktail napkin from the diner and groaned.

Her workload had just increased substantially.

Chapter 24

THE RULE BOOK

THE NEXT MORNING, the niece and her cat-filled stroller set off on their regular trek to City Hall an hour early. She'd spent the previous afternoon sorting through the details for Monty's upcoming America's Cup event, but she'd made only a small dent in the related to-do list before heading home.

Monty's constant pestering, questioning, and additions to the project hadn't helped matters.

Navigating through the security line, she heaved out a weary sigh. She'd tossed and turned the night before thinking about the peculiar perfume that had infiltrated the mayor's office suite.

She couldn't stop wondering what had generated the odor, why it had suddenly disappeared, and if it would reoccur.

The most critical question, of course, was whether this signified the return of the Knitting Needle Ninja.

DESPITE THE NIECE'S early arrival, she still found herself sharing an elevator with Wanda Williams.

I can't catch a break, she thought as the woman's hand stopped the door at its half-closed position and forced it to reopen.

Wanda had something more on her mind than her regular beef about cats being brought into City Hall. Once inside the elevator car, the niece's self-appointed rival didn't even glance down at the stroller.

Rupert appeared not to notice that he was being ignored. While passing through the security scanners minutes earlier, the guard had repeated his tease about fried chicken donuts. The cat had a dreamy, faraway look in his eyes as he smacked his lips, trying to imagine the taste.

The niece smiled ruefully. One day, she would have to take on the difficult task of explaining to Rupert that this food item simply did not exist.

Alert in the carriage next to her distracted brother, Isabella sniffed her offense. It was poor form for Wanda to deprive the cat of the opportunity to win another staring contest.

The elevator door finally closed, sealing them all inside. Wanda shifted her weight, focusing her attention squarely on the niece, who squirmed before offering a forced greeting.

"Morning, Wanda."

The niece sensed she'd walked into a premeditated ambush. Wanda must have been hanging out downstairs—for who knew how long—waiting to pounce.

Wanda cut to the point.

"Isn't it time you hired an intern?"

"An intern?" the niece sputtered. She'd guessed Wanda had some sort of agenda that morning, but she hadn't expected this. "Why would I hire an intern?"

Wanda blew out a dismissive *pfft* as if the answer was obvious. "Every mayor has at least one intern. It's in the rule book, dear."

Ah, the rule book, the niece thought sourly. *Of course.*

The oft-cited rule book was trotted out any time the niece did anything outside the norm or, more specifically, failed to follow Wanda's interpretation of the established protocol. Despite making several requests, the niece had never actually seen the vaunted text. She suspected the rule book only existed in Wanda's head.

In past conversations, the niece had struggled to counter Wanda's rule book trump card. Being a newcomer to the ranks of City Hall's administrative staff, she was at a distinct disadvantage in such debates.

But in this instance, the niece figured she had an irrefutable exception.

"Yes, well, uh, we've decided to put off getting an intern for now . . . you know, because of what happened to the last one."

The elevator opened to the second floor, and the niece shoved the cat stroller out into the foyer.

Surely the specter of the last murdered intern would put a stop to Wanda's meddling, at least on this issue.

Not wanting to extend the discussion, the niece sped to the front entrance of the mayor's office suite. As she pulled out her key to unlock the door, she looked over her shoulder and gave the other woman a limp wave.

Wanda shot back a pout before stomping off toward the supervisor's wing on the opposite end of the building.

THE NIECE WHEELED the cat stroller into the reception area, unzipped the net cover, and got to work on the preparations for Monty's event.

She assumed she'd successfully deflected Wanda on the intern issue—until Monty walked into the office an hour later.

He stopped to visit briefly with Rupert (who was asleep) and Isabella (who gave him an icy stare), before turning toward the niece's desk. He twiddled his fingers in the air, as if searching for the appropriate words to convey his wishes.

It was then that the niece realized she had underestimated Wanda.

The other secretary had done an end run around her and targeted the mayor directly—through her own boss, the president of the board of supervisors.

Monty was nothing if not highly prone to suggestion.

He pumped his thin eyebrows and leaned across the desk. "So . . . when are we going to hire an intern?"

Chapter 25

CUTTHROAT COMPETITION

INFORMATION TRAVELED FAST through City Hall's marbled corridors. Spats between supervisors, the forging of secret political alliances, even the day's selection of soups that would be available in the rotunda vendor cart—all of these details circulated efficiently among the inhabitants of the domed building.

Word of the mayoral intern opening disseminated at lightning speed.

By midafternoon, the niece had received a six-inch-high stack of résumés from interested applicants.

That the last person to hold the job had been brutally murdered had done little to dampen interest in the position. Short-term memory was apparently an innate survival instinct for those with political aspirations.

The niece flipped through the pages of carefully typed cover letters, marveling at the candidates' qualifications. Even for such a minor, entry-level position, the competition was cutthroat.

For the first time, she began to appreciate how skillfully

Mabel had sifted through her potential victims. She must have surveyed hundreds of intern applications to find individuals with just the right combination of personality and social circumstance so that his or her later disappearance might be easily explained away.

BEYOND THE GRUESOME precedent of the murdered interns, there was another factor that might have deterred applicants from applying for the new position. The niece was surprised that so many intelligent and apparently well-respected people were putting themselves forward to work for Interim Mayor Carmichael.

Monty's, ahem, eccentricities were known far and wide. He had been criticized in the local newspapers and on television news shows. Entire websites were devoted to Monty-related satire and mimicry. The Internet was littered with embarrassing photos and video clips.

No one—except the interim mayor himself—gave Monty any chance of success in the next election.

The niece puzzled over the résumé pile.

Surely, all of these applicants could find better things to do than spending the next couple of months working for Monty.

The niece grimaced at this last thought.

She certainly could.

"I DON'T KNOW, Isabella," the niece said as she plowed through the stack. She looked up at the filing cabinet. "We don't even have a job description. What am I supposed to do with this intern once we hire him or her?"

Isabella had draped her body over the cabinet's top edge so that she could peer down at the papers. In response to the niece's question, she sat upright and looked pointedly toward the America's Cup poster on the reception wall.

"Yeah, okay," the niece replied, pondering the suggestion. "You might have something there."

Isabella emitted a disgruntled warble at the implication that her idea might be anything less than extremely useful.

Issuing a series of sharp clicking sounds, Isabella hopped down to the desk to assist directly in the résumé review. She pawed through the papers, her pink nose sniffing the smells associated with each sheet as she spread them across the desk.

The niece threw her hands up, capitulating.

"Okay, I guess this is one way we could handle the selection process."

After a lengthy sorting guided by Isabella's expert analysis, the pile was narrowed down to three candidates who would be brought in for interviews.

The niece picked up the phone and began to dial the first number on the short list.

"Well, here goes nothing."

Chapter 26

THE LOTTERY WINNER

THE FIRST INTERN candidate was camped outside the mayor's office suite when the niece and the cats arrived the next morning—even though her interview wasn't scheduled until later that afternoon.

The excited young woman raced up to the niece as soon as she exited the elevator. She had light brown skin, full lips, and thick black hair wound into a heavy braid that fell midway down her back. Her floor-length sari swished with each hurried step.

The niece wondered how she'd been recognized as the mayor's administrative assistant—until she realized that she was likely the only person walking through City Hall pushing a cat-filled stroller.

Regardless, she was unprepared for the encounter.

"Well, hello," the niece managed to get out before the eager woman began her pitch.

"Hi, my name's Alberta. Alberta Conway—I've applied for the intern position. I'm a big fan of Mayor Carmichael. I've been following his career for years, all the way back to his life coaching days. He's a wise man, a wise man indeed."

The niece looked down at the stroller. She almost laughed out loud at the expression on Isabella's face.

"Ah, hmm, yes, I suppose he is."

Alberta didn't seem to pick up on the sarcasm in the niece's voice.

"I thought I might discuss the intern opening with you so that I'll be prepared for my interview this afternoon."

The niece shrugged her shoulders. "Uh, well, there's not much to say . . ."

"How many other applicants are you considering for the post? How long will it be until you make your decision? I have seven references lined up. Do I need more?"

"Seven?" the niece repeated, eyes widening. She sensed Alberta Conway would not be easily dissuaded.

"Come on inside. We might as well do the full interview right now."

ALBERTA GLANCED ONLY briefly at the cat cage as Rupert waddled into the litter box and began his morning routine. The sounds of spastic digging soon filled the office, but nothing could disrupt the young woman's intensity.

Alberta fell into lockstep behind the niece as she rolled the stroller to the side of the room. Turning, the niece almost ran into the intern candidate. The two performed an awkward dance, trying to avoid the collision.

"Sorry."

"That's all right."

"So sorry."

The niece pulled up a spare chair, positioned it in front of the desk, and then deliberately slid it a few extra feet toward the wall.

"Please, Miss Conway, take a seat," she said, escaping to her chair on the opposite side of the desk.

Isabella hopped onto the filing cabinet. Her front paws curved over the edge as she scrutinized the applicant.

The niece shuffled through her papers and pulled out the woman's résumé.

"So, uh, Alberta," the niece said, scanning the information on the top sheet. She'd planned to spend the morning preparing questions for the afternoon interviews, but now she was forced to ad-lib. "That's an interesting name. Are you from Canada?"

She had hoped to lighten the mood, but the comment had the opposite effect.

Alberta shot her a suspicious look. "Why would you say that?"

There was a long moment of silence. The intern candidate leaned toward the desk, staring intensely at the niece. The niece stared down at the woman's résumé, trying to determine if she'd asked an offensive question.

Isabella lorded over them both, her blue eyes sharply interpreting the scene.

"Mao-wao."

Looking up, the niece followed Isabella's gaze across the room to the poster hanging from the reception wall. She latched on to the cat's suggestion.

"What do you know about sailboats?"

Alberta straightened her shoulders. "I have a Coast Guard–approved captain's license for small watercraft."

"And, uh, how about experience in event planning?"

The applicant sat even straighter in her chair. "I was the lead organizer for my high school prom and three consecutive homecoming weekends for my sorority at Fresno State."

The niece looked up at the filing cabinet to check for a final ruling. Isabella rotated her head, as if considering. Then she gave her person a solemn stare.

"I guess that's a go, then." The niece slid the résumé into a file. "When can you start?"

MOMENTS LATER, THE niece escorted Alberta to the reception door and watched the woman bound toward the elevators, ecstatic. Isabella sat on the floor at the office suite entrance, her orange ears turned sideways. With a wide yawn, Rupert peeked around his person's legs, curiously pondering the jubilant display.

With the elevator's *ding*, the new intern threw her hands in the air, celebrating as if she'd won some sort of lottery.

She had no idea of the grim prize that awaited her.

Chapter 27

ALBERTA

ONCE AGAIN, ALBERTA was waiting outside the mayor's office suite when the niece stepped from the elevator the following morning.

This time, the niece was relieved to see the young woman. She was anxious to hand over the preparations for Monty's upcoming America's Cup event, and she'd been afraid the applicant might have changed her mind.

The niece needn't have worried. Alberta's enthusiasm hadn't waned. If anything, it had intensified.

"Good morning, Ms. Conway . . ." was all the niece got out before being verbally run over.

"I brought my sailing gear and equipment. It's in my car in the parking garage." Alberta pointed to a loaded duffel bag on the floor beside the office door. "And my training manuals." She looked up at the niece with an overeager smile. "In case I need them today."

The niece maneuvered the stroller around the bag and unlocked the door. She exchanged looks with Isabella through the mesh netting.

"That's great." The niece shoved the stroller through the entrance. "But hopefully, all of today's activities will be on land."

TO THE NIECE'S delight, Alberta dove into the event-planning project. The young intern was a perfect fit for the job. Her designated cubicle in City Hall's basement office space soon became a command center.

Alberta scoured the basement supply closets until she found a bulletin board. After polishing it up, she covered its flat surface with three-by-five note cards. Each card was filled with dense text and highlighter markings. Pieces of color-coded yarn connected the cards to one another in a complicated network of intersecting lines.

The niece had no idea how to interpret the elaborate spider's web diagram, nor did she seek out an explanation.

She was just relieved to have delegated the task to someone else.

More important, she was thrilled to direct Monty's many inquiries on the matter to the new intern.

WHILE RUNNING ALBERTA ragged with his many changes and additions, Monty was pleased with the way the America's Cup event was shaping up. He could hardly wait for Saturday night's gala. He had purchased a brand-new tuxedo that he would debut at the soiree along with a special pair of custom-crafted cuff links.

Over a hundred VIP guests were expected to attend the affair, which would be held on the Baron's yacht.

Monty was well on his way toward ingratiating himself with the local sailing community, step one in his dubious plan to shore up his prospects for the fall election.

The niece smiled as Alberta entered the mayor's office suite, chatting busily into her headset with a caterer. The intern waved absentmindedly to the niece, but didn't in any way slow her ongoing conversation as she crossed the room to Monty's office.

Isabella's brow furrowed at the woman's behavior, but the niece didn't mind.

In her view, Operation Intern had turned out far better than expected.

"I don't know why I ever resisted hiring an intern," she said as she returned her attention to the history book spread open on her desk.

Isabella was far less convinced of the initiative's success. *"Mrao."*

ALBERTA EMERGED FROM Monty's office still talking into her headset, this time to the company who would be providing the event's floral arrangements.

The niece looked up, expecting another distracted walk-by.

"I was very specific in the purchase order. The carnations must be white with either red or blue striping . . ."

The intern fluttered a few fingers in the niece's direction, reserving the bulk of her attention for the caller on the other end of the line.

The woman's demeanor changed dramatically, however, when the reception door opened and Hoxton Finn poked his head inside. Seeing the niece at her desk, he strode into the room.

He only made it halfway across before a sari whirlwind nearly knocked him over.

"Hoxton Finn," Alberta gushed, dropping the caller on the other end of the line as she rushed up to shake his hand.

"This is Alberta . . ." the niece started, but the rest of her words were drowned out.

"I've read every article you've ever written. What an impressive career. Have you ever considered hiring an intern to work with you?"

It took the concerted efforts of Hox and the niece—along

with a firm hiss from Isabella—before the intern was ushered out the door.

The reporter looked quizzically at the niece.

"Alberta? Is she from Canada?"

The niece crinkled her nose. She'd just detected a whiff of the lemony-sweet perfume coming down from the ceiling.

Tucking her skirt around her knees, she climbed up onto her desk and stretched her head toward the ceiling tiles. As she sniffed the air, trying to discern the origin of the scent, she mumbled her reply.

"Don't ask."

Chapter 28

TUXEDO-CLAD FROGS

SATURDAY AFTERNOON BROUGHT wind and rain to San Francisco's waterfront. The drenching was predicted to last through late evening—and the mayor's elaborate cocktail party.

Not even superintern Alberta could organize away the weather.

The niece stood in the Green Vase showroom, staring out at the rain. She and the cats were ready to depart for the Embarcadero pier that was under renovation to host the America's Cup. The Baron's megayacht was docked at the platform, where it would host the night's festivities.

Beneath her raincoat, the niece wore the only garment from her closet that classified as formal attire. The black dress had last seen service a few years earlier at a benefit for a local cat shelter held in the Palace Hotel ballroom. That event had featured a special "cat"-walk for Rupert and Isabella to model cat costumes crafted out of diamond-studded chains.

The niece had been assured no such shenanigans would take place this evening.

She knelt to the stroller and peeked beneath a nylon attachment that stretched over the passenger compartment to prevent rain from soaking the feline cargo.

Instead of diamond outfits, the cats were dressed in stylish but much more practical collars, Isabella's in velvet pink, Rupert's in satin black.

A car stopped in the street outside, flashed its headlights, and honked its horn. Pulling her hood over her head, the niece swung open the door to the Green Vase and pushed the stroller through.

She had made a onetime exception to her regular transportation policy and agreed to ride to the cocktail event with Monty. He'd requested a larger limo so there would be plenty of room for the cats and their stroller.

The driver helped the niece and the carriage into the back seating area. Monty leapt into the car from the opposite side, having run out from his art studio across the street.

The niece wiped the rain from her face, thankful for the car's warm interior. The only downside to the luxury accommodations, she mused, was putting up with the human company.

Monty held out his wrist and pulled back the sleeve of his jacket, showing off his new cuff links: little gold frogs dressed in tuxedos.

"What do you think, eh? Stylish, huh?"

He took the niece's silent eyebrow pump as approval.

"I know. I think these have just become my favorite pair."

From the stroller, Isabella voiced her opinion loud and clear.

"Mrao."

IT WAS A short drive along San Francisco's soggy waterfront to the event location.

Fifteen minutes later—and not a second too soon for the niece—the limo turned into the cavernous opening for piers Twenty-seven and Twenty-nine. The arched entranceway

led into a rickety warehouse that up until recently had been
used as valet parking space for a nearby restaurant. The two
docks merged together to form a triangular platform that
stretched out into the bay.

Renovation work to prepare the pier for the summer's
regatta was well under way. Sealant had been applied to the
cracked concrete base, and scaffolding rose to the warehouse
ceiling where attempts had been made to shore up the structure's leaky roof.

The niece peered up through the limo's rain-spattered
moonroof. Given the amount of water still dribbling through
the rafters, the latter task was proving to be a challenge.

Reaching the opposite end of the warehouse, the limo
exited out onto the open pier where the bulk of the regatta
infrastructure would be assembled. The framework for
several temporary structures flashed in the limo's headlights.

There were no existing water or sewage facilities on the
platform, so design-arounds had been devised to support
the planned food and beverage services. When finished, the
area would resemble a high-tech, high-end campsite, complete with a network of several hundred luxury Porta-Potties
that would be set up inside the warehouse.

Alberta had obtained a landscape model of the planned
pier facilities, so the niece had a sense of what the area
would look like once the grandstand and associated buildings were completed.

There was still much to be done before the pier would be
ready for the summer's activities. An event of this magnitude
would require a monumental effort from its organizers. The
evening's cocktail party, by comparison, was but a minor
gathering.

The niece glanced across the limo at Monty. Even without
his hindrance, there was still a risk the regatta might fall
apart or implode under the weight of its own ambitions.

Monty showed no sign of concern. He saw only upside.

No matter the odds, failure was not an option.

THE LIMO STOPPED at the far end of the pier. A string of lights surrounded a gangplank that led up into the biggest yacht the niece had ever seen.

The massive structure was a floating mansion, an over-the-top display of wealth. The niece counted at least four separate living levels rising above the waterline. Even through the evening's dusk and whipping rain, every inch of white on the hull and paneling gleamed.

The cocktail party was being held on the first floor. Glass windows revealed a number of fancily clad guests sipping from champagne flutes and nibbling appetizers from clear plastic plates.

A smaller—more exclusive—group had convened on the boat's top deck, chief among them, the Baron. The business mogul leaned over the railing, a martini glass in one hand, a cell phone in the other.

Monty was the first to hop out of the limo. He was already halfway up the gangplank by the time the niece lifted out the cat stroller and straightened its nylon rain cover.

She could hear him showing off his new cuff links to the first waiter he encountered on the yacht's front deck.

"Take a look at these, will you? Frogs—with tuxedos!"

The niece wrapped her raincoat around her dress and proceeded up the ramp at a more measured pace.

A wet wind blew across the pier, sprinkling raindrops sideways into the carriage. Rupert dove beneath the blankets, trying to stay dry, but Isabella remained vigilant. The hairs along the center ridge of her back rose in a slight hackle.

The niece looked at the crowd of people mingling in the boat's ballroom-sized entertainment area and, farther up, the Baron.

She couldn't put her finger on it, but something felt odd. And it had nothing to do with Monty's wacky cuff links.

Chapter 29

APPETIZER DELIGHT

RUPERT ROUSTED HIMSELF from the blankets as the niece pushed the stroller up the gangplank and into the yacht. Gripping his claws into the sheets, he peered up through the screened netting, but the nylon rain cover over the passenger compartment blocked most of his view.

The carriage wobbled back and forth on the uneven planks as Rupert's narrow window of sight tilted upward. He caught a brief glimpse of the yacht's front ballroom area and the private balcony above. The Baron took a sip from his champagne flute as he stared curiously down at the stroller.

Rupert felt the wheels bump beneath him, causing him to jostle Isabella. Luckily, she had braced herself before the carriage reached the end of the gangplank. With an apologetic look at his glaring sister, Rupert scrambled back onto his side of the passenger compartment.

His person wasn't near as good at guiding the stroller as she thought.

No matter. Rupert would let the matter slide. Nothing

could diminish his anticipation for the night's event. He'd taken an extra nap on the car ride to the pier to ensure he'd be fully rested for the festivities. He'd even agreed to wear this silly bow tie collar.

From his slumbering position in the mayor's office, he'd overheard Alberta's phone conversation with the caterer about the elaborate food that would be served.

If ever there was a place where he might seek out a fried chicken donut, this was it.

The stroller's front bumper slammed into a door facing as the niece tried to maneuver through to the yacht's ballroom.

Rupert righted himself and rolled his eyes up at the green nylon cover.

Seriously, the woman needs to have her glasses checked.

ONCE INSIDE THE yacht, the niece removed the stroller's rain canopy and surrendered it and her raincoat to a valet manning the entrance.

Rupert spun a tight circle, taking full advantage of the unobstructed line of sight above the passenger compartment.

He watched as his person slipped the paper number corresponding to her coat's hanger into one of the stroller's side pockets and nudged the carriage toward the edge of the crowd.

Pivoting on his round rump, Rupert returned to a forward-facing position. The view was now dramatically more interesting. Pushing his head against the net cover, he could make out the ankles and shins of the nearest guests. Women's toned legs flirted out from beneath dresses of various lengths, while men stood in dress slacks, for the most part neatly pressed. Rupert identified a few pairs of pants whose owners had skimped on the week's dry cleaning.

Shifting his focus upward, Rupert saw a number of waists and midsections, many accompanied by a handheld appetizer plate or plastic champagne flute.

Most of the attendees were unknown to him, but he picked out a handful of familiar torsos that he recognized from the past few weeks he'd spent at City Hall.

The president of the board of supervisors had scored an invite, along with several members of his staff. If his nervous hand gestures were any gauge, the seasoned politician was a bit unsure whether he should have attended this soiree. Rupert heard him laugh—far too loudly—at a joke made by one of his colleagues.

The prickly secretary from the elevator walked past the stroller. Rupert shuddered as Wanda Williams glared down at him, giving him a full view of her scowling face. In the carriage beside him, Isabella stiffened with affront.

Seeking to distance herself from Wanda, the niece shoved the stroller toward the opposite side of the ballroom.

Grumbling about the niece's driving capabilities, Rupert again regained his footing. As he peered up through the netting, he spied the City Hall wedding coordinator, the woman with the bouncy chest and the blond wig that looked like a bird's nest.

Birds, he thought, his mind transitioning to food.

Waitstaff scurried about with trays of hors d'oeuvres and champagne glasses. The servers whipped their trays in front of guests, hovered for a few seconds while selections were made, and then zoomed on to the next group of nibblers. It was an elaborately choreographed dance of decadent food, capped off by a constant stream of empty trays being ferried back to the ship's kitchen.

Rupert's head swung back and forth, trying to follow the action from his restricted stroller seat.

The niece dodged a tray of mozzarella and tomato crostinis as Alberta rushed past, a blur of a rustling silk sari, clicking high-heeled sandals, and a fluttering clipboard. She waved hurriedly at the niece while speaking into the handheld device for the mobile phone secured around her ear.

"T-minus seven minutes until the second course of

appetizers is due out to the ballroom. Kitchen rep, please confirm the plating is on schedule . . ."

The niece muttered something under her breath. Rupert couldn't make out the words, but he could easily interpret the expression on her face.

Thank goodness for interns.

Rupert was reserving judgment on the new intern until he learned whether Alberta had included his favorite item on the night's menu.

He snorkeled in a deep volume of air and began sorting through the various smells. The confined space had captured and concentrated a number of odors.

First, he filtered out the various personal scent enhancers. A shindig of this nature attracted a wide array of perfumes and colognes—including one rather familiar lemony-sweet scent . . .

His orange ears turned sideways in consternation. *What an overpowering, offensive aroma.*

Just then, Hoxton Finn stepped up to the stroller. The loud *pop* of his notepad against his left leg rang in Rupert's sensitive ears.

"Monty really thinks this is going to win him the next election?"

Before the niece could answer, a waiter swept in with a tray of goat cheese–stuffed mushrooms.

"Oh, you've got to try these," Hox said, reaching for the tongs.

Mushrooms, Rupert thought with disdain as he studied the brown lumps from the underside of Hox's clear plastic plate. The slimy fungi ranked right up there with diet cat food on the list of foods he refused to eat.

He glanced at his sister, who delicately licked her lips. Isabella, on the other hand, loved roasted mushrooms.

Before Rupert could broach the subject of whether mushrooms were appropriate for the feline diet, another pair of legs approached the group standing around the stroller.

The Baron had descended to the yacht's first floor to greet his guests. Humphrey, the news station's stylist, was admiring the business mogul's outfit.

"The cut of that suit fits you perfectly, sir." Humphrey touched the Baron's wrist and lifted his arm upward. "I'm wondering—have you tried mohair? The fabric would accent your shoulder blades." He nodded, affirming his expert opinion. "It's the wooliness."

Rupert's brow furrowed as he tried to imagine the garment Humphrey had described, but his attention was soon drawn to an elderly waiter at the edge of his periphery.

The man walked with a noticeable limp. He steadied himself with a cane whose rubber-tipped end thumped against the ballroom's wooden floor. From his floor-restricted angle, Rupert couldn't see up to the man's face. His viewpoint cut off at the sizeable paunch around his waist.

Rupert homed in on the tray the waiter carried in his free hand. The cat's stomach rumbled as he breathed in a delightful scent.

Fried chicken!

But wait. There was a slight modification.

Rupert's eyes crossed as he processed the complex concoction of aromas.

Could it be true?

The niece failed to notice as the waiter knelt toward the stroller and unzipped the net cover. Rupert bounced up and down at Oscar's conspiring wink—and the food item displayed on his tray.

Oscar slid a plastic plate into the stroller's passenger compartment. The dish contained tiny pieces of fried chicken—each one encapsulated in a doughy crust.

The waiter disappeared as Rupert dove into the delicacy. Isabella pawed a sample to her side of the stroller and tasted it, munching critically.

Before the cats could finish their treat, Alberta swung back through the ballroom, diligently checking that everything was in order.

The Baron held up a crunchy brown morsel and called out, "Love the fried chicken donuts, dear. Excellent selection."

Alberta's eyes widened in panic. She stared in horror at the piece of food in the Baron's hand. "Fried chicken what? That's not on the menu!"

Spinning around, she bustled off to the kitchen, intent on rectifying the menu aberration.

Still munching, Rupert shook his head as he watched her depart.

The intern had just received a failing grade from the feline contingent.

• • •

WITH THE GUESTS congregated in the ballroom, the Baron motioned for the mayor to officially start the evening's proceedings.

Monty raised a champagne flute and clinked his fork (ineffectively) against the plastic stem. He improvised (just as ineffectively) with one of his cuff links.

"Ladies and gentlemen," he called out grandly. "If I could have your attention, please."

The crowd turned toward the center of the ballroom. Monty scanned their faces and frowned. Leaning toward the niece, he whispered urgently in her ear.

"Where's Alberta?"

The niece had just taken a bite of stuffed mushroom. Still chewing, she shrugged.

"She's supposed to bring out the scale model," Monty hissed. "The one of the event pavilion."

Swallowing her mouthful, the niece left the stroller in place and scampered through the crowd to the doorway at the far end of the ballroom, where the waitstaff—and Alberta—had been trafficking in and out.

A narrow hallway separated the ballroom exit from the kitchen entrance.

The moment the niece crossed over the threshold, she felt a sickening sensation, an instinctive response to the lemony-sweet scent of perfume—and the blood spatter thrown across the wall.

Hox nearly ran into her from behind as she skidded to a stop.

The pier model lay upended on the floor—next to a clipboard, a wireless headset, and a blood-soaked, sari-wrapped heap.

In the ballroom behind them, someone called for a doctor. Hox stepped forward to press his index finger against the intern's neck.

Grimly, he shook his head.

A physician came forward from the ballroom, and Hox stepped aside. The man quickly checked the woman's vitals. Second later, he came to the same conclusion.

Sirens wailed in the distance as the niece stared in disbelief at the gouging stab wounds in the intern's chest—and the knifed knitting needles discarded next to the body.

On Board the *San Carlos*

*Anchored off Angel Island
in the San Francisco Bay*

August 1775

Chapter 30

THE CAPTAIN'S QUARTERS

CAPTAIN AYALA SAT at a wooden desk in his quarters on the *San Carlos*, writing up his report on the events of the last twenty-four hours.

He propped his left foot on a stool in the hopes that the elevation might alleviate the intense throbbing in his injured toe. A long day of standing at the ship's helm had left the area around the amputation swollen and sore. But he soon forgot about the foot pain as he recapped the day's adventures.

Most of his reports were factual and to the point, but tonight's write-up warranted a few extra flourishes. From the ship's journey up the coast and its epic battle against the tide to the immense size of the protected inlet where the ship was now berthed, this summary was more than just routine record-keeping.

Even through the darkness, he could sense the magnitude of the newfound bay. There was no doubt about it. This port would inevitably overshadow the other established harbors along the Pacific's west coast. It was a mariner's dream assignment, charting virgin territory with such unmatched potential.

The captain's quill scribbled late into the night, a constant flow of indigo ink across pages of parchment. At the corner of the desk, close to the lantern's heat, Petey the parrot curled up on one of the captain's shirts. Every few minutes, the bird cooed, comforted by the scratching of the stylus and the warmth of his comfy bed.

The ink-covered pages piled up as Ayala related the journey's many ups and downs, the valiant efforts of his crew, the invaluable assistance of his first mate, Humphretto, and, of course, his own cunning and courage.

As for Isabella's role in the sighting of the bay's opening, he was forced to make a tactical omission. While he was grudgingly grateful for the feline's assistance, he couldn't credit a cat with providing insight into the bay's hidden location. He would find himself in the same mental institution as the previous captain of the *San Carlos*.

Of course, it would have been even worse if he'd sailed past the passage and reported the negative finding back to the head of the armada.

Ayala cringed, thinking of the ridicule he would have received when the bay was later discovered.

He shook his head, imagining the Commodore's response to such a revelation.

"I'd have lost my commission for sure."

AFTER MORE THAN an hour's worth of diligent note-taking, Ayala pushed back from his desk and stared up at the ceiling. He often found that the act of writing down his thoughts helped him to organize and make sense of his observations. It was a process that was needed far more tonight than on any previous evening.

With a heavy *thump*, he dropped his foot from the stool. There was one more item from the day's travails he had yet to describe in his notes: the slaying of the deckhand minutes before the ship's celebration feast.

Ayala scowled, rubbing his chin. The murder was a black mark against an otherwise successful journey. It was the type of event that would be followed up with scrutiny by his superiors when he returned to Mexico City.

The body of the murdered deckhand had been moved into the ship's brig for the night. They didn't have the resources to keep the corpse chilled for the return trip to Mexico, so the next morning the deceased would be buried on the island where they had dropped anchor.

The passengers and crew were understandably on edge.

Among the ship's occupants, the prevailing theory was that a stowaway had sneaked on board at San Blas and that this heretofore unseen person had murdered the deckhand.

Ayala had dismissed this notion as ridiculous, but he had personally conducted a top-to-bottom search of the *San Carlos*—if for no other reason than to appease his shipmates. He'd seen no indication that the ship carried an unauthorized passenger, particularly one with such a carnal bloodthirst.

This provided no assurance to his sailing comrades.

Cabin doors were now securely locked. The men who slept in the boat's long bunkroom had assigned shifts to keep watch through the night.

Humphretto had posted himself outside the captain's quarters. The tiny lieutenant wouldn't be much of a deterrent against a murderous attack, but he had insisted on protecting the captain as a matter of duty.

Ayala glanced across the room and smiled. Humphretto's boots were visible in the wide crack beneath the door. The little man's snores drifted through the wood barrier.

The captain wasn't worried about a surprise attack. He was a light sleeper, and Petey could be trusted to squawk out a warning if an intruder slipped into the room.

But this was the type of event that could quickly erode morale.

The sooner the culprit was identified, the better.

CAPTAIN AYALA RETURNED his attention to the pile of parchment on his desk. He picked up a sheet written in a slightly different color of ink. This page represented his private notes on the killing. It was a less organized writing, one that he would burn at the end of the trip. Here he had summarized a few pieces of information that he had decided not to share on the official record.

The top of the page contained the bullet points he had gleaned from the ship's chef earlier that evening.

This was presumably the source of the stowaway rumor.

Oscar had told the captain he'd caught a glimpse of a shadowy figure in the hallway outside the galley kitchen, right before the start of the dinner service.

Not much help in terms of identification, Ayala mused. He would have disregarded the chef's testimony altogether, if not for the second part of his statement.

The nebulous presence had been accompanied by a distinctive scent—that of a lemony-sweet perfume.

Perplexed, Ayala shifted his thoughts to the last item on his unofficial list of observations.

Taking care not to disturb the parrot, he reached across his desk and picked up the bloody knitting needle that had been left at the scene of the crime.

During their earlier visit, the captain had asked Oscar to opine on the deckhand's wounds. Given his culinary skills, he was the closest they had to a knife expert.

Oscar had examined the weapon, curiously turning it over in his hands. After several minutes of silent observation and a few speculative air jabs, he'd concurred that it was the likely cause of the man's injuries.

Gingerly, Ayala held the knitting needle up to the lantern's light. Oscar thought he might have seen similar weaponry in an antique shop down south, but the captain had never come across anything like it.

A cap had been removed from the needle's curved end, exposing a razor-sharp blade.

Sniffing the needle, Ayala thought he detected the faintest trace of a lemony perfume.

Chapter 31

UNQUALIFIED

THE NEXT MORNING dawned clear and bright, sending a waking warmth through the ship's wooden walls. Captain Ayala jumped out of bed and threw open a window. He poked his head outside, eager for the first daylight view of his surroundings.

He could see only a narrow angle of the bay, but even the limited scene exceeded his expectations. He leaned farther and farther out the hole, marveling at the breadth and beauty of the boat's surroundings—until he nearly slipped and fell through.

Dragging his body back inside, Ayala hurriedly dressed and crossed the room to unbolt the door. Wincing at the pain in his foot, the captain stepped over Humphretto, who'd fallen asleep at his post, and hobbled down the hallway to the main deck.

Ayala whipped out his binoculars and scanned the shoreline, slowly pivoting to capture the full extent of the bay. Rolling hills cupped the harbor like a giant green hand, sealing it off from the beastly Pacific. It was just as he had suspected the night before. Despite the difficulties the *San*

Carlos had encountered navigating the entrance, once the tides and currents were properly mapped, the area would become a haven of first resort for every ship passing along the continent's west coast.

The binoculars remained plastered to Ayala's face as he admired the scene.

The captain shook his head in disbelief. None of the previous maps or reports had come close to suggesting the size of the bay. Even Portola and his bumbling overland crew had failed to convey the importance of this find in their descriptions. They must have been in a hurry to get back to Monterey before they ran out of provisions.

It was a wonder the bay had gone undiscovered all these years. If he himself hadn't had such a difficult time both identifying the opening and navigating through its mouth, he wouldn't have understood how so many of his predecessors could have missed it.

Finally, Ayala dropped the binoculars. Hands on his hips, he gazed out at the panoramic vista.

"Amazing."

CAPTAIN AYALA WAS itching to begin exploring the area, but first, he had to attend to the serious matter of the deckhand's burial.

Groggy crew members and passengers soon joined him on the ship's main deck. Many reported hearing suspicious bumps and noises in the night, but Ayala chalked this up to overwrought nerves. No new victims had been identified. He hoped that with the burial, they could put the unfortunate incident of the deckhand's death behind them and move on with the ship's mission.

The kitchen gong sounded, a makeshift announcement that the funeral was about to commence.

Petey swooped down from the mast and settled on Ayala's shoulder as the captain turned to watch the solemn procession carrying the body out of the brig.

The corpse had been wrapped in a shroud of white linen and laid on a long board, which was then hefted on the shoulders of designated crew members.

Little was known about Alberto. A quiet fellow of Indian descent, he'd been a diligent worker who kept mostly to himself.

He had been the last to sign on to the newly constituted crew at San Blas, and there hadn't been time for him to bond with his fellow shipmates during the short voyage up the coast.

Nevertheless, the crew was shaken by his death. Such a gruesome murder, however anonymous the victim, reminded the men of the many perils they risked at sea.

It was a sailor's grim reality. At death, he would likely be buried in an unmarked grave, thousands of miles from home, at a site his family and loved ones would never reach to mourn. In the worst-case scenario, his body might be dumped in the ocean to be consumed by fishes.

Even the most hardened crew member had moments of lonesomeness and regret, never more so than when faced with a stark reminder of his own mortality.

It was a situation that called for a leader who could provide calming reassurance, solid emotional guidance, and a grounding of place and purpose.

Into this fraught atmosphere stepped the ship's designated religious counselor, Father Monty.

AYALA COULDN'T IMAGINE a clergyman less qualified for the job.

He had attended dozens of Catholic funerals in his lifetime, many of them conducted out of necessity on ships.

Never had he seen one performed so ineptly.

How Father Monty could have completed his liturgical training without mastering this critical skill was a mystery to the captain. Perhaps, he reasoned with a shrug, that was why they'd been able to secure a last-minute priest for the journey—the sole available candidate had flunked out of seminary.

Ayala frowned at the robe Monty had donned for the ceremony. It was made of a glimmering gold fabric—more like something you would see at a carnival than in a church. The garment's loose sleeves dangled dangerously close to the incense ball Monty had started to swing awkwardly back and forth.

While no expert in the ritual, the captain had the distinct impression that the incense had been heated to too high of a temperature. Smoke billowed out of the ball's metal chamber, clogging the air and making it difficult for Monty to see the area around his feet.

The priest stepped clumsily onto the gangplank, tapping the toes of his shoes as if trying to feel his way forward. He turned sideways, aiming the smoking incense ball at the corpse's head. The crew members carrying the body followed a short distance behind, warily eyeing the swinging ball.

Anticipating disaster, Ayala glanced at the observers lined up beside him. He wasn't the only one who sensed a pending calamity.

The chef's niece winced at Father Monty's unsteady footing. On the ground at her person's feet, Isabella stood alert, her blue eyes sharply concerned. Rupert hid behind the woman's legs, afraid to watch.

Two steps down the gangplank, Monty's heel caught on the walkway's ridged footholds, and he stumbled toward the pallbearers.

Trying to avoid a collision with the priest, the crew members carrying the front end of the body board jerked sideways. The sudden movement upset the board's center of balance, and the dead cargo slid off its platform.

The linen shroud unraveled as the corpse plunged head-first into the water.

Monty lurched backward, overcorrecting in his attempt to regain his footing. He wobbled back and forth for several seconds, his arms helplessly flailing the air.

The gold chain slipped from his grasp, and the incense ball soared in a perfect arc before landing with a steaming *plink* in the water.

A meek "oops" signaled Monty had lost his battle with gravity. He tumbled over the side of the gangplank and hit the water with a splash.

The niece and her two cats peeked over the railing. (At this point, even Rupert couldn't suppress his curiosity.)

Monty soon surfaced, the gold robe billowing around him as he struggled to tread water.

"I wonder if he knows how to swim," the niece said, furrowing her brow.

Isabella warbled out a dubious reply.

"Wrao-wra-wra-mrao."

Ayala crossed his arms and grunted.

"Guess we'll find out."

Chapter 32

A MURDERER AMONG US?

THE PASSENGERS AND crew of the *San Carlos* gathered on Angel Island to complete the burial of their deceased—and dunked—comrade.

After the accidental overboarding, the body was retrieved from the water and carried onto the beach. There, the linen shroud was rewrapped and the corpse returned to its support plank.

With the dignity of the procession somewhat restored, the funeral party proceeded up a short hill from the beach to the burial site.

The clear morning carried a crisp breeze—one felt most keenly by Father Carmichael, now wrapped in a wet blanket, who shivered while he spoke the last rites.

AS SHOVELS PILED heavy clods of damp earth on the burial mound, the niece glanced uneasily at the assembled ship members.

She'd always felt safe accompanying her uncle on his

oceangoing commissions. A tomboy, she dressed in man's clothes and kept a low profile. The ships' military commanders had made clear that she was not to be touched or harmed in any way.

But now, she sensed a growing lawlessness, a dark nebulous force that, if left unchecked, threatened everyone on board the *San Carlos*.

She studied the surrounding mourners, wondering who among them was a murderer.

FIRST, THERE WAS Captain Ayala, she mused, formulating a list of suspects.

He was a grim man, and his intensity was somewhat frightening, but she didn't detect any malice within him. And besides, she thought, looking down at the two cats seated at her feet, for some reason, both Rupert and Isabella seemed to like the captain—even if he didn't outwardly reciprocate their affection.

He must secretly harbor feline sympathies, she concluded. In her book, that made him unlikely to commit murder.

The niece moved on to the first mate, Lieutenant Humphretto.

The dapper little man had a cheerful personality and gave every indication of being the most harmless soul on the ship. On the other hand, she had seen his dexterity with haircutting shears. His sewing proficiency made him the person with the closest link to the knitting needle knife that had been left next to the murdered deckhand.

No, Humphretto couldn't be discounted, much as she doubted his involvement. He remained a suspect based on his skill set, if nothing else.

The niece shifted her focus to the Baron, who stood, as usual, apart from the rest of the group.

His presence on the boat was an anomaly in itself. In all of the years she'd spent on Spanish ships, she'd never encountered a person of such privately accumulated wealth. Her initial impression was of a calculating, conniving individual who no doubt planned to use the bay's discovery to his personal advantage, but nothing in that agenda gave him motive to murder a deckhand.

The Baron was aloof and, it seemed, intentionally mysterious. For this reason, she determined, he remained on the suspect list.

THE LAST SHOVELFULS of dirt fell on the grave as the niece concluded her assessment of the crew members gathered around the burial site.

There were a number of deckhands and other low-level workers whose names she hadn't yet learned. Even a ship as modest in size as the *San Carlos* required a sizeable team of able-bodied sailors to man the complicated rigging system. They were kept busy constantly adjusting the sails to take advantage of the wind. The rigors of daily maintenance took up any free time that remained.

Some of the faces were familiar, sailors that she had seen on previous ships. Others were completely foreign to her.

Any one of the crew members, she reasoned, could be harboring a murderous secret.

THAT LEFT FATHER Monty, a suspicious character if ever she'd met one. She watched as he doused the fresh dirt with a drenching of holy water.

The priest clearly lacked basic clerical skills. She was convinced he hadn't been officially ordained.

More likely, she reasoned, he was an impostor who had hopped on board the *San Carlos* as a means of skipping town. She wouldn't be surprised if he was wanted by the authorities in San Blas for some sort of ill-conceived scam or poorly executed theft.

I'd put my money on him.

A gust of wind whipped across the hillside, tearing the blanket from Monty's shoulders, revealing the sparkling gold robe beneath.

That can't be an authorized uniform, the niece thought, vowing to keep a close watch on the inept priest.

As she stared across the gravesite, she realized several of the surrounding faces reflected speculations similar to her own. The ship members were all conducting the same analysis: Who among them was the murderer?

She wondered what conclusions they had drawn about her.

A fuzzy figure stirred on the ground at the woman's feet. Isabella lifted her head, sniffing the breeze floating in from the water.

A second later, the niece detected the uncanny scent of a lemony-sweet perfume, and she was forced to second-guess her entire analysis.

At the time of the murder, everyone on her suspect list had been seated at the table on the ship's top deck, waiting for the fried chicken feast to begin. All of the ship's passengers and crew had alibis, verified by multiple witnesses—all except for her uncle, who had been wrapping up the last meal items down below in the galley kitchen.

She refused to even contemplate the notion that he might be guilty of such a crime.

Nose crinkling at the strange odor, she glanced nervously over her shoulder and down the embankment toward the—supposedly—empty ship. Only her uncle had remained on board so that he could prepare the morning meal.

Perhaps it was time to consider the bizarre rumor that the *San Carlos* harbored a psychopathic stowaway.

Chapter 33

TAUNTED

RUPERT RODE IN his person's arms as the passengers and crew of the *San Carlos* returned to the ship for a post-funeral brunch.

It had been an entertaining morning, Rupert thought, glancing over at the tall priest in the gold robe. That Father Monty was a funny fellow, what with all of his tripping, falling, and dunking. Highly amusing stuff.

Rupert hadn't paid much attention to the actual funeral ceremony. He'd quickly tired of listening to Monty's incomprehensible Latin phrases. In his view, the burial ritual could have done with someone tumbling into that big hole before they filled it in—a little excitement to jazz things up. And he couldn't understand why he hadn't been allowed to dig in that tempting pile of fresh dirt.

After Monty nearly splashed holy water in his face, Rupert had wandered off a short distance to a bluff overlooking the bay.

Several flocks of birds had swooped past the location, some of them directly over his head. He'd taken a few running leaps into the air, but the targets had easily eluded his attempts at capture.

He hadn't realized he looked like a plump bunny rabbit with pointed orange ears until his person rushed over and scooped him up, shooing off the hawk that was diving toward him, talons extended.

Birds, Rupert thought with a frustrated sigh. They always got the best of him.

But as the niece climbed up the ship's gangplank, Rupert caught sight of a huge plate of leftover fried chicken on the deck dinner table.

The sigh transformed into a delighted squeal.

He could always depend on Uncle Oscar's cooking to save the day.

• • •

SOON RUPERT AND Isabella were seated on the floor beneath their person's chair, munching on their servings of chicken. Given his loud smacks and slurping, Rupert could barely hear the voices of the humans seated at the table above.

Isabella, however, listened closely to the conversation, even while eating her portion of the leftovers—and making sure her brother didn't steal any food from her plate.

With the somber business of the burial completed, Captain Ayala was eager to organize teams for the day's surveys and reconnaissance.

As the crew sat down to eat, he began barking out orders.

"Humphretto, you'll be in charge of the ship while I lead a launch party to the bay's south shore."

Isabella stared thoughtfully at the captain's wounded foot, which he had propped on a short block beneath the table. Ayala had been limping on the walk back to the ship. The injury was far worse than he let on. Perhaps the captain was in denial about the extent of his incapacitation.

Regardless, he had no business tromping across the wetlands that afternoon.

Plus, she needed him to stay on board and guard his ship.

No offense to Humphretto, but he was no match for the Knitting Needle Ninja.

Isabella's eyes narrowed as she devised a plan.

• • •

A FEW MINUTES later, Rupert licked the last greasy residue from his dish and, with a contented sigh, lifted his head from his plate.

He blinked drowsily, contemplating a nap—but then suddenly returned to full wakefulness at the sight of his sister's abandoned plate about a yard away. She'd pushed it to the other side of their person's chair, but he could see a few chicken morsels had been left unattended.

Odd for Isabella to be so careless, he thought, stealthily sneaking around the chair. But he didn't hesitate to gobble up the remaining bits.

His sister's plate was centered beneath the end of the table. As Rupert swallowed the stolen bites, he heard a familiar rustling above his head: the distinctive sound of parrot claws gripping the wooden table.

I'm ignoring you, Rupert resolved with determination.

A shiny red head with a green collar peeked over the table's edge. Petey blinked a teasing yellow eye at the plump feline.

Nope. Rupert kept his face firmly planted in the plate. There wasn't much left other than a greasy film, but the parrot didn't need to know that. He wasn't going to get drawn into another one of the bird's pranks. Not this time.

No matter. Petey knew how to provoke his furry friend.

The parrot dipped under the table, pinched his beak around a clump of fluff from Rupert's tail, and yanked. Carrying off his prize, the bird disappeared into the sky over the ship.

Rupert jumped into the air and spun around, upending the now-empty dish. *Where is that parrot? That's it. I'm eating him for dessert!*

Emitting a loud *squawk*, Petey swooped down from the heavens, a feather-coated missile. He aimed his trajectory at a narrow opening between two chairs. With fighter pilot precision, the parrot dove through the gap and glided beneath the length of the table.

Rupert charged after the bird, slamming into table legs and human shins in his effort to catch his feathered tormentor.

A chain reaction registered in the startled faces of the seated crew members. Knees banged against chair legs and the table's bottom surface, generating a rolling wave of clinking plates and glasses.

Halfway down the table's length, Rupert knocked over the wooden block supporting the captain's tender foot.

The wounded appendage hit the ground with a *thud*—immediately followed by a deafening roar of pain.

ONCE THE COMMOTION died down and Captain Ayala's foot pain subsided, the crew members regrouped for the afternoon's mission. It was clear Ayala was in no condition to lead the exploratory team to the bay's south shore. Reluctantly, he switched assignments with Humphretto.

Retrieving Rupert from the mêlée, the niece discreetly wrapped him in a blanket, hoping against hope that the captain hadn't realized the cause of the ruckus that led to his intense foot pain.

As the canoes for the launch party were lowered down the sides of the ship, Ayala monitored the preparations from a comfortable chair that had been set up on the top deck. A pillow-topped stool propped up his foot, a steadier and more comfortable brace than the wooden block he'd tried to hide beneath the table.

Petey perched on the pillow next to the captain's swollen foot. The parrot preened his feathers, diligently running his beak through the quills, not looking the least bit guilty for his role in the earlier caper.

Father Monty sidled up to Ayala's chair.

"I'd like to do a little exploring myself, Captain." He coughed into his fist. "If you don't mind."

Ayala raised a weary eyebrow.

The priest pointed at the island where they'd buried the deckhand. "Here, on Angel Island."

With a grunt, Ayala shrugged his shoulders. "Why not. Let me know what you find."

The niece watched this interchange, wondering what Monty aimed to accomplish. Was he just hoping to spend a few hours on land or did he have an alternative agenda?

She recalled her earlier pledge to keep an eye on the suspicious priest.

From the ground beneath the table, Isabella nudged the niece's hand, encouraging her person to act on the impulse.

"I'll come along. I could use a walk."

Ayala grimaced his response. He glared at the orange and white bundle curled up in the woman's lap.

"Fine. Take that thing with you."

Affronted, the niece stood and turned toward the stairwell leading to the kitchen and her lower-level quarters. Isabella followed as her person stomped down the steps to prepare for the outing.

Maybe Ayala wasn't a secret cat sympathizer after all.

He had just moved up a notch on her suspect list.

Chapter 34

WELCOME WARRIORS

WARY OF THE hawk she'd seen earlier, the niece secured Rupert and Isabella inside a wicker stroller that her uncle Oscar had crafted for cat transport. Typically, she used it to maneuver the cats when they were changing ships or taking a shopping day in port (in addition to the cat compartment, the contraption had plenty of cargo storage).

Rupert spent most of his carriage time curled up asleep in a pile of blankets, but Isabella insisted on being able to see out so she could issue navigational instructions. This was a problem with the carriage's initial design. The cat compartment was vented for air flow, but had no clear viewing portal.

After the first usage—when the stroller's interior cavity was almost destroyed by Isabella's irate protest—Oscar made the cat-suggested modifications.

The stroller now featured a visor-like view hole that encircled the cat compartment's top rim. The gap provided just enough space for Isabella to see out. Other than the spots blocked by intermittent connecting bands of wicker,

she had an almost three-hundred-sixty-degree vantage of
the stroller's surroundings.

And so, when the niece pulled out the carriage from its
kitchen storage closet and unlatched the lid, Isabella hopped
readily inside.

The niece scooped up Rupert and dropped him in beside
his sister. Tuckered out from the morning's parrot chase, he
quickly fell into a deep slumber, even as the niece bumped
the wooden wheels up the stairs to the main deck.

Father Monty slapped his hands together, as if he welcomed their addition to his walk.

"I'm so glad you decided to join me."

The niece smiled her response, but internally, she found
the priest's actions highly suspicious.

From the stroller, Isabella issued a forward command.

"Mrao!"

THE UNLIKELY EXPLORERS set out from the *San Carlos* with Father Monty in the lead. The priest paraded down
the gangplank and onto the beach, chattering like a tour
guide as the niece and the cat-laden carriage followed several wary steps behind.

Trying to recover his gravitas from the earlier mishaps
during the burial ceremony, Monty strode confidently across
the beach. His flat-soled shoes left narrow exclamation
point–shaped imprints on the sand.

"I believe I hear the song of a whipper-willowed warbling
wren," he announced, cupping a hand to his ear.

It was but the first of many dubious birdcall identifica-
tions. The niece suspected he was just making up names,
but she let him continue the charade.

She was far more concerned about the non-avian creatures that might be lurking nearby.

So far, theirs were the only markings on the beach. But as
the niece maneuvered the stroller around a clump of seaweed,
she glanced nervously at the scrubby bushes that crowded

their inland flank. Out of sight of the boat and without any defensive weapons, they were ill prepared for an ambush.

The breeze changed direction, cutting across the beach from the island's interior, pushing away the sounds of the lapping water.

In the subsequent lull, the niece thought she heard a twig snap in the trees to her right.

Her hand gripped the stroller's wooden handle as she stopped and scanned the dense greenery.

The niece checked the carriage for a cat reading on the noise. If Isabella had sensed any movement in the forest, she didn't show it. Her blue eyes were trained on Monty's brown robe. His tinny voice floated back to the stroller, this time commenting on a purple-throated mocking jay.

The niece pushed the stroller forward, but she remained on alert.

She had the distinct impression that they were being watched—and that the unseen observers weren't yellow-chested woodpeckers.

AS THE GROUP proceeded around the next bend, the niece noticed an object on a bluff about a hundred yards ahead. At first, she thought it was an odd-shaped tree. It wasn't until they were almost directly underneath the bluff that she realized the landmark was man-made.

A piece of driftwood had been upended and planted into the dirt so that its roots stuck up into the air. The trunk's upper portion had been decorated with a thick red paste, a few seashells, and several feathers.

Father Monty blew out a derisive *sfft*.

"Looks like some sort of pagan ritual," he said, peering up at the roots. He pointed at a curved arc painted on one of the roots. "Likely done by the local heathens . . ."

The niece returned her gaze to the woods.

They weren't the only ones who had been performing a ceremony that morning, she realized uneasily.

And they definitely weren't alone on Angel Island.

Just then Isabella trilled out a warning.

The niece jumped. There on the beach, she saw the danger that had triggered the cat's alarm.

Gulping, she pointed at Monty. He looked briefly puzzled—and then turned to find himself face-to-face with the aforementioned "heathen."

Monty let out a high-pitched screech, which he immediately stifled, in spite of his fear.

The Indian's muscled body was decked out in leather hides, a feather headdress, and a number of sheathed knives. Dabs of paint decorated his cheekbones and forehead.

The niece drew in her breath, freezing in place, afraid that any sudden movement might be misinterpreted by their new acquaintance—and his similarly clad colleagues who had now encircled their location.

Only Rupert remained oblivious to the danger.

Brow furrowed, the Indian strode around Monty—who had fallen into a catatonic state—and cautiously approached the wicker stroller.

The niece gulped as the man bent to the cat compartment, unlatched the lid, and peered curiously inside.

Isabella sat stiffly in place. Her blue eyes glittered as she stared regally up at the stranger.

Rupert simply rolled over and exposed his furry round stomach for a belly rub.

Chapter 35

A WARNING

THE EXPLORATION PARTY from the *San Carlos* stood on Angel Island's south shore, surrounded by local inhabitants.

The niece was unsure how best to proceed—or whether they were about to be sacrificed on the driftwood altar Father Monty had derided a few minutes earlier.

The priest's skin had blanched to a sickly shade of green. His pale lips quivered, perhaps reciting a prayer—or perhaps cursing the curiosity that had spurred the day's venture—the niece couldn't tell which.

The tribe conferred in a language she couldn't understand. The words seemed to replicate a low threatening rumble. She felt her palms sweat as she gripped the stroller's wooden handle.

Isabella sat protectively next to her brother, tensely watching the Indian who looked down into the cat carriage. She wasn't growling—yet.

Only Rupert offered a welcoming gesture. True to his nature, he always expected the best from everyone he met.

He was forever hopeful that a newcomer might be carrying a container of freshly cooked fried chicken.

And so, when the Indian reached his hand into the cat compartment, Rupert rolled onto his back to expose his fluffy white stomach. The cat wiggled, and his front feet playfully prodded the air.

As the Indian leaned forward, the afternoon sun flashed on a hunting knife hanging from a belt secured around his waist.

Father Monty managed a feeble whisper. "We're all going to die."

Then his legs crumpled beneath him. There was a light *thud* as his body hit the sand.

"No!" the niece cried out, lunging forward to protect her cat.

But before she could intervene, the Indian's face broke into a broad smile.

His weatherworn fingers tickled Rupert's belly, generating a friendly feline coo.

IT TOOK SEVERAL splashes of cold water to revive Father Monty.

Once the wet chill kicked in, his lips sputtered and the color returned to his cheeks.

Then, as if suddenly remembering the previous danger, he tried to scramble to his feet. The niece clamped her hands down on his shoulders, restraining him until he processed her whispered message that the Indians had decided to treat the group from the *San Carlos* as guests.

The Indians had been wary of Monty's flapping robe and his strange chattering voice, but the cats had won them over.

The tribe built a campfire on the beach and began to assemble the fixings for a meal of roasted fowl and fish.

It wasn't exactly fried chicken, Rupert noted with a critical twitch of his whiskers. But when the Indian chief dished out cat-sized portions of both entrees into carved wooden bowls and offered them to the cats, Rupert immediately dove in. Even Isabella, who had eaten a full meal just an hour earlier, gobbled down her serving.

With stomachs sated and Father Monty momentarily quiet, the chief motioned for the niece to join him by the water's edge. Isabella accompanied her person, her tail stretched up with interest as she walked across the beach.

The chief picked up a pointed stick and began to draw figures in the sand.

The niece soon recognized the *San Carlos*, depicted with its sails billowing in the moonlight as it passed through the mouth of the bay. The Indians had been watching their progress for some time, she realized.

Isabella pawed the air, as if communicating her understanding.

Nodding, the chief shifted to a clean spot of sand and started on a new image. This sketch, too, was of the *San Carlos*, but this time, the ship was shown in a magnified perspective, with its hull filling the entire cleared area.

This version contained far more detail of the boat and its occupants. The niece watched as the chief drew Captain Ayala and Lieutenant Humphretto standing on the ship's top deck, the latter wearing his favorite horsehair coat. On the center mast, far above the deck, he drew a tiny parrot representing Petey. Then, in the galley, one level below, he positioned her uncle, cooking at his stove.

The chief looked up from the sketch, checking that the niece had followed his meaning.

"Yes," she said, hoping the tone of her voice conveyed confirmation.

The chief returned to the drawing, this time focusing on the bottom of the ship's hull. It was a dank rank-smelling area, a place she had visited only once during her few days on board.

Here, the chief drew yet another stick figure, a human with a bent back and wild, scraggly hair.

The niece shook her head, unable to make the correlation.

Seeing her confusion, the chief marked a symbol next to the mysterious ship member.

It was a curved arc, the same as the one Father Monty had pointed out on the altar they'd seen earlier.

The niece squinted at the image and then looked up at the chief. His previously pleasant expression had transitioned to one of fear and foreboding.

She shook her head, perplexed.

"Does he mean the dead crew member? The lowest deck is where they stored his body . . ."

Isabella trilled out a rebuke. The niece glanced down at her cat and then returned to the picture—and the meaning of the chief's message suddenly hit her.

"Oh."

Isabella confirmed the translation.

"Mrao."

The chief nodded again, as if he understood the cat perfectly.

The niece frowned with concern. The Indians were giving them a warning.

Something evil lurked on board the *San Carlos*.

More specifically, she reasoned, some*one*.

Modern-Day San Francisco

Three Months Prior to the America's Cup Regatta

Chapter 36

UNFLAPPABLE

MAYOR MONTGOMERY CARMICHAEL breezed up the central marble staircase inside San Francisco's City Hall. The soles of his dress shoes slapped against the polished stone floor as he strode around the second-floor hallway overlooking the rotunda. Whistling to himself, he danced up to the mayor's office suite and swung open the reception's main doors.

"Good morning, all!"

The niece mumbled a distracted reply. The lemon-scented perfume had once again permeated her desk. Isabella sat on her filing cabinet perch, offering warbling comments of assistance while the niece searched for the source of the smell.

Neither paid much attention as Monty paraded through to his open office door. His regular refrain echoed back to the reception.

"It's a fabulous day to be mayor!"

"If you say so," the niece muttered, crawling beneath her desk to inspect the underside paneling.

It had been a busy couple of months for the accidental administrative assistant. After Alberta's murder on the Baron's yacht, she had been loath to hire a replacement intern for fear of triggering another Ninja attack.

Even if she'd sought a new candidate, the pool of applicants had immediately dried up. The specter of two murdered interns in a row was too big of a coincidence to be ignored. The city's politically minded career builders had fallen back on innate self-preservation.

No matter how prestigious the position, no internship was worth being killed—especially when the slot was in Mayor Carmichael's office.

Unfortunately, this meant that the niece was left doing the bulk of the organizational work for Monty's ongoing America's Cup activities.

As she settled back into her chair and glanced at the pile of the day's paperwork, she thought wistfully of the deceased Alberta. No one had mourned the zealous young woman's passing more than the niece.

The next big event was coming up at the end of the week. As if tempting fate, this, too, would be held on the Baron's yacht.

For the last several days, the niece had been busy tracking down RSVPs from local political leaders, coordinating with the media, and reviewing the final catering details. She felt as if her head were permanently attached to her telephone headset. If she never made another phone call, it would be too soon.

To top it all off, each morning when she returned to the office, she was met by the horrid perfume smell—the Knitting Needle Ninja, mocking her by odor.

As the niece dug determinedly through a side drawer she had searched several times before, Rupert trotted out of the igloo-shaped litter box and fell in line behind the interim mayor, slipping through to the next office before the heavy wooden door closed behind him.

His person didn't notice his departure.

Isabella decided to look the other way.

• • •

"WHAT DO YOU think of my digs, eh, Rupert?" Monty asked, pleased to have someone with whom to share his exalted mood.

The pair walked the circumference of the square room, with Monty pointing out several of the paintings that he had brought in from his art studio—and Rupert wondering if Monty by chance had a secret stash of those fried chicken donuts the downstairs security guard was always talking about.

Unfortunately, they reached the mayor's desk at the far side of the office without any sign of poultry-laden pastries.

The large bureau that had occupied the space for several mayoral administrations had been impounded by the police as evidence in their stalled Ninja investigation. The bloody knitting needles used in the Ninja's assault on the intern last fall had been wrapped in a plastic bag and taped beneath the previous desk's center console.

Monty had replaced the confiscated desk with a far more delicate piece of furniture. The elegant design featured spindly carved legs and a minimalist center shelf. There was no room for anyone to hide a packet of bloody knitting needles in this desk—he'd made sure of that.

Rupert nosed at the nearest wooden leg with disinterest.

The desk's small size also meant there was little chance it held any hidden fried chicken donuts.

AFTER A DISAPPOINTING perusal of the desk, Rupert turned his attention to the decorative chairs by the floor-to-ceiling windows that fronted the balcony. Hopping onto one of the plush velvet seat cushions, the cat gazed out at the Civic Center plaza, an open green space that fronted City

Hall. The public library's main branch, a couple of muse-ums, and several other city and state government buildings also flanked the plaza.

"It's a nice view, don't you think?" Monty sidled up beside his furry friend and reached for the handle to one of the top windowpanes. "If you like, I can open this up for some fresh air."

Rupert's wobbly blue eyes crossed with intrigue as the pane swung open. He lifted himself up on his haunches, curiously sniffing the spring breeze.

Just then, a fist-sized bullet of green feathers zoomed through the opening and into the office.

"Wha-ha-ha!" Monty hollered, ducking as a redheaded parrot swooped toward his face.

The bird was the least of the mayor's problems. Rupert's feline instincts took over, and he leapt into the air, his front paws swatting at the fast-moving object—without regard for their eventual landing point.

"Ahh!" Monty screamed as Rupert's claws accidentally dug into his shoulder blades.

The parrot circled the room, keeping well out of reach. Rupert romped from one chair to the next, finally landing on the desktop, his tail swishing with intrigue.

The parrot's red head cocked to one side as he eyed the cat, sizing up his opposition. He was a cagy bird and not easily intimidated.

Hearing the commotion, the niece threw open the office door. The parrot zoomed through the opening, flying over her head and into the reception area.

Rupert bounded after the bird, running between his per-son's legs.

"What's going on in here?" the niece demanded, peering under the desk where Monty had crawled in an attempt to hide from the chase.

"Bird," he replied in a traumatized whisper.

Turning, the niece looked through the open doorway. She spotted the green intruder perched at the top of a coatrack.

The parrot appeared far less confident in his new surroundings. He had escaped the mayor's main office, but picked up an extra feline.

Isabella stood on top of the filing cabinet, her blue eyes focused on the prey, her back legs tensed for a takedown leap.

The parrot sensed that his odds had now diminished. The once-confident smirk had been replaced by an expression of genuine concern.

Before Isabella could launch her attack, the reception door opened, and a young man stepped inside.

He opened his mouth to introduce himself, but was cut off by the niece's hollered command.

"Close the door!"

It was a testament to the newcomer's sharp wits and quick reaction time that he managed to maneuver around the door and close it behind him without mishap.

The parrot slipped through unscathed, leaving two disappointed cats skidding to a stop at the man's feet.

Unaffected by the feline and avian charge, the unflappable fellow turned to the niece and smiled.

"I'm here for the intern position."

Chapter 37

THE VOLUNTEER

"YOU'RE HERE FOR the intern position?"

The niece couldn't believe her ears.

"The *mayoral* intern position?"

The young man pointed across the reception desk to a sign posted over the door to the mayor's office. Muffled howls emanated from within as Monty applied disinfectant and antibiotic cream to the deep scratches on his shoulders.

"This is the mayor's office suite, isn't it?"

The niece plopped down in the chair behind her desk. "You know what happened to the last two mayoral interns, right?"

The man nodded, unconcerned.

The niece decided to be blunt. "They were both murdered."

The remark caused no dent in the man's armor of confidence.

"By the Knitting Needle Ninja."

He smiled, undeterred by the prospect of being gored through the chest with an antique sewing weapon.

"Hmm." The niece stared at the potential intern, searching for the catch.

Isabella resumed her position on the filing cabinet. The cat leaned forward, her blue eyes gleaming with intensity.

He seemed like a nice enough guy, the niece thought, puzzling over the man's suicidal interest in the treacherous intern position. He wore his hair in a buzz cut, trimmed so short she couldn't tell whether the color was a dark blond or light brown. Fit and athletic, he had a pleasant smile and a casual demeanor.

He didn't *look* like a disturbed individual—nor did he resemble an overzealous political type.

Further questioning was definitely in order.

Before she could speak, Hoxton Finn strode through the reception entrance. Popping his notepad against his left thigh, he grunted at the man who had just volunteered for intern duty.

"Hello, Officer."

THE WOULD-BE UNDERCOVER intern crumpled into an office chair, blushing at how easily he'd been revealed. He grimaced up at Hox.

"I didn't think you'd recognize me that easily." He pointed to his short hair. "I got my hair shaved off and everything."

Hox whapped the notebook against his leg. "I've been telling you to cut that mop for years. Five pounds of hair removal is hardly a disguise. If I recognized you, Mabel surely will."

The officer held up his hands, trying to deflect the criticism. "It was unlucky, running into you first thing. Before I had a chance to perfect my role. You won't tell anyone at the station, will you, Hox? I'll never hear the end of it."

Hox huffed noncommittally. "They should have told me they were sending you over here."

"Well, hey, no harm done," the man said with an impish grin. "You're in the know now."

The notepad took another beating. "Surely you're not serious about going through with this?"

The officer straightened his shoulders. "Of course I am. We can't let the Ninja continue her killing spree."

"You're underestimating this woman. You think she's nothing but a little old lady with a knife problem."

Solemnly, the officer unbuttoned his shirt, revealing a Kevlar vest. "I'm prepared for anything . . ."

But Hox wasn't finished. "Or maybe you're just trying to advance your career." He bent over the man's chair. "Accolades aren't much use if you're dead."

The officer rebuttoned his shirt. His expression remained steadfast. Hox's warnings were not having any effect.

"What's your alias?" The reporter crossed his arms over his chest. "So I know what I'm supposed to call you."

"Toronto. James Toronto." He paused before adding with a wink. "In honor of Alberta."

Hox groaned and turned away.

The niece had remained silent throughout this exchange, occasionally looking up at the filing cabinet to visually confer with Isabella. As Hox paced a circle around her desk, however, she leaned in for a question.

"Can you do event organization?" she asked. "Some routine filing, perhaps make a few phone calls?"

At his nodding shrug, she shoved a stack of papers across the desk.

"Great. You're hired."

With an apologetic glance at Hox, she added, "And, uh, please try not to get yourself killed."

Chapter 38

CAPED CRUSADERS

THE FRISKY PARROT shot into the second-floor foyer outside the mayor's office suite, relieved to hear the reception door *thump* shut behind him, sealing the two pursuing cats on the opposite side.

The bird took a relaxed swoop through City Hall's ornate rotunda, his red head bobbing as he surveyed the building's open center.

He had strayed almost two miles from his regular roost on Telegraph Hill, but the morning light streaming through the stained glass windows felt warm and inviting—and there was something familiar about the stenciled image of the *San Carlos* etched into the windows' center panes . . .

The parrot circled the enormous interior, casting a moving shadow across the multiple marble surfaces.

Office workers traversing the second-floor corridor shuffled from side to side, trying to avoid the dark object sliding across their feet. Someone realized the source of the shadow and called it out to the others. Soon, groups began to gather, staring up at the unusual sight.

Despite the vast open space beneath the dome, City Hall rarely entertained avian visitors. Occasionally, a stray pigeon or two managed to sneak through the front doors before being corralled out the exit, but no one could recall ever having seen a parrot inside the building.

Pointed fingers traced the bird's path through the rotunda. Excited whispers bounced off the stone walls as the collected watchers lost track of the green body and then picked it up again.

Unaware of all this attention, the parrot glided into the ceremonial rotunda at the top of the central marble staircase and landed on the polished bronze head of the Harvey Milk bust.

Making himself at home, he reached over his shoulder and casually preened his feathers.

• • •

MEANWHILE, THE MORNING'S first wedding party gathered in the first-floor foyer outside City Hall's licensing office.

The couple had decided to turn their nuptials into a theme party. The bride was dressed as Wonder Woman, with a red and gold corset, a short star-spangled skirt, and knee-high red leather boots. The groom had donned a shiny blue Superman suit, complete with flowing cape. Members of the wedding party were clad as various comic book characters.

Everyone cheered when the wedding coordinator rounded the corner, applauding with delight at her over-the-top Marilyn Monroe getup. Her blond wig, stuffed bosom blouse, and bouncy white skirt fit right in with the rest of the group.

The groom whooped his approval.

"Man, I can't wait to see our wedding pictures."

With a demure smile, the coordinator ushered the eager couple and their entourage toward the inner dome area.

But at the entrance to the rotunda, she looked up and across to the top of the central staircase where the soup vendor stood with the parrot perched on his arm. Raising her hand, she halted the wedding party.

"There you go, Petey. Let me give you a ride." Oscar's voice echoed down to the rotunda's lower level as he began to descend the steps. "What are you doing so far from home? Come along with me. I'll take you back where you belong."

The wedding coordinator pursed her heavily painted lips. She wasn't sure why, but she felt a strong aversion to the bird.

Pivoting, she turned her clients toward the elevator bank in the foyer wing.

Preoccupied with the antics of a Green Lantern–impersonating groomsman, the group didn't notice the sudden diversion.

But after a discussion about their various superhero powers, the conversation turned to the recent City Hall crimes.

"Is it true the Ninja killed another intern? On the billionaire's yacht during an America's Cup shindig?"

"Do you think she's hanging out here in City Hall?" The caped crusader shuddered at the thought. "That would be creepy."

"Well," Marilyn replied as the elevator doors slid open, "that's what they say . . ."

Chapter 39

THE CAPTAIN OF A
TROUBLED SHIP

REPORTER HOXTON FINN returned to the newspaper's Mission Street office building that afternoon, perplexed by the latest development in the Ninja case. He'd spent several hours at the police station, arguing with the chief detective about the risks of Officer Toronto's undercover assignment—to no avail.

It had been three months without any leads. The investigators were desperate for a break.

With a grunt, Hox swung open the door to the third-floor conference room that he had commandeered last fall after the murder of intern Spider Jones.

He had an assigned desk in the main office area, but he rarely used it. Whenever he worked in the newspaper's building, he closed himself up in this conference room. Here, he was the captain of a troubled ship, surrounded by files, boxes, newspaper clippings, and other various documents related to the Knitting Needle Ninja.

Everything the reporter had gathered about the most recent episode was piled in the center of a long wooden table.

Alberta's murder on the Baron's yacht had generated a stir in the local press. Once the signature knifed knitting needles had been spotted, there had been no doubt as to the murderer's identity. Despite a thorough search of the massive boat, the Ninja had eluded capture.

Alberta's beaming smile had been plastered across every news outlet. Word had quickly spread, generating gruesome headlines.

THE NINJA TAKES ANOTHER

BAY AREA ASSASSIN
SKEWERS CITY HALL INTERN

NAUGHTY KNITTER
NOTCHES ONE MORE VICTIM

Conventional wisdom now assumed that the Ninja had taken up a disguise—leading to a second series of bold-type banners.

NINJA GIVES SLEUTHS THE SLIP

HOW WELL DO YOU KNOW
YOUR NEIGHBOR?

NURSING HOME KNITTING CIRCLE
NEEDLED BY COPS

Hox grunted as he flipped through the pages. Each round of publicity, he sensed, only increased the likelihood of another kill.

He had a bad feeling about the police department's covert intern operation. He leaned back in the conference room's creaking chair, surveyed the cluttered table, and wondered how long it would be until the next slaying.

"You'd better watch your back, Toronto."

Angel Island, near the Anchored *San Carlos*

August 1775

Chapter 40

POSSESSED

"THAT'S PREPOSTEROUS!"

Father Monty shook his head, refusing to accept the niece's interpretation of the images the Indian chief had drawn in the sand. He absolutely rejected the notion that something evil had invaded their ship.

They were on their way back to the *San Carlos*, having bade good-bye to their new friends at the campfire. Father Monty led the way down the return path. The niece followed several feet behind, pushing the cat-filled stroller.

"Absolutely ridiculous!"

Father Monty's ranting could be heard all along the beach.

"I'm a priest," he said, stopping to turn and wag his finger at the niece. "Trust me, I would know if the ship was possessed."

He resumed his pace, no less agitated. "I have specific training in this area." He threw his hands in the air. "No respect, I tell you."

The niece glanced down at the stroller and exchanged looks with Isabella.

A discreet warble of skepticism floated up from the carriage.

"*Mrao.*"

BY THE TIME Father Monty reached the gangplank that had been left propped down to the beach, he'd nearly lost his voice.

While the niece still viewed the priest with suspicion and distrust, those feelings were now evenly matched—if not surpassed—with that of annoyance.

Thankfully, the buzz on board the *San Carlos* drowned out Monty's last hoarse complaints.

Humphretto and his team had just returned from their exploration of the bay's south shoreline, and the lieutenant was eager to share what they'd found.

As the niece hefted the cat carriage up the slanted walkway, Humphretto began his enthusiastic report.

"Unbelievable find, Captain. You could not imagine a better port. Yes, yes, okay, it's a bit marshy there along the shore, but we can work with that."

A few muttered grumbles rumbled up from the men who had paddled the canoes.

"Okay, yes, there were some issues with the current," he said defensively. "But nothing like what we experienced coming in from the Pacific."

Ayala listened to the discourse, vaguely amused and secretly jealous of the excursion. It had been difficult for him to remain on the ship while watching Humphretto and the other crew members through his scope. Frustrated, the captain pressed down on his injured foot, an action that sent a shot of pain up through his leg, a reminder of why he had been forced to stay behind.

The captain hadn't spent the whole afternoon with his foot propped up. Restless, he'd taken advantage of the lull to conduct another search of the ship.

The few crew members still on board had been busy

swabbing the deck, cleaning the rigging, and checking the intricate network of ropes for nicks or frays. Down below in his galley, Oscar had hummed while chopping up ingredients for the night's meal. But beyond these areas of activity, the captain had been able to inspect the *San Carlos* unimpeded.

He'd scoured every available inch, hoping to find some previously overlooked clue to the deckhand's murder—or to the phantom stowaway widely believed to have killed him.

Everything had been disturbingly normal.

He'd found nothing but his own increased unease.

STILL PONDERING THE mystery, Ayala turned to greet Father Carmichael, who had just stepped off the gangplank and onto the deck.

"How was your walk?"

"Indians," Monty croaked hoarsely.

Ayala thumped his left thigh with his spyglass. His face registered concern.

"Were they friendly?"

Monty threw his hands in the air. "Witchcraft-practicing heathens . . . uncivilized barbarians . . ." Then he stomped down the stairs toward his quarters.

Puzzled, the captain shifted his attention to the niece. With his free hand, he grabbed the front rim of the wicker stroller and helped her lift it over the top of the gangplank.

"Well?"

The niece shrugged. "They fed us a nice lunch."

Ayala sensed there was something more. "And?"

From the cat compartment, Isabella called out her response.

"Mrao."

The niece translated the remark for the captain.

"The Indians think the *San Carlos* is cursed."

Chapter 41

THE MORNING ROUTINE

OSCAR ROSE THE next morning at his regular predawn hour. Rolling out of his bunk, he dressed and yawned his way to the kitchen.

Coffee was the first order of business.

He crouched in front of the stove, wrenched open the blackened metal door to access the lower grate, and stirred the coals. With an expertise honed over many years of repetition, he puffed on the glowing embers and fed in tiny pieces of kindling until a flame flickered and began to grow.

With the stove warming, he prepared for his least-favorite task of the morning: pulling his arthritic body into a standing position after starting the fire.

He wasn't one to delay a necessary but painful endeavor. Both hands gripped the nearest countertop as Oscar heaved his body upward. A loud *creak* signified the popping of joints. Panting, he gripped the small of his back and waited for the ache to subside.

The niece would gladly have started the fire for him each morning, but he didn't like to wake her. And besides, he wouldn't be able to carry on his cooking duties much longer. Best to keep up his mobility for as long as he could. At some point, the niece would have to take over. He wanted to delay that inevitability for as long as possible.

Pulling open a cabinet door, he reached inside for the container of coffee grounds. He held the open tin under his nose and let the rich smell engulf his senses.

"Ahh." His scruffy eyebrows pumped as he soaked in the aroma.

Feeling much more awake, Oscar dumped a spoonful of coffee into a metal percolator, topped the container off with water, and set it on the stove to heat.

A ROOSTER'S MUFFLED crow summoned Oscar to the opposite side of the ship.

He reached for a basket and hobbled out of the kitchen to the main corridor. With a grimace at the snores emanating from behind the chapel door, he proceeded down the hallway, stopping at the end farthest away from the steps leading to the main deck.

Here, the chicken chatter was much louder. Behind a grated metal door, Oscar entered the ship's small chicken coop.

A well-known figure among the coop's feathered residents, the chef was greeted with disgruntled clucks and defensive hunkering.

Thus began the morning's regular testy exchange.

Oscar approached the first nest and tentatively slid his hand out.

"Now, then, Bessie. I'm only taking what I need . . ."

Bessie was unmoved by this assurance. Her beak jumped out and pecked Oscar's skin.

"Ow!" He rubbed the sore spot on his finger. "I'll remember that, little lady. There'll be another feast before we pull up anchor and head out of here." He gave the chicken a meaningful stare.

"A good excuse for me to use my big skillets."

MUTTERING ABOUT FRIED chicken revenge, Oscar returned to the kitchen with a basketful of eggs.

Pouring himself a cup of fresh coffee, he cleaned his hands and started on the biscuits. He poured flour and water into a large bowl, still grumbling to himself as he eyed the amounts.

With a wooden spoon, he folded over the mixture and then tested the consistency with the tip of a finger.

The eyebrows pumped again as he adjusted the balance by adding a tad more flour.

A dash of salt, a dollop of lard, a spoonful of baking soda, and a few other secret seasonings topped off the ingredients. Once the components were evenly distributed, he turned the bowl sideways and rolled the resulting sticky lump out onto his flour-dusted counter. Minutes later, a greased pan full of circular-cut mounds was ready to slide into the oven.

Turning to the next portion of the meal, Oscar sliced up several dozen links of sausage and began heating them in a pan.

While he waited for the meat to cook, he glanced through the galley to the quarters he shared with his niece. The young woman was still asleep in her bunk, her arms wrapped around Rupert, whose furry head shared her pillow.

Isabella emerged from the covers and hopped onto the floor. She stretched her legs in a deep lunge and sauntered into the kitchen.

She and Oscar shared a good-morning gaze—before they both froze with alarm. Back arching, Isabella let out a hissing growl.

A foreign odor had entered the kitchen, overriding the combined smells of the coffee, the baking biscuits, and the sausage.

It was the lemony-sweet scent of a woman's perfume.

Chapter 42

TORONTINO

OSCAR FINISHED PREPARING breakfast, trying to forget about the perfume. The scent had vanished as suddenly as it had appeared. The kitchen had quickly returned to its robust breakfast aroma.

Neither he nor Isabella shared the most recent perfume intrusion with the niece as she and Rupert woke and drowsily joined them.

The cooking team was soon caught up in the busiest segment of the morning's meal preparation. An industrial-sized pot of coffee bubbled on the stove. The biscuits reached a flaky golden shade and were rescued from the oven just before burning. Sausage links were rolled into a serving dish; their skillet was then used to cook a heap of scrambled eggs.

But the task of simultaneously bringing multiple dishes to completion wasn't enough to fully distract Oscar—or Isabella—from thoughts of the portentous perfume.

TOO SLEEPY TO pick up on her uncle's anxiety (and not keen enough to notice Isabella's masked unease), the niece began carrying trays of food up to the ship's top deck.

Hungry sailors lined the dining table, thirstily passing around the vat of coffee. A full day's exploring was on the agenda and the men were eager to fill up before heading out on the canoes.

The platters of sausage and biscuits were met with cheers. The arrival of the scrambled eggs received another round of applause.

The niece grinned at the antics. "I'll pass your approval on to the chef."

From his seat at the head of the table, Captain Ayala leaned back and stroked his chin, relieved at the improved morale. The ship was back on track. His foot felt immensely better after being elevated all night while he slept. He might even join the day's outing.

Between mouthfuls, one of the crew members called out. "Hey, where's Torontino? Somebody should pull him out of bed."

Humphretto swallowed a bite and politely wiped his mouth with a napkin.

"Torontino. What a pleasant chap. I sat him down for a haircut last night. Shaved off that mullet and left him with a trim buzz cut. You'll hardly recognize him. I think it suits his face. So much easier to maintain while on ship."

The niece arrived with the last menu item, a saucer of gravy. No sooner had she delivered the dish to the table than a horrified shriek rose up from below.

Concerned, she raced back to the steps, worried that something had happened to her uncle.

She clasped a hand to her chest, thankful to see him standing—unharmed—at the opening to the lower corridor.

Oscar grimly shook his head.

The shriek had emanated from Father Monty. The priest

had gone back to the chapel to fetch his cuff links, which he'd forgotten to put on before breakfast.

He'd found a body on the floor by the confessional.

Another crew member had met a grisly end. A man whose head had been freshly shaved in a stylish crew cut lay facedown in a pool of blood.

A collective gasp rose from the deck as the news circled the table.

It's Torontino.

Ayala jumped from his chair and raced down the stairs. His left foot was once more throbbing with pain by the time he pounded into the chapel.

On the ground a few feet from the body, he spied a pair of bloody knitting needles. The curved points had been fitted with a sharp blade. They were exact replicas of the first murder weapon.

Father Monty stared down at the body. He was fixed to the spot, his expression unreadable. He hadn't moved since making the gory discovery.

Suddenly, he slapped his hands together.

"Right then." He looked up at the captain and added briskly, "I'd better get started with that exorcism."

Modern-Day San Francisco

One Month Prior to the America's Cup Regatta

Chapter 43

INTERNSHIP INTERMINABLE

OFFICER TORONTO WAS soon immersed in his intern duties at City Hall.

The niece had immediately put him to work. The better to make his undercover intern role convincing, she'd assured him.

Toronto quickly found himself up to his ears in paperwork, phone calls, e-mails, and errands, all in support of Mayor Carmichael's never-ending activities with the America's Cup organizers.

After a few weeks of intern duty with no sign of the Ninja—other than the occasional blitz of lemony-sweet perfume—he'd begun to have second thoughts about his assignment.

The concept of sailing as a competitive sport was completely foreign to him. His feet had never left the solid comfort of land—truth be told, he didn't even like boats. But having grown up in San Francisco and worked its steep streets for years as a beat cop, he'd grown used to the bay's constant presence, a corner of blue peeking around the next corner, the wide expanse that popped into view at the top of a hill.

Trapped inside the claustrophobic confines of the intern cubicles in City Hall's dreary basement, he felt restless and utterly inept.

Toronto flipped open a file folder and began wading through the specifications for yet another sailing-related promotional event. With a restless sigh, he ran his hands over his crew cut's fuzzy bristle.

Waiting for a seasoned serial killer to make her next move was not near as glamorous as he'd thought it would be.

He was an overworked paper pusher, a secretarial sitting duck who could be picked off at any moment by a knitting needle–crazed nanny.

This assignment was starting to wear on his nerves.

And he really missed his long hair.

• • •

ONE MONTH BEFORE the start of San Francisco's America's Cup, two months into Officer Toronto's interminable internship, Mayor Carmichael threw open the door to his office, startling both the niece and the undercover intern, who were discussing the latest promotional project.

Isabella calmly shifted her gaze to the doorway. The filing cabinet perch, she'd found, transmitted excellent acoustics. Even through the thick wooden door, she'd heard Monty's footsteps crossing the inner office.

As for Rupert, he merely yawned from his sprawled position on the pillowed cat bed. Few events warranted disruption of his midmorning nap, especially when he'd been dreaming about fried chicken donuts. He smacked his lips together and rolled over, covering his face with his paws.

Monty snapped the collar of a black overcoat he'd pulled on over his suit.

"I've just had a call from the Baron," he announced dramatically.

The niece and Toronto exchanged weary looks, afraid of what might be coming next.

The America's Cup had been Monty's primary focus since he took office in January, but in recent weeks, the upcoming sailboat race had garnered his full attention. He had no interest in anything else—including any issue remotely related to his actual mayoral duties.

In any other instance, such negligent behavior by a sitting mayor would have been met with censure and rebuke. But given Monty's eccentric reputation, the rest of City Hall had decided that a distracted mayor was preferable to one with potentially misguided activism. The board of supervisors had carried on with the city's business, leaving Monty to his regatta fixation.

"Come along, team," he said with a flourish that included Rupert and Isabella. "We've been invited to the pier for a tour of the pavilion."

The niece held up the file she and Toronto had been discussing.

"We've got too much work to do. Can't you go without us?"

Monty rushed forward and snatched the file from her hands. "They've just finished the pier renovations—you'll want to see that—and . . ." He drew the last word out into a dramatic pause.

"I'm going for a ride on the official team racing boat!"

The niece shrugged. "That should be entertaining." She began loading the cats into their stroller.

"Count me in!" Eager for the chance to escape City Hall, Officer Toronto scooped up a clipboard with his latest notes, gave the ringing telephone a surly look, and helped the niece through the main door with the cat carriage.

Quiet fell upon the mayor's office suite.

Then a surge of lemony perfume swilled down from the ceiling and onto the niece's desk.

Chapter 44

MAN OVERBOARD

MAYOR CARMICHAEL AND his staff weren't the only invites to the Baron's tour of the newly completed America's Cup facilities and a preview of his team's racing sailboat.

The mayor's town car dropped his group off at the pier's Embarcadero entrance. As the niece stood on the sidewalk, gripping the handle to the cat-filled stroller, she heard the familiar *pop* of a reporter's notebook.

Hoxton Finn strode up, accompanied by Humphrey, his ever-present hairstylist. A full news crew followed shortly behind.

The Baron had promised exclusive behind-the-scenes access, hoping for favorable television and newspaper coverage.

The billionaire greeted the crowd as they walked inside the main warehouse.

"We have our latest prototype pulled up to the dock out front." He motioned toward the far end of the pier. "The team has been practicing in her all morning. She's giving us great speed out and back to Angel Island." Cocking an eyebrow, he turned toward Monty. "You ready to take a spin, Mayor?"

Monty leapt forward, apparently eager to begin, but the niece knew he'd skipped out on his sailing lessons. Despite his frequently cited desire to gain nautical expertise, she suspected he secretly feared the water. If the prospect of setting sail on the bay caused him any anxiety, he didn't show it.

"I thought you'd never ask!" he replied with gusto.

As the rest of the group caught up to where the boat was tethered at the far end of the pier, the niece stared with concern at the sailboat bobbing in the water. She instantly sensed that this was a bad idea.

She'd seen numerous photos of the racing boats over the past few months. But even the massive America's Cup billboard fronting Union Square had failed to capture the vessel's enormous height—and fragile instability.

Isabella shared her person's misgivings about Monty's upcoming boat ride. She warbled skeptically from the stroller.

"Wrao."

The camera crews whipped out their equipment and began filming as the racing team marched out of a nearby warehouse, fully kitted in their sailing gear. Each sailor was covered from head to toe in a heavy-duty wet suit, the fabric reinforced throughout with patches of nylon sheeting. The men began strapping on state-of-the-art plastic helmets, shin guards, and elbow protectors.

The Baron nodded at the team's outfits.

"First, Mayor, you'll have to suit up."

The niece thought she detected a slight trepidation in Monty's voice as he gulped out his answer.

"Lead the way, sir!"

TWENTY MINUTES LATER, Monty emerged from the changing room.

The rubber costume, it seemed, had not been an easy fit.

A teetering chuckle ran through the crowd on the pier, which had grown to at least thirty. The niece recognized most as members of Hox's news organization. In addition, several members of the board of supervisors and their staff had made the short trek from City Hall. This event had clearly been staged for maximum publicity.

She was beginning to think it was the Baron who was using Monty for his own personal gain, and not the other way around.

Monty had been filmed in a wet suit before—while being chased by a hungry albino alligator.

This wet suit would have provided better protection against the gator's snapping jaws, the niece thought as she studied the thick insulating material.

But standing next to the athletic crew members, with their toned muscles and chiseled expressions, Monty did not compare favorably.

Officer Toronto leaned toward her shoulder. "Should we tell him that he looks like a rubber-coated toothpick?"

The niece shook her head, trying to suppress a grin. Monty's audacious self-belief had taken him this far in life. He was unlikely to abandon it now.

"He wouldn't believe you anyway."

THE RACING CREW piled onto the sailboat, nimbly crawling over the webbing that connected the craft's two slender hulls. Ropes spun in their pulleys as the sails were tightened and maneuvered into position.

Isabella pawed the passenger compartment cover, demanding to be let out so she could watch the spectacle without the hindrance of the netting.

"I don't know, Issy." The niece squinted at the racing boat. "This might get ugly."

At the cat's stern look, the niece relented. She slipped a

harness around Isabella's chest, hooked a leash into the top center hook, and helped her onto the pier.

Rupert took advantage of the extra space to stretch out into a full-body sprawl. He appeared unconcerned about Monty's prospects on the water—that, or Monty's impending peril couldn't compete with his latest musings on fried chicken donuts.

If Rupert had confidence in Monty's ability to survive the sailboating endeavor, he was one of the few.

The observers' faces had quickly turned from jocular to tense. Hoxton Finn scribbled furiously in his notebook, grunting with increasing frequency. Beside him, Humphrey fiddled nervously with his jacket, a stylish if somewhat unconventional horsehair assembly.

The extra crew member himself was now visibly ill at ease. Monty's long legs wobbled precariously as he tried to steady himself on the craft. His thin lips pinched with worry.

The sailboat was primarily composed of flexible moving pieces. There was little in the way of fixed support. As the mayor struggled for a foothold, his slim body bowed back and forth, failing to find its center of gravity.

"I wonder if Monty knows how to swim," the niece murmured.

Sitting on the pier at the woman's feet, Isabella twitched her whiskers dubiously.

A passing ferryboat kicked out a wave that promulgated toward the pier. The rocking motion combined with a gust of wind to throw Monty completely off balance. He fell onto the slick shell that covered the nearest hull. Before a fellow crew member could grab him, his feet popped up into the air and he disappeared, headfirst and backward, over the side.

Isabella and the niece stared down at the swirling water beside the boat. There was no sign of the city's interim mayor.

After a moment, Isabella looked up at her person, offering a matter-of-fact assessment.

"*Mrao.*"

• • •

WITH ATTENTION FOCUSED on the sailboat and the submerged mayor, none of the many spectators on the pier noticed that Officer Toronto had disappeared.

Chapter 45

ANOTHER ONE BITES THE DUST

OFFICER TORONTO SHOOK his head as he watched Mayor Carmichael climb onto the racing sailboat. It was clear from the outset that Monty was destined for a dunking. The awkward display was painful to watch.

This will not end well, Toronto thought to himself.

It was a sadly prophetic statement.

Distracted by the fiasco unfolding on the water, he loosened his grip on the clipboard.

A gust of wind pushed in from the bay, blowing a wall of air across the pier. Jackets flapped, the sailboat tipped sideways, the mayor splashed into the water, and the top sheets attached to Toronto's clipboard flew off and scattered down the pier.

"Bah! Come back here."

Toronto clamped his hand down on the clipboard, securing the remaining pages. Then he scurried after the lost papers, dodging a pair of squawking seagulls as he scrambled across the windswept platform.

He caught the last sheet by the entrance to the sailing team's locker room.

Stepping into the doorway, he bent to scoop it up.

"From paper pusher to paper chaser. Man, I've gotta get back to my regular beat . . ."

The edge of the building blocked the bay breeze. In the stillness of the doorway, a second puff of air filled the vacuum—one laden with a lemony-sweet perfume.

Officer Toronto dropped to the floor, reaching for the service weapon strapped to his lower calf.

His instincts had kicked in a second too late.

Avoiding the encumbrance of the bulletproof vest, Mabel aimed for his neck. Stepping up behind him, she reached around his shoulders and deftly slid the knitting needle's knife across his jugular.

It was a quick and efficient maneuver.

Toronto gasped his last breath as the Ninja tossed the bloody needle on the concrete floor.

She surveyed the results of her handiwork. Then she exited the warehouse, her footsteps echoing calmly across the pier.

Chapter 46

UNINVITED

"**WHAT DO YOU** mean I've been uninvited?"

Monty's indignant howl echoed through the reception area. The protest could be heard outside the mayor's office suite, all the way to the elevators.

"Sorry, Monty." The niece shrugged apologetically. "They said they just couldn't risk it."

Minutes earlier, she had received a phone call from the Baron's administrative assistant.

In the wake of Officer Toronto's death, many race sponsors had raised concerns with Cup organizers. The corporate entities were wary of having their brand names associated with yet another murder.

After careful deliberation, the organizers had respectfully asked that the mayor limit his public involvement with the race, for fear it might incite the Ninja to make another attack, potentially sinking the whole event.

The Baron felt he had no choice. Monty's VIP credentials had officially been revoked.

The niece relayed the explanation, but it didn't help Monty accept the Baron's decision.

"Revoked?" Monty repeated, incredulous. He threw his hands in the air. "I'm the mayor of this city, for Pete's sake." He leaned over the niece's desk. The veins in his thin neck pulsed with anger.

"San Francisco has put a substantial amount of money into this event." After an anxious swallow, he added tensely, "I've got a lot at stake here. He can't just uninvite me."

The niece slid a pencil behind her ear and glanced down at her notes. "I believe the exact terminology the admin used was 'decommissioned.'" She scanned her handwriting and looked up. "Your position on the event team has been decommissioned."

Monty's cheeks turned a strange shade of purple. Pushing away from the desk, he pivoted toward his office, stomped inside, and slammed the door shut.

Seconds later, he stormed back into the reception area to the spot where he had hung the sailing poster months before. Lifting the frame from the hook, he turned the poster face inward against the wall and returned to his office.

The niece looked up at the filing cabinet where Isabella had silently observed the exchange.

"Well, that's that, then."

The cat gazed thoughtfully at the back of the poster before issuing her cryptic reply.

"*Mrao.*

On Board the *San Carlos*

Anchored off Angel Island

August 1775

Chapter 47

VERY SUPERSTITIOUS

"SUCH A SHAME about Torontino . . . he was a good man."

The sentiment reverberated through the ship as the crew member's death sank in.

The first killing had disrupted the *San Carlos* and left everyone on edge, but the associated shock had quickly passed. The victim had been a virtual unknown. His passing was, sadly, anonymous.

The second murder was far more damaging to morale. Torontino was well known to everyone on board. The sorrowful murmurs could be heard in every quarter.

"I know his mother back in Barcelona. The poor woman will be devastated."

"My cousin married his sister. He was the best man at my wedding . . ."

"I sailed with his brother a few years back. He was a good mate." The speaker heaved out a heavy sigh. "They were both good mates."

Beyond the painful round of grieving, however, the new death raised an issue of far greater concern for Captain Ayala.

Sailors were a notoriously superstitious lot, constantly on the lookout for omens that might predict their fate. They read meaning into everything. The most innocuous observations could be twisted into portentous warnings. Odd-shaped clouds, irregular waves, or even a disturbance in the flotsam and jetsam that floated on the water's surface—any one of these sightings could raise irrational alarm.

Most sailors kept talismans for good luck. The treasured trinkets were secured to their body the moment they boarded ship and not relinquished until they returned safely to port.

Even Captain Ayala wasn't completely immune to the practice.

He carried in his luggage a special pair of socks that he wore while navigating difficult passages—he'd put them on the night the *San Carlos* sailed through the Golden Gate. They were hanging on a hook in his stateroom, airing out so they'd be ready for the return maneuver.

But the captain drew the line at footwear.

Superstitions related to weather formations, water turbulence, or seaweed debris were, in his book, just plain silly.

AFTER TORONTINO'S DEATH, Captain Ayala was a lone voice of reason on a boat full of hysteria.

Rumors of what had happened to the ship's previous captain and crew had been circulating since the vessel set sail from the Mexican coast. The newly assembled team had at first ignored the dark whispers they'd heard in San Blas. They'd welcomed the opportunity to jump on board a new ship. But what had initially been dismissed as nonsense was now being taken much more seriously.

The warning conveyed by the Angel Island Indians had spread rapidly—despite Ayala's attempts to quash it.

The niece swore she'd told only her uncle Oscar and the captain about the scenes the Indian chief had drawn in the sand.

That left Father Monty as the likely gossip.

Captain Ayala groaned at the thought of the chatty priest. Monty's so-called confessional in the ship's chapel had become a popular venue for information exchange.

The captain shook his head in frustration. He couldn't very well shut down the chapel, but its role in amplifying rampant speculation wasn't helping morale.

Vivid tales of the Indian's warning and the curved symbol the chief had drawn—combined with the second knitting needle murder in as many days—had led many to believe that the ship was cursed.

The sailors feared they would be picked off, one by one. Panic was setting in. Crew members were staring at one another with distrust and suspicion.

The situation could easily descend into a crazed mutiny.

The only way the *San Carlos* could be cleared of this cancerous angst was with a spiritual cleansing by a respected religious official.

It was a feat unlikely to be pulled off by Father Carmichael.

Grumbling bitterly, Ayala tromped down the steps to the ship's lower level.

He had better check on Monty's exorcism preparations.

Chapter 48

THE MEDIATION

CAPTAIN AYALA HEARD Monty's voice inside the chapel as he approached. The captain stopped in the corridor, across from the entrance to the kitchen, and listened to the priest's one-sided conversation.

"Now, gentlemen. Let's discuss the nature of your dispute."

Frowning, Ayala leaned in closer. He wasn't aware of any specific frictions among his crew—and he was leery of Father Monty getting involved in such a conflict if one did exist. Surely, Monty's meddling would only make the problem worse.

The next comment appeared to support this conclusion.

"He pulled your hair?" Monty tutted his disapproval. "That doesn't sound very nice."

There was a long pause, followed by Monty's summation of the rebuttal.

"I see. And you say he chased you up the mast pole?" Finger tapping echoed out into the corridor. "That sounds a bit extreme."

Ayala pressed his ear against the hallway's wooden paneling, straining to hear. Try as he might, he couldn't pick up anything from the voices of the two men who were participating in the counseling session. Monty's words, however, continued to come through loud and clear.

"Well, there's no reason why you two can't be friends."

The suggestion was met by an awkward silence, broken only by Monty's blustering *pshaw*.

"You think he's trying to *kill* you? Oh, surely not."

At the loud *squawk* that followed this last statement, Ayala charged into the chapel.

"What's going on in here?" he demanded loudly—and then stopped short.

He squinted at the feline and feathered pair seated in front of Father Monty: a fluffy orange and white cat and a green parrot with a bright red head.

Rupert and Petey turned to look at the room's intruder.

"Captain Ayala," Monty said, standing from his chair. "I was just gathering a few tools for the exorcism."

He nodded to the animals seated next to him.

"Gentlemen, I think we can pick this up later." He added sternly, "I trust you can put aside your differences until then."

Ayala stood speechless as the bird and cat filed, one after the other, out of the room.

THE CAPTAIN WAS still staring at the empty doorway when Monty leaned toward him and whispered in his ear.

"So, Captain, about this exorcism . . ."

Ayala immediately snapped his attention back to the priest.

Monty stared sheepishly at the ground. "I have to confess, I haven't performed that particular ceremony before."

The captain tensed with alarm.

"What?"

Monty stepped back, self-consciously straightening his

brown robe. "Well, of course, I studied the procedure at seminary." He reached beneath his robe to fiddle with a cuff link. "And I did see it done once . . . on a rabbit."

The captain's head ached with the same intensity as his left foot.

"Listen here . . ." Ayala's face skewed up as he suppressed an expletive. With effort, he instead used the priest's name. "Father Carmichael." He drew in a steadying breath and continued. "We've got an emergency situation on board this ship. My men have bought into this crazy notion that the *San Carlos* is cursed. If we don't get this thing under control, there's going to be a mass exodus—or worse."

He placed a hand on the priest's shoulder to emphasize the seriousness of the matter. "You've got to go out there, do your hocus-pocus, and convince the crew that whatever evil spirit they think has invaded this ship has been exorcised." He clenched his grip through the brown robe. "I mean totally and completely gone."

Monty twisted the hem of the ceremonial collar he'd draped around his neck.

"You know, I really should have permission from my bishop before trying this."

Ayala gritted his teeth. "I'll cover for you."

With that, the captain turned and headed for the exit. At the threshold, he stopped and looked back.

"Just make it believable."

Chapter 49

INEXORABLE

FIFTEEN MINUTES LATER, Father Carmichael emerged from the second floor stairwell carrying a velvet bag and a book that detailed the steps for performing the exorcism ritual. On his head, he wore a pointed hat whose purple fabric matched that of the velvet bag.

Captain Ayala stopped him at the top of the steps. He grimaced at the hat, pursed his lips as if he'd just swallowed something distasteful, and hissed, "Remember, Father. Be convincing." With that, he shoved the priest forward.

The passengers and crew had gathered on the ship's top deck for the ceremony. The observers' faces reflected a mix of curiosity, bemusement, religious fervor, and skepticism. The niece and Isabella fell into the last category, while Rupert landed decidedly in the first. He could hardly wait to see what entertainment Monty had up his sleeve this time.

The niece stood with her arms crossed over her chest; the corners of her mouth pinched with concern. Isabella sat at her person's feet, her orange ears turned sideways. Rupert bounced up and down beside them, trying to see around the surrounding sea of legs.

With a solemn nod to the assembled audience, Monty set the velvet bag on the deck, pulled out several wooden crosses, and arrayed them in a circle at his feet.

Standing, he opened the book to a marked section. The pages were yellow and frail with age, the edges gilded with a crusty gold paint. Holding the book up to his face, he ran his index finger down a column of text, as if reviewing a checklist, and then began to read out loud.

He appeared to be reciting some sort of incantation, but the words were (perhaps intentionally) difficult to discern.

"rom . . . tus . . . ettya . . . mmm . . . nnn . . . nus . . ."

The audience edged closer, straining to listen. A sailor whispered at the back of the crowd.

"If we can't hear him, how will the demon?"

Monty raised the volume of his voice.

The niece soon concluded he would have been better off masking his words. She'd never heard Latin spoken in such a garbled and unmetered manner.

"romulus terribulus, adieus supplicamus . . ."

She looked down at Isabella. The cat's expression conveyed utter disdain.

The performance continued to deteriorate as the chant droned on. Monty still held the book up to his face, but he had clearly stopped reading the text. The ad-lib became obvious.

"exitus the boaticus you evilus spiritus . . ."

But things really went downhill when he began tapping the toes of his shoes. Before long, he was swaying wildly back and forth, as if a lively music played inside his head.

Even the true believers in the crowd started to question the ritual's authenticity.

Monty finished off the recitation with a few dancing pivots. Scooping up one of the crosses at his feet, he used it to make a series of wild flourishing gestures, first at the audience, then at the stairs leading down into the hold, and, finally, up at the ship's masts.

Petey squawked offense at the last action and fluttered off his cross-pole perch.

With a deep sigh, Monty wiped the sweat from his forehead and took a bow.

"Well, folks, that should do it."

The crew members exchanged glances and a few disconcerted shrugs.

Moments later, the first splash was heard.

Several sailors had untied a canoe from the ship's side and were fleeing for the shoreline in the hopes of trekking south to Monterey.

The unmarked land route was fraught with its own dangers, but the men had decided to take their chances on foot. No one wanted to stay on board a boat haunted by a murderous spirit.

Captain Ayala watched the canoe paddle away from the *San Carlos* and shook his head. Scowling, he turned to Father Monty, who was sliding the crosses back into their velvet bag.

"Good job, Father," the captain said sarcastically. "You really nailed it at the end."

Isabella chimed in with her own assessment.

"Mrao."

Modern-Day San Francisco

The Week Before the America's Cup Regatta

Chapter 50

SACRIFICIAL LAMB

THE FIRST COUPLE of weeks following the sailboat debacle were tough on Mayor Carmichael. Monty arrived at City Hall each day, moody and out of sorts. He spent hours sulking behind the closed door to his office, lamenting his ouster from the America's Cup promotional team.

Not knowing what to do with all of his free time, Monty brought in a stack of blank canvases from his Jackson Square art studio. He set them up on easels and began painting dark, calamitous scenes of sailboats sinking in a stormy San Francisco Bay.

When the niece dared to peek inside the office to check on him, his only words were muttered curses about the upcoming regatta.

Oh—and, of course, he was also sad about Officer Toronto's death.

MEANWHILE, THE POLICE were at a loss on how to proceed with their case against the Knitting Needle Ninja.

The serial killer had stymied their best investigators—and murdered one of their favorite officers. They'd been unable to recruit another volunteer to fill the undercover intern position.

Whatever disguise she had adopted was eluding detection—even, apparently, in the corridors of City Hall.

Simply put, they were out of leads.

As for the lemony-sweet perfume that randomly swamped Mabel's old desk, the odor disappeared every time the detectives were summoned to the mayor's office to investigate. After several fruitless aroma alarms, they had dismissed the niece's smell reports.

After all, who ever heard of a serial killer haunting her victims by scent?

THE NIECE HAD just received another fragrance bombardment when the reception door opened and the secretary for the president of the board of supervisors marched inside.

Wanda Williams crinkled her nose and frowned with disapproval.

"You should really cut back on your perfume, honey." She tapped her neck. "Just a light touch is all you need."

The niece opened her mouth to protest, but held back as a second entrant moved into the room.

"Can I help you, sir?" she asked, leaning to see around Wanda.

She soon realized that she needed to look up instead of sideways. The man was nearly seven feet tall. He was a gaunt fellow with graying temples. His face carried a wispy, far-away expression—as if he were permanently lost.

"This is my nephew." Wanda turned and grabbed the man's wrist, pulling him forward. With her free hand, she plopped a résumé on the desk. "He's here for the intern position."

The niece glanced up at the filing cabinet, exchanging wary looks with Isabella.

She returned her attention to Wanda and her nephew. "You know that the last three interns have been murdered?"

The tall man cleared his throat. He spoke with unwavering self-assurance—that or he had been well coached by his aunt, the niece wasn't sure which.

"I am not afraid."

"Umm." The niece tapped her pencil against the desk as she skimmed the résumé. Then she sniffed the air, puzzled. The perfume smell had suddenly disappeared.

"I have faced great challenges in my life," the nephew said. He began pacing back and forth in front of the niece's desk. He appeared to be reciting a well-practiced speech, and his voice took on a vaguely familiar drone. "Recently, I rode my bike across the country."

"Just California," Wanda broke in, correcting. "And it was almost fifteen years ago."

The man continued his spiel without flinching. He obviously had practice tuning out criticism. "The trip was a treacherous experience, one that pushed me to the limits of my abilities."

"To be clear, it was the width of the state, not the length," the aunt cut in testily. "He rode from the Golden Gate Bridge to Lake Tahoe. Not more than two hundred miles."

"Along the way, I was chased by a bear."

Wanda sighed testily. "I heard it was a cat."

"I'm writing a book about my experiences," the man persisted.

"He's only written the first chapter."

"These things can't be rushed."

"In the meantime, he needs a job."

"Well, I have a small part-time position."

Wanda shot her nephew a sharp look. "But it's not enough to pay his bills."

Throughout this tit-for-tat, the niece's gaze bounced back and forth between the aunt and the nephew. She wasn't sure how the minimal intern salary would help the man's finances, but at the momentary break in the verbal traffic between the two, she jumped in and tried to steer the conversation toward the applicant's résumé.

"I see you have experience in the fast-food industry?"

The nephew began another pacing circle. "I spent several years exploring the complicated science of nutrition and how the body processes food. I was a line chef . . ."

The aunt interrupted. "At a burger joint."

"Ahem." He raised a bony finger. "At a restaurant geared to speed-optimized consumption."

"I see." The niece squinted at the next line in the employment history section. "It says here you have master-level skills in recreational management?"

The man beamed proudly. "Ah yes. I'm a certified outdoor practitioner."

Wanda folded her arms over her chest. "It means he likes to ride his bike through the forest."

The niece glanced up from the résumé. Wanda and her nephew both stared down at her, she with intensity, he with a laid-back—and inexplicable—confidence.

"There's no address listed. Do you live in San Francisco?"

"I prefer to camp, mostly. I live in the spiritual care of the stars." He tilted his head toward the ceiling, reflecting. "Or sometimes in my car, if it's raining."

The aunt cut in. "All of his stuff is in his parents' garage. Most of the time, he sleeps there."

He gave a casual shrug. "To use their Wi-Fi."

The niece looked over her shoulder. Isabella tapped the tip of her tail against the filing cabinet. As if sensing that the cat was the real decision-maker, the tall man shifted his attention to the cabinet.

The niece couldn't interpret the visual exchange that passed between them, but Isabella soon chirped out an approving comment.

"Mrao."

The niece looked up at the strange man, trying to figure him out. "So why are you interested in this internship?"

He smiled cheekily. "It seemed like a short-term commitment."

The niece sighed her capitulation. "Okay, then. The job is yours."

She reached into a desk drawer for a file folder. "Sorry, I didn't catch your name."

"It's Van." He grinned. "My parents met up north. It's short for Vancouver. You know, Vancouver, Canada."

Wanda left the mayor's office suite as the niece began writing the name on the folder tab.

"Of course it is."

Chapter 51

UNCUNNING

THE NIECE WAS about to take the new mayoral intern downstairs to show him his basement cubicle when the office printer connected to Monty's computer began to hum.

The machine kicked out a sheet of printed paper as the mayor's office door swung open. Monty swept into the reception area and danced up to the printer. For the first time in weeks, there was a grin on his narrow face.

The niece looked at him with concern. While the sunny disposition was welcome, the sudden change in attitude was cause for alarm.

Monty scooped up the sheet from the printer tray, scanned the inked side, and beamed triumphantly.

"It's a fabulous day, isn't it?"

"I suppose . . ." The niece craned her neck, trying to see what was on the printout. "We, uh, have a new intern."

Van gave the mayor a slanted salute. "Nice to meet you, sir."

"Oh, hello," Monty said, stepping forward to greet the intern. He stared at Van's chest and then adjusted his head upward. He was unaccustomed to looking up to someone taller than himself.

Both men were enthusiastic hand-shakers. The result was a wild, bouncing clasp of hands.

The niece managed to stand clear of the flailing body parts as she called out, "This is Van."

"Welcome, Mr. Van." Monty waved the paper in the air. "Perfect timing. Things are about to get busy around here. We're going to need the extra help."

The niece nearly tripped over a chair, trying to get a glimpse of the printing on the paper. She couldn't imagine what could be written on it that would have inspired such a dramatic shift in circumstances—but she was afraid she was about to find out.

"Ahem." The mayor assumed a solemn expression. "I have a cunning plan."

The niece cringed at the announcement. Despite having a fondness for the phrase, Monty was not known for devising brilliant strategy. And besides, she reflected, no self-respecting plan that was truly cunning in nature would have allowed itself to be branded as such.

Truth be told, most cunning plans were smart enough to keep away from the likes of Montgomery Carmichael.

She heaved out a reluctant sigh, and then, because she knew she had no other choice, asked warily, "All right. Let's hear it."

Monty pumped his eyebrows. "I'm going to perform an exorcism."

Van nodded his head approvingly. "Cool."

The niece had a far less supportive reaction. "You're going to do what?"

"I'm going to perform an exorcism," Monty replied succinctly, speaking as if this was a regular everyday occurrence. "In order to rid my office, my persona, my *aura* of this serial killer woman and get myself reinstated to the America's Cup publicity committee."

Nothing about this proposal struck Van as odd. "Sounds good," he said with another nod. "I'm in."

The niece looked back and forth between the mayor and the intern, struck by the many similarities in both body type and personality. Van could have been Monty's long-lost— and decidedly weird—cousin.

Oh no, she thought with horror. *I hired a Monty.*

The niece looked up at the filing cabinet. As if denying responsibility, Isabella uncharacteristically averted her gaze.

The cat issued a feeble defense.

"Mer-rao."

Chapter 52

ORDAINED

THE NIECE COULD see that she faced an uphill battle to stop the mayor from making a fool of himself.

"Monty, you can't perform an exorcism. You're not a priest."

"I am now!" With a flourish, he turned the paper so she could read it. "I just took an online course and paid a small fee. It's all official."

"How small a fee?" she asked suspiciously.

Pursing his lips, Monty flipped the document around and read the scrolling font. "It says here that I've just been ordained in the Church of Vincent Santa Maria." He squinted at the address line. "From the Stargazing Chapel on the Miracle Mile."

"The what on the where?" The niece tried to grab the paper from Monty's grasp, but he held it over her head and continued reading.

". . . by the power and blessing of Father Aaron E. Presley, I hereby confer upon Mayor Montgomery Carmichael of San

Francisco, California, the highest order of ordainment . . ." He paused, reflecting. "Hey, we should frame this."

The niece remained unconvinced. "And this new church of yours does exorcisms?"

Monty lowered the document and puffed out his chest. "They do now!"

She tugged the paper from his hands and studied the certificate.

"Monty, this isn't real. That man's an Elvis impersonator— from Las Vegas!"

"Sure it's real," Monty replied. "Real enough for my purposes, anyway." He tapped the desk. "The exorcism ceremony only has to be good enough to satisfy the entrepreneur that I'm not jinxed, so he'll let me back into the regatta."

Van peered over the niece's shoulder at the certificate. "Looks legit to me, dude."

The niece scowled up at the intern. The last thing Monty needed was encouragement.

Pushing the intern aside, she returned her attention to the artificially ordained interim mayor.

"Is the Baron Catholic?"

Monty thunked his chin, pondering. "Presbyterian, I think."

Van chimed in from across the room. "Close enough!"

The niece handed back the document.

"You've got your work cut out for you, Reverend."

Chapter 53

A SÉANCE ... OF SORTS

MONTY AND VAN spent a couple of hours working on the computer inside the mayor's inner office, researching exorcisms. They consulted several online resources, reviewed materials from various religious websites, and pooled their combined recollections of fictional depictions they'd seen in movies and on television.

Having devised an overall plan of attack, they then headed out into the streets of San Francisco to search for the necessary supplies.

They returned to City Hall later that afternoon with several large shopping bags.

Isabella and Rupert inspected each item as it was removed from its sack.

"What's with the hat?" the niece asked, pointing at the purple pointed item Monty had just placed on his head.

"Ooh, I've got one, too," Van said, lifting up a rainbow-colored tie-dye version and setting it on his noggin.

She grimaced at the intern's headgear. "Have you also been ordained?"

"I appointed him my associate bishop," Monty replied. He gave the niece an impish grin. "I would have offered you the title, but you declined to join our purchasing expedition."

The niece rolled her eyes. "Thank goodness for small blessings."

WITH THE PROPS unpacked and laid out across the floor, Monty and Van began to assemble an array of incense-burning devices they'd picked up in Chinatown.

Soon several candles, votives, and ceramic containers of sandalwood and sage were organized in a circle in the middle of the floor. Van offered his cigarette lighter to ignite a foot-long wooden match, which Monty then used to spread the flame among the incense units.

The niece crinkled her nose as a musky aroma spread through the room. "Maybe all this will get rid of the perfume."

"Hold up!" Monty exclaimed. He ran into his office and brought back a digital video camera. "Here." He thrust it at the niece. "Make yourself useful."

"You want me to film this?"

Monty blew out an exasperated *sfft*. "Of course. That's the whole point. How am I going to convince the Baron I performed an exorcism if I don't have video evidence?"

Reluctantly, the niece took the camera and flipped on the recording switch. She aimed the lens at Monty as he finished lighting the various incense containers.

"Oh!" He skipped over to the wall and turned the America's Cup poster around so that its front once more faced into the room. "Make sure you get this in the video, too."

The stage now set, it was time for the ceremony to begin.

Van sat on the floor, cross-legged, his arms folded in front of his chest, nodding and humming supportively.

Monty stepped into the center of the ring of smoking canisters, straightened his purple hat, and held up a plastic crucifix purchased earlier from a tourist shop.

"I, Reverend Interim Mayor Montgomery Carmichael, of the Church of Vincent Santa Maria . . ." He paused to take a breath—and choked on the incense smoke.

Still coughing, he continued. "I, Reverend Carmichael, command the evil spirit of the Knitting Needle Ninja to leave this building and to permanently disassociate herself from San Francisco's mayoral office."

Van stopped humming. He cleared his throat in a prompting manner.

With a nod to his assistant, Monty added, "And I forbid you to do any harm to anyone employed as a mayoral intern."

The niece turned her head away from the camera's viewfinder. She and Isabella exchanged dubious glances.

Rupert, however, looked on in fascination. He remained hopeful that one of the shopping bags might contain yet another package—perhaps a box of fried chicken donuts.

A sudden screech caused everyone to jump.

It wasn't the reply of the Ninja's demonic spirit. The clouds of incense smoke had triggered the fire alarm.

Seconds later, the sprinkler system lowered from the ceiling, and metal spigots began shooting water onto the floor.

Humans and cats ran for cover. The ring of burning materials sputtered and hissed.

The niece hovered with Isabella under the desk. Rupert zoomed inside his domed litter box.

Monty and Van hopscotched around the room, dodging water spigots while holding on to their respective pointed hats.

The reception door opened and Hoxton Finn stuck his head inside.

The reporter took one look at the scene and threw up his hands.

"I don't want to know," he muttered, before retreating back outside and shutting the door.

AFTER THE SPRINKLERS finally shut off, the niece and Van began mopping up puddles of water from the reception room's carpet. As the smell of wet incense began to dissipate, she stared up at the holes in the ceiling where the spigots had descended, pondering.

Isabella waved a paw in the air, concurring with her person's hunch.

The perfume smell had just returned.

"Van," the niece said. "You're tall enough to reach up to those sprinkler heads, aren't you?"

On Board the *San Carlos*

San Francisco Bay, August 1775

Chapter 54

A MAN OF THE WOODS

CAPTAIN AYALA SAT at his desk in his ship quarters, adding notes to his sheath of papers, both to the official registry and to his personal reflections.

This evening, the latter log had received the bulk of his attention.

The desk lantern sent out a warm glow, casting a small circle of light in an otherwise dark room. It was a quarter past midnight and most of the passengers and crew on the *San Carlos* were asleep—that is, those who remained on board.

At last count, nearly half of the sailors had abandoned ship, relinquishing their posts rather than risk falling victim to the evil spirit who had already murdered two of their number. No longer an unsubstantiated rumor, the men were now convinced that the ship was haunted and that none of them would make it back to Mexico alive.

Despite exhaustive searching, Ayala had failed to find any evidence linking one of the crew members to the killings. Nor had he seen any indication of the elusive stowaway widely believed to be responsible for the murders.

The ship was in a state of all-out panic. Without a dramatic change in circumstances, he faced the near-certain prospect that the *San Carlos* would be left stranded here in this remarkable bay—which, if they all perished, might remain undiscovered for another decade or more.

The captain set down his quill. He pressed his fingertips against his temples, trying to quell the headache that had intensified during his lengthy writing session.

Sighing wearily, Ayala shifted his gaze to the green parrot curled up in the discarded shirt that had become his nighttime nest. Snuggling in the warmth generated by the nearby lantern, the bird wheezed out a contented coo.

The captain wished he could emulate the parrot's peaceful sleep. With a groan, he returned to his log:

"Crew morale affected by . . ."

He held the quill in the air for several seconds, searching for the right words. Finally, he dipped the tip in the inkwell and added: "motivational challenges."

As early as the eighteenth century, but human language had already been corrupted by corporate-speak.

AYALA LOOKED UP at a knock on his door.

"Humphretto?"

The door cracked open and the ship's chef leaned inside.

"Captain, if I may?" The chef nodded toward the captain's desk. "I saw the glow of your light from the hallway."

"Oscar. Please, come in." Ayala yawned his exhaustion. "I don't think there's any chance of sleep for me tonight."

"I have an idea that might help with your . . . uh . . . situation," Oscar said, stepping into the room.

Ayala grunted his response. "Not another exorcism."

"No." Oscar smiled. "I have a much more nuanced approach in mind."

The captain turned his chair away from the desk. He looked up at Oscar expectantly.

"Well, don't just stand there. Spit it out, man."

Oscar pointed to the captain's paperwork. "It might be better if you don't know the specifics, given your reporting obligations."

Ayala nodded his understanding. "Just give me the general gist."

"I'll need a canoe and a man to help me paddle it," Oscar replied with a wink. "Humphretto if you can spare him. We'll leave at dawn."

Standing, the captain shook his head. "Oscar, we cannot survive if the ship's chef abandons us. That would be the last straw. The men have to eat."

"Trust me, Captain. I'll be back by sundown."

Ayala was unconvinced. He paced a nervous circle around the room.

"I'll leave my niece here," Oscar said. "I'm sure you know I would never abandon her."

Ayala tapped his quill against his left thigh. "Where are you going?"

"The north shore." Oscar began retreating to the exit. He paused at the threshold and looked back. "I saw a plume of smoke in the hills the other night. I think a friend of mine is camped there."

The captain sensed he wouldn't get any more details, but he pressed with a last question as Oscar stepped out of the room. "Is your friend an Indian?"

"He's not an Indian, but he is friends with them," Oscar replied. "He's a man of the woods. A rustic."

Oscar chuckled to himself as he disappeared down the hallway.

"The Indians are far more civilized than Samuel Eckles."

Chapter 55

THE TRUCE

WHILE CAPTAIN AYALA and Oscar were discussing the ship's dire situation, a furry white creature with orange-tipped ears and tail slipped unnoticed through the half-open door.

Rupert padded silently across the captain's stateroom—a short, fluffy shadow.

The cat kept out of the lamplight, carefully timing his movements to avoid detection. He waited until Ayala stood from his chair and began pacing the room. Then he slinked toward the captain's empty seat.

Throughout all this subterfuge, Rupert kept his focus trained on the snoring lump of green feathers curled up by the lantern on the top of the desk. His feather-duster tail swished back and forth as he hunched on the ground below, waiting for the right moment to pounce.

Ayala stopped pacing, stared curiously at Oscar, and asked, "Is your friend an Indian?"

Rupert bounded up into the seat. A second leap took him to the desktop. He crept silently across the paper-covered surface, parking himself within inches of the dozing parrot.

Perhaps sensing the encroaching danger, Petey woke with a start. He'd been caught napping—literally. It looked to be a fatal error, a deadly checkmate. The bird froze in place, his yellow eyes widening with terror. The cat could finish him off with a single swipe of his claws.

But then a surprising and unlikely thing occurred. Instead of moving in for the kill, Rupert sidled up to the parrot and licked the feathers on the back of his neck.

Petey remained still, unsure of how to process this strange gesture from the cat he had spent the last week tormenting. Was the feline just getting in a premeal taste or was he making a peace offering?

Rupert's next action provided an unequivocal answer. He sprawled his hefty body across the desk and cuddled up next to the bird.

• • •

AS OSCAR DEPARTED down the corridor, Ayala turned back toward his desk—and gaped in alarm at the pile of feathers and fur by the lantern.

"No . . ." he whispered, his anger rising. On top of everything else, must he also lose his beloved parrot to a flea-bitten feline?

He stomped toward the desk, prepared to grab the cat by the scruff of his neck and toss him out the nearest window into the bay.

Halfway across, however, he noticed a movement.

The bird was very much alive. Rupert had wrapped a front paw around his new friend. The parrot nuzzled his head into the cat's fluffy white chest.

"Well," Ayala said, peering down at the snoozing pair. "Hmm."

He crossed to a cupboard and pulled out a soft blanket. Tiptoeing back to the desk, he tucked it around the unlikely duo and quietly snuffed out the lamp.

Chapter 56

THE PORTAL

A FEW HOURS before dawn, Oscar rose from his bed and lit a lantern.

The *San Carlos* was on the verge of calamitous ruin. It was time for him to take action or they would never get back to their home port.

The ship wasn't haunted. He had no doubt of that. It was, however, under siege by a deranged stowaway.

Each morning since they left San Blas, he'd detected a small amount of food missing from his pantry. At first, he'd chalked the petty thievery up to a hungry crew member sneaking into the kitchen for a late-night snack.

But after several days, a distinct pattern had emerged.

Given Captain Ayala's diligent searches of the ship, Oscar reasoned the killer must have some sort of hidden closet or secret room, a niche where she resided during the day—that is, when she wasn't hunting her next victim.

The middle of the night, when she might be foraging for food, was the best time to surprise her and get the upper hand.

QUIETLY DRESSING, OSCAR wandered into the kitchen.

He rubbed his scruffy eyebrows, trying to jolt himself awake. He would have to accomplish this task without the help of caffeine. It would make too much noise to roust the fire to cook a pot of coffee on the stove.

As he gazed longingly at his empty percolator, a second figure entered the room.

"You coming with me?" he whispered down to Isabella.

He grunted as she rubbed her shoulder against his shin.

"That's probably a good idea."

His expression grew somber.

"I might need backup."

OSCAR LIT A lantern, and the pair moved cautiously into the hallway outside the kitchen.

Isabella's sharp eyes scanned the darkness as Oscar held the lamp up to the walls, inspecting the woodwork. He ran his free hand over the rough surface, feeling for hidden seams in the joints. Every couple of feet, he rapped his knuckles on the paneling, hoping to discern the presence of a hollow cavity beneath, anywhere a person might hide to avoid detection.

The *San Carlos* was just over five years old. Since the boat's initial construction, she had received regular maintenance at San Blas, but the constant tug and pull of storms, wind, waves, and rain had wrenched the ship's rigid form. A number of small gaps could be seen in the wooden wall, but Oscar found none that weren't easily explained by the natural contortion of the surrounding boards.

He and Isabella continued to the next level down, descending on a much narrower flight of stairs than the one that led up to the ship's top deck. The lantern flickered a dim halo of light as they resumed their search in the hallway directly beneath the kitchen.

The ridge of hair along Isabella's spine stood on edge. She could sense danger in the dark, damp air.

As they reached the end of the corridor and turned a sharp corner, she let out a low growl—at the faint but unmistakable scent of a lemony-sweet perfume.

• • •

THE CORRIDOR REMAINED silent for several seconds after Oscar and Isabella passed, but there was a noticeable change in atmosphere. The perfume scent now carried with it a dash of expectancy.

The ceiling creaked. Then an opening appeared in the top wood paneling, no more than a half-inch slat, just large enough for a single beady eye to peek through.

The eye blinked, adjusting its focus. It stared down onto the hallway for a long moment before pulling back from the hole. After a brief shuffling, the eye returned, this time at a different angle. The watcher wanted to confirm that the area below was clear.

Finally, the boards surrounding the modified slat began to move. A square section of the ceiling slid back on a hidden hinge, creating a square portal.

A human's feet, legs, and torso squeezed through the hole, and a curious figure dropped nimbly onto the floor.

It was an older woman dressed in a rumpled gunnysack. Her white hair was knotted and tangled; her skin was mottled and dirt-stained.

But her feet were clad in a pair of sturdy women's shoes.

A cloth bag looped around her left shoulder held an assortment of knitting equipment and supplies, yarn, scissors, and a bundle of specialized needles, each one curved in shape, with the tip adapted to accommodate the fittings for a sharp blade.

The stowaway set off down the corridor, her bowed legs

walking with an odd limp as if they'd been cramped in a tight-fitting space for several hours.

She followed after the chef and the cat with the orange-tipped ears and tail—leaving behind a scented trail of lemony-sweet perfume.

Chapter 57

A FEARSOME BEAST

JUST BEFORE DAYBREAK, Humphretto readied a canoe for launch. It was the last remaining transport vessel on board the *San Carlos*. The rest had been taken by fleeing crew members and left beached along the bay's south shore where the men had continued on foot, hoping to make it south to Monterey.

It took every bit of Humphretto's meager strength to heft the canoe over the ship's side, but once he had the hull clear of the railing, the rest of the canoe's descent to the water was easily controlled by a series of pulleys and ropes that ran through hooks attached to the boat's side.

The lieutenant had been dragging the canoe around for the last twenty-four hours—ever since the first crew members began abandoning the *San Carlos*. He'd kept it secured in his cabin, which was the only reason it was still available.

When Captain Ayala alerted him to Oscar's covert mission, Humphretto was glad he'd taken the precaution. He'd jumped at the chance to participate in the plan, eager to play a role in saving the ship.

He just wished he knew why they were headed to the bay's north shore.

He couldn't see how that would help return the men fleeing to the south.

THE SUN WAS but a faint glow on the horizon when the canoe touched down on the water.

Humphretto jumped at a tap on his shoulder. With difficulty, he managed to stifle his instinctive yelp.

Oscar stood on the deck behind him with a large rucksack slung over his shoulder. The chef had left the ship's breakfast preparations in the hands of his niece, to be closely supervised by Isabella.

"Everything ready to go?" Oscar asked quietly.

Humphretto nodded enthusiastically. "Yes, sir."

Oscar smiled at the salutation. Humphretto clearly outranked him. The "sir" was merely out of respect for his advanced age. "Let's get to it, mate."

The lieutenant led the way, shimmying down a rope ladder attached to the ship's side. Oscar followed at a much slower pace and not near as nimbly.

Wobbling precariously, Oscar managed to transfer first his pack and then his body into the canoe's front end.

Humphretto had taken up the rear steering seat. There was only one paddle, so the lieutenant insisted on providing the manpower.

Moments later, they slipped into the morning's half-light, undetected by the remaining crew.

Oscar glanced over his shoulder at the panting lieutenant. Humphretto had paused his paddling to remove his horsehair jacket, which was too warm for the morning's strenuous exercise.

"That's a truly stunning coat. I've been admiring it the whole trip."

"Well, thank you, Oscar. I was going to leave it behind today, since the weather's been so pleasant, but the captain said you wanted me to bring it along."

"Yes," Oscar replied, returning to a face-forward position. "You never know when such a piece of apparel might come in handy."

Humphretto shrugged. Right now, the bulky coat was more of a burden than a blessing. He paddled a few more strokes and then called out to the front of the canoe.

"Why did you ask me to bring my sewing kit?"

WITH HUMPHRETTO HUFFING and puffing at the stern, the canoe slowly picked up speed, gliding away from the *San Carlos*.

The rising sun glistened on the water, shining across the faint ripples generated by the tiny boat.

The bay's north shore was calmer and noticeably warmer than the south, where Humphretto had explored the day before. As the canoe slid onto the beach, the lieutenant gazed up at the gentle green hills and sighed.

In the presence of such natural beauty, he could almost forget the urgency of their visit.

The tranquil scene was broken by a husky voice that called out from the woods.

"Oscar!" The bushes along the hillside rustled. The movement in the leaves indicated a large disturbance. "I thought that was you!"

Despite the warning signs, Humphretto was unprepared for the sight—and size—of the creature who emerged from the greenery.

As Oscar hobbled across the wet sand, the lieutenant stood by the canoe, awestruck.

"Oh my."

Humphretto had heard tales of Neanderthals living in the great forests of the north. A few of his fellow Spaniards had speculated that the species represented offshoots from mankind's early predecessors. Others swore the beasts were artifacts of the devil, pure evil spewed up from the depths of hell. He'd been cautioned to guard himself when traveling in the woods, lest a wooly demon drag him off to its lair.

Humphretto had always eschewed these stories as creative fiction told around a campfire, but right now, he was having second thoughts.

The specimen running onto the beach—whatever it was—was downright terrifying.

The creature was covered in hair, much of it orangish-red, some of it human, some of it animal. Humphretto thought he recognized a cured hide or two in the mix. A raccoon tail swung wildly from the back of a roughly hewn cap. It was a brutish assembly of lumbering limbs and muscle.

And it had just tackled Oscar with a frightening bear hug.

His hands shaking, Humphretto reached for the musket attached to his shoulder belt. He had never actually fired the weapon. He didn't even know how to aim it. But he couldn't stand by and let the ship's chef get mauled by this . . . this . . . *thing*.

"Come on, Humphretto." Oscar broke free of the friendly embrace and waved for the lieutenant to join them. "Let me introduce you to my friend Sam."

Humphretto stared in awe as Oscar walked up the shoreline, laughing chummily with the hairiest man the lieutenant had ever seen.

After a few steps the chef turned and called back to the canoe.

"And don't forget to bring the coat."

Still perplexed, Humphretto reached for the horsehair jacket. Coat in hand, he started to follow Oscar and his strange companion.

But the lieutenant abruptly stopped as he noticed two small green figures riding on the burly man's shoulders.

His brow furrowed.

"Are those frogs?"

Chapter 58

THE BEAR

TRUE TO HIS word, Oscar returned to the *San Carlos* that afternoon, before any of the remaining crew members noticed his absence and in plenty of time to prepare the evening's dinner. He and Humphretto left the canoe tied in the water. The lieutenant scampered briskly up the rope ladder, leaving Oscar to lumber up on his own.

Once he reached the top deck, Oscar proceeded immediately to the kitchen. Due to the recent departures, the dining table's head count had been dramatically reduced, but Oscar assembled enough ingredients to feed a full ship.

Captain Ayala stepped into the galley for an update on the day's excursion. He frowned, noting the amount of food laid out on the counter.

"You must have worked up an appetite, Oscar. There's hardly anyone left. We won't make a dent in this. It'll go to waste."

With a grin, Oscar confidently *thunk*ed the counter with his knife.

"Captain, I guarantee all of this food will be devoured by midnight—by your regular crew members."

Unconvinced, Ayala ground his left foot into the floor. He winced from the pain as Oscar reached for a large pot hanging on the wall.

"Humphretto's assistance was invaluable."

The captain scowled his frustration. "I haven't seen him since you returned."

"I believe he retired to his quarters." Oscar paused and then pumped his scraggly eyebrows. "He's in mourning."

Ayala's face registered alarm. "Who died?"

Oscar tossed a handful of vegetables into the pot.

"His coat."

CAPTAIN AYALA FOUND his lieutenant a few minutes later. He knocked on the open doorway to Humphretto's tiny cubicle and leaned inside.

The little man sat at his desk, staring down at his various sewing and shearing tools. The implements were covered with tufts of reddish-brown fuzz that carried a rank animal scent.

Ayala tried to draw the lieutenant's attention. "I understand you made an enormous sacrifice today. Thank you, my friend."

Humphretto shuddered as if reliving a painful memory. His gaze remained fixed on the desk's wooden surface. After a moment of silence, he finally spoke.

"I have never seen such hair on a man." With a disturbed sigh, he picked up a pair of scissors and wiped the handle with a felt cloth. "If you need me, Captain, I'll be sharpening my shears . . ."

Scratching his head, Ayala quietly left the room. He closed the door and stood in the hallway, puzzling.

He was still unclear exactly what had gone on during Oscar and Humphretto's excursion.

What's the old man up to? he pondered. He limped down the corridor, his brow deeply furrowed. *And how is all this going to bring my crew back?*

DINNER WAS A somber and lightly attended affair. The huge spread brought up to the top deck went largely untouched.

The few sailors still on board clumped together in nervous groups, staring at the empty chairs that lined the table. Even the Baron hunched uncomfortably in his seat.

It seemed unlikely that the last canoe, tethered at the bottom of the rope ladder, would remain empty for long.

Ayala stared at the near-empty table with grave concern. He had little appetite, and his foot throbbed with as much pain as ever.

Oscar, however, appeared untroubled by the sparse showing. He and his niece wrapped up the leftovers and carried the food back downstairs to the kitchen.

AS THE SUN went down, a tense quiet settled over the ship. Captain Ayala retired to his room, defeated. If the men were determined to leave, he was helpless to stop them.

A couple of the remaining sailors headed to their bunks; the others convened in the shadows, discussing their options. The Baron joined the conversation, forking over a substantial sum of cash to ensure himself a seat on the next departing vessel. The lone canoe soon filled to capacity and, under the power of its one paddle, disappeared into the night.

Humphretto watched the last group leave and then sadly rolled up the rope ladder. It was too late, he feared, for Oscar's plan—and his hairy friend—to do any good.

A few hours later, a desperate splashing could be heard in the shallows by the ship's hull.

With a groan, Ayala struggled from his bed and hobbled onto the deck.

This was it, he thought grimly. His first commission in command of a ship would end with its pitiful abandonment in an unknown port.

He lifted his lantern to look over the railing, expecting

to see the last hapless traitors swimming toward shore—and then gasped with surprise.

The splashing was not the sound of crew members jumping ship, but of the missing sailors clambering to return.

"Throw down the ladder! Let us back on board!"

Hearing the commotion, Humphretto rushed to the captain's side. He unfurled the ladder down to the water. A flotilla of canoes had converged on the *San Carlos*, including the tiny craft that had departed just hours earlier.

One by one, the sheepish faces climbed over the railing and onto the deck. They rushed to the table where a full spread of leftovers awaited them.

Oscar looked on with approval as the hungry men dug into the food. Almost fifty famished sailors gorged themselves at the dining table. For the men who had left immediately following Monty's disastrous exorcism, it was their first decent meal in over a day.

After the initial food orgy, nutritional intake slowed to allow stomachs to catch up with digestion. As more and more crew members leaned back in their chairs, rubbing their swollen guts, the men recounted the terror that had driven them to return to the ship.

While wandering through the marshy woods on the bay's south shore, they had encountered a fearsome creature, one so horrific and terrifying that they had decided the phantom spirit on board the *San Carlos* was less dangerous.

"A demon beast, that's what it was. I've never seen anything like it."

"Bigfoot, I tell you. Sasquatch."

"Naw, I think it was a bear."

AYALA LISTENED QUIETLY to the dinner conversations. Then he motioned for Oscar to join him in the stairwell leading down to the ship's lower level.

Now that the crisis had abated—at least temporarily—and there was a chance the ship might actually make it back to Mexico, Ayala wanted to hear more about the territory on the bay's north shore.

"What can you tell me about the habitat where Mr. Eckles is camped?"

Oscar stroked his chin, reflecting. "Sam quite likes it. He says it's far more pleasant than the south side of the bay. Less fog, warmer weather. He's got a floating platform in the harbor that he lives on most of the time. It's a funny-looking thing. He calls it a houseboat."

"Interesting. I'll make a note of that in my observations."

Oscar opened his mouth, as if to caution against a direct quotation, but Ayala waved him off.

"Anonymously, of course."

"Thank you, Captain."

"The thanks are all mine to you, Oscar."

• • •

THROUGHOUT THE RAUCOUS late-night dinner, the fantastic tales from the satiated sailors, and the hushed conference in the stairwell, one observer remained hidden, revealing nothing more than a slit of an eyeball in the ship's wood paneling.

As the stowaway watched the festivities, she fumed over the chef who had thwarted her plans. Intent on revenge, she pondered her next move.

Two Days Before the America's Cup Regatta

Modern-Day San Francisco

Chapter 59

SLEPT OUT

AFTER THE EXORCISM-TRIGGERED fire alarm and sprinkler soaking, the first few days of Van's internship passed without incident. He'd been unable to identify any scent-making device in the ceiling sprinklers—and the perfume had yet to return to the reception area or the admin's desk.

The niece had begun to think the Knitting Needle Ninja might have moved on to other interests. Maybe she'd grown bored with killing mayoral interns. Perhaps she'd developed a new hobby—one that didn't involve knife-edged crochet needles.

But when Van didn't show up for work one morning, the niece feared the worst.

"Oh, Issy," she said, wincing as she glanced from the clock over the door to the cat's filing cabinet roost. "I'm afraid we've lost another one."

Isabella showed no concern for the missing intern. Her

blue eyes were focused on the ceiling. Her radar ears had picked up on a mysterious sound above the room.

Van's rudimentary sprinkler search hadn't satisfied Isabella. She was convinced the source of the perfume scent was hidden somewhere, somehow, in the ceiling.

And so, to the niece's worried pondering, the cat provided an absentminded reply.

"Mrao-rao."

The niece tapped a pencil against her desk.

Hmm.

WHEN AT NOON, Van still hadn't appeared, the niece called the phone number he had listed on his emergency contact form.

An elderly woman answered the line.

It must be Wanda's sister, the niece surmised. The voice sounded similar—as did the tone.

The mother was surprisingly unbothered about Van's disappearance. He hadn't slept in the garage the previous evening, but that wasn't unusual. Her feral son rarely stayed indoors on a clear night. He'd never been able to pass up an opportunity to enjoy prime camping weather.

She was, however, worried that Van might have lost yet another job.

"We were so hoping that this would work out for him," the mother fretted over the phone. Her voice sank into a frazzled whimper. "Please don't send him back here. Not just yet."

The niece frowned at the phone after the conversation ended.

"He's not *that* bad."

Isabella's warbled response wasn't exactly a concurrence.

"Wrao-rao."

The unlikely intern was starting to grow on the niece. He was kind of like Monty in that regard.

Despite his eccentricities, she preferred not to think of him skewered by one of Mabel's knifed knitting needles and lying dead somewhere in the woods.

It looked like she was one of the few who held that opinion.

THE CLOCK TICKED past one.

"That's it." The niece picked up the phone. "It's time to call the police."

Just then, the reception door opened and Van walked sleepily through. His hair was ruffled, and stray pine needles poked out of his rumpled clothing—the same outfit of jeans and T-shirt that he had worn the day before. With a yawn, he waved to the niece.

"Howdy."

He reached toward the filing cabinet to pat Isabella on the head. A short hiss warded off the gesture. Rupert, dozing on the cat bed on the floor below, was more than happy to accommodate a belly rub.

It turned out the intern had just slept in—or, to be more specific, out.

Like Monty, the niece's irritation with him returned with his presence.

"Van, you really shouldn't be wandering in the woods by yourself right now. You're just asking for trouble. Aren't you afraid Mabel might track you down out there and kill you in your sleep?"

Van shrugged with his typical nonchalance.

"I think that exorcism thing must have worked. I would have noticed if she was following me." He tapped his ears. "I'm very observant."

The niece doubted Van had any visual capabilities associated with his ears—or that the exorcism had had any effect on Mabel's murderous intentions.

As for Monty's hopes that the exorcism ceremony would

convince the Baron to reinstate him to the America's Cup promotional committee, that initiative appeared to have also failed.

He and Van had edited the video to remove the portion showing the sprinklers raining down on the mayor's reception area. Following Monty's insistent orders—and against her own better judgment—the niece had e-mailed the video clip to the Baron's assistant.

To Monty's intense frustration, there had been no reply.

"Are you sure they got it?" he'd asked persistently.

"I called to check." The niece had pursed her lips, deciding the less she relayed about the conversation, the better.

"And?"

"They got it."

THE NIECE WAS far more concerned with her intern's security precautions, or lack thereof, than Monty's failed attempts to reinsert himself into the America's Cup activities.

She tried to find the right words to convince Van to be more cautious. She opened her mouth, drew in her breath as if to speak, and then abandoned the effort as an exercise in futility.

Oblivious to her frustration, Van started his regular pacing on the floor in front of her desk. He tucked his hands behind his back and looked up toward the ceiling.

"But you know, if I could pick a place to die, it would be the forest . . ." He stared dreamily off into space. "My feet would become flowers and from my heart would sprout a clump of grass . . ."

As if inspired by the speech, Rupert began rummaging inside his litter box. The igloo-shaped hood rocked back and forth as the cat dug enthusiastically through the sandy composite.

The niece stared up at the tall man, pondering his strange existence.

Isabella restricted her insights to a cryptic one-syllable assessment.

"Mrao."

Chapter 60

DEAD YET?

VAN SOON DISAPPEARED downstairs to his basement cubicle—at the urging of the niece, Isabella, and even Rupert.

Another cloud of Mabel's perfume would have been preferable to the stale sweaty smell emanating from the unshowered intern.

With Monty still on the outs with the America's Cup organizers, there was little actual work for Van to do. The niece suspected he would spend most of his time in the basement pontificating to the unlucky occupants of the other cubicles about the wonders of the great outdoors.

Better them than me, she thought wearily.

Relieved as she was that he hadn't been hunted down and speared by the Knitting Needle Ninja, and disturbed as she was by his own mother's lack of compassion, there was only so much Van she could take in a single session.

After all, she still had Monty to contend with.

She looked at the door to the mayor's inner office, which had been firmly shut since his arrival that morning.

The start of the regatta was just two days away. America's Cup advertising had been plastered all over the city. It had taken over bus stops and BART stations. Full-page ads filled the local newspaper. The event's promotion was impossible to escape.

For several months, the marquee billboard in Union Square had been occupied by a larger-than-life version of the (now slightly water-stained) poster hanging in the reception area. Monty glared at it each time he walked past, but so far, he had declined to turn it back toward the wall.

The niece suspected he was still holding out hope that the exorcism video would sway the Baron.

She shook her head at the closed door.

She didn't have the heart to tell him there was no chance of that happening.

It was a fine line between self-belief and delusion.

WITH VAN SAFELY located and Monty sulking in his office, the niece slipped downstairs to the rotunda to pick up lunch from the soup vendor.

She got the last servings of the day's special, a delicious-smelling chicken noodle concoction, and carried it back upstairs to share with the hungry eaters in the mayor's office suite.

Rupert bounced around at her feet, beside himself with anticipation as she sorted through the paper containers. Isabella inched to the edge of the filing cabinet, almost falling off in her eagerness to supervise. The cat soon joined her brother on the floor, where the pair waited for their midday snack.

As the niece poured a serving of broth into each cat's bowl, she heard Monty rustling inside his office. She was ready when he burst into the reception, hungrily sniffing the air. With a smile, she handed him a spoon and a paper container full of soup.

Monty leaned against the corner of her desk and lifted the lid.

"This makes everything better," he said between slurps.

Nodding, the niece sat in her chair and dug into her cup.

For several minutes, the room was quiet, save for reverent sipping sounds.

Until the reception door swung open and Wanda Williams swept in.

AT FIRST, THE niece thought Wanda's sister had alerted her to Van's late arrival and the aunt was there to check on her nephew's well-being.

She was sorely mistaken.

Wanda glanced around the room. Not seeing Van among the human and feline mix, she approached the desk, pushed Monty out of the way, and scowled at the niece.

"Is he dead yet?"

Monty nearly choked on a spoonful of soup. "Who?"

Wanda sniped out her response. "Van."

Monty nearly dropped his soup in alarm. Then he paused and, holding his spoon midair, reflected on the implications. "Does that mean the exorcism didn't work . . ."

The niece cut in. "Van's fine. He just slept in. Or out, rather. Anyway, he's downstairs in the basement."

Disappointment flooded Wanda's face. "When I heard he didn't show up for work this morning, I thought maybe . . ."

"No." The niece set down her soup. "He was just late."

Sighing in frustration, Wanda pushed away from the desk. She walked toward the door, as if to leave, and then turned back.

"How long does it usually take?" she asked impatiently.

"I'm sorry." The niece smiled tensely. "What do you mean?"

Wanda drummed her fingers against the door frame. "How long does it take this Ninja woman to do her business? Surely, you expect her to make a move on him before too much longer?"

The room fell silent. Rupert shoved his head under his cat bed. Even Monty had nothing to contribute.

Finally, Isabella issued a polite but curt hiss.

The niece rose from her chair. "I think you should leave."

She crossed the room as Wanda stomped out. Closing the door behind Van's aunt, the niece found herself immensely disliking the woman.

Almost as much as she disliked the Ninja.

Monty sucked down another spoonful of soup and loudly smacked his lips.

"That is one evil secretary," he said with a shudder.

For once, Isabella chimed in with agreement.

"Mrao."

But then the cat's furry face paused for reflection. After a moment of deep thought, Isabella issued an amendment to her previous comment. This statement was far more nuanced in tone.

"Mrao."

The niece looked at Monty as she silently considered Isabella's remark.

While she had never actually wished Monty harm, there had been many times over the years when her pesky neighbor had severely tried her patience.

She wasn't a murderous person, but she couldn't say with absolute certainty that—during one of those particularly trying circumstances—if she'd seen him stepping off a curb in front of a runaway bus, she might not have muted her shout of warning.

She didn't condone the behavior of Wanda Williams, but then, she had to admit, she wouldn't necessarily object if Mabel switched the target of her attacks from mayoral interns to the mayor himself . . .

Isabella blinked as if reading her person's thoughts.

Wickedness came in many shades. Motivations couldn't be easily slotted into simple categories.

One person's evil was another's opportunity or convenience.

"What's that?" Monty asked. He glanced up at Isabella, trying to interpret her second *Mrao.*

The cat shifted her gaze and looked innocently up at the ceiling.

The niece shuffled some papers on her desk.

"Um, yep. Horrible woman."

Chapter 61

THE TIPPING POINT

THE NEXT MORNING, Mabel stood in her Geary Street studio apartment, gazing at her reflection in a full-length mirror nailed to the outer surface of a closet door.

San Francisco's Theater District included a number of older multistory apartment buildings, many of which rented rooms by the week. Mabel's cash deposit for six months' accommodation had been accepted without question. The building manager didn't raise an eyebrow at the alias she provided for the rental agreement. As far as he was concerned, Marilyn Monroe's cash was as good as any.

Mabel compared her reflected image to that in a small picture pinned to the side of the mirror, searching for any differences between her appearance and that of the woman she was trying to emulate.

She had almost finished assembling her outfit.

The model was far curvier and a bit more top-heavy than Mabel's natural build. Adjusting the inflated chest strapped to her torso, she straightened the top sweater layer and fastened its center row of buttons.

There, she thought, pleased with the result. *A near-perfect match.*

She'd already completed her face makeup. It was time for the wig.

This was the most difficult aspect of the costume. It seemed she could never get the wig in the right orientation. Carefully, she lifted the hairpiece from its mannequin post, set it on her head, and pinned it in place.

Stepping back, she turned a pivot, painstakingly checking every detail in the mirror.

Not bad, she thought, twitching her mouth critically.

The Theater District apartment had been an excellent location from which to launch her daily surveillance on the mayor's office suite. That dim-witted woman and her mangy cats had no idea that the Knitting Needle Ninja paraded through City Hall each day.

Not even Oscar had detected her disguise.

As Mabel leaned into the mirror, conducting one last check, she couldn't help but note the similarities between this and her previous life.

Like before, her daily existence had fallen into a regimented routine, a constant repetition of memorized steps designed to allow her to hide in plain sight.

Pausing, she thought back to how it all began.

BOREDOM, THAT WAS the trigger.

By her late thirties, Mabel had developed an overwhelming dissatisfaction with life's dull predictability. Each day had become a replay of the one that came before. She was desperate to inject some variety into her calendar's blank white squares, some means of discerning one twenty-four-hour cycle from another.

She searched the newspaper for activity ideas. An advert for a neighborhood knitting class caught her eye, and one day after work, she introduced herself to the group.

By the second week, she was hooked. The initial foray quickly grew into an obsession.

Far from breaking up her life's previous pattern, the new hobby only drew her deeper into compulsion, closer to the brink.

Fascinated, she found herself staring for hours at the rows of knotted yarn, the intricate bumps and gullies lined up in rigid formation. She slipped deeper and deeper into the patterns until, as if triggered by an overdose of structure, she suddenly veered to the opposite direction, once more feverishly craving dissonance.

It was while researching esoteric crochet stitches that she discovered a reference to an antique weapon of self-defense. The device had been popular during the Gold Rush with the few women who dared to brave San Francisco's Barbary Coast. To the unsuspecting observer, the ladies appeared to be carrying innocuous knitting needles. But when faced with intimidation or unwanted male attention, the needle's tip was quickly removed to reveal a sharp deterring blade.

Mabel was beside herself with intrigue.

At the outset, she had no intention of doing any harm. She simply longed for the uniqueness of the item.

This was a tool she must possess.

IT WAS NO small feat to locate a set of antique knifed knitting needles. They weren't commercially available in any of the typical knitting outlets where she shopped.

The rarity only made them that much more desirable.

Mabel expanded her search, querying several Bay Area antique shops, to no avail. Finally, someone suggested she try the Green Vase in Jackson Square. If anyone would have such an item, it was the elderly proprietor, a grouchy guy named Oscar.

The next day, she arrived at the Jackson Street address, a decrepit three-story building with tarnished brass columns and a crumbling brick façade. It was an anomaly on the otherwise highbrow street. The storefront seemed intentionally designed to scare away shoppers, not to welcome them in.

Mabel peered inside the cracked front window. The dimly lit interior was filled with a jumbled assortment of boxes and crates. The place appeared to be abandoned. She couldn't see that anyone was manning the store.

Tentatively, she tested the door.

To her surprise, the rusted iron frame swung open.

She stepped inside and looked around. The showroom looked even worse up close. Surely, this Oscar fellow was long gone.

But as Mabel turned to leave, she heard a sound at the rear of the building.

A portly man in a blue collared shirt and navy slacks shuffled toward the storefront. He grunted out a greeting as he approached.

Mabel stared at his short, rounded shoulders and the grease stains and dustings of flour on his shirt. She almost turned in hasty retreat. Summoning her courage, she stuttered out her request.

"Hello. You must be Oscar. I'm . . . I'm looking for an antique."

The store owner's bristly eyebrows furrowed as she described the knifed knitting needles she'd read about in the old knitting manual.

"Hmm." Oscar scratched the stubble on his chin. Then he wandered off into the showroom, casually digging through various piles of junk.

Mabel waited patiently. After a while, she thought perhaps the store owner had forgotten she was still there. But at last, Oscar pulled out a slim wooden case from a crate and brought it up to the cashier counter.

Opening the case, he removed several curved needles and arrayed them on the counter.

"These actually go back to before the Gold Rush," he

explained. "They came up from Mexico in the late 1700s on a ship called the *San Carlos*."

Mabel was entranced.

"Careful," he said as she picked a needle up and removed its tip. "The blade is sharp."

She rolled the curved rod in her hand, instantly enamored.

"You wouldn't want to knit with these," he added as she practiced a stitching maneuver. "I'd be afraid the cap would slip off and you'd accidentally lose a finger."

"Oh, I assure you," she replied, her eyes gleaming. "I'm quite skilled."

MABEL BOUGHT THE entire stock of antique needles.

If not for their acquisition, the rest of her murderous mayhem—the deaths of all those unlucky interns—might never have happened.

She took the needles home and began to practice. It took some time for her to adjust to each rod's specific curvature. As the yarn slid through her fingers and around the capped needles, she began to wonder what it would feel like to master the object's other skill set.

Once she started thinking about killing with the needles, she couldn't stop. She knitted through skeins of yarn, meticulously planning her first attack, all the while uncertain if she could go through with the deed.

It was a dangerous, inherently unstable situation. For several months, she teetered back and forth.

But with the slaying of the first intern—followed by the easy disposal of his corpse and the total lack of consequence for her grisly action—she set off down the irreversible path to becoming one of San Francisco's most notorious serial killers.

On Board the *San Carlos*

San Francisco Bay, August 1775

Chapter 62

O' CANADA

THE RECENTLY RECONSTITUTED crew of the *San Carlos* scurried about the boat, checking the rigging lines and mending rips in the masts.

Captain Ayala paced the ship's top deck, monitoring the flurry of activity. He wanted to set sail as soon as possible—before anything else happened that might derail their departure. If all went according to plan, they would lift anchor that night and take advantage of the tide to give them an extra push through the Golden Gate and out into the Pacific.

Ayala's tense face cracked a smile as Petey swooped across the deck with his new feline friend romping playfully behind. Rupert took a flying leap through the air, clearing enough space for the parrot to dive beneath the cat's furry white belly.

Maybe the cross-species camaraderie was a sign his luck had changed and that the ship would make it back to San Blas without further incident.

The captain's expression grew somber as he remembered that he didn't believe in portents or, for that matter, chance.

No matter how unlikely the pairing of the parrot and the cat, it was nothing more than an odd occurrence, completely unconnected to the likelihood of any future success the ship might enjoy on its passage home.

Ayala stroked his chin. Perhaps he should make an exception . . . just this once.

With a shrug, he hollered for Humphretto.

"Where are my special socks?"

. . .

DOWNSTAIRS IN THE galley, Oscar and his niece prepared the kitchen for transit. Anything left unsecured risked falling to the floor during the return trip south to Mexico. Pots, pans, and cooking utensils—every loose piece had to be tied down or tucked into a locked cabinet or drawer.

During the last few days' anchorage, a number of items had been pulled out of their regular stowage spots—and not returned. As happened every time the ship transitioned from a stable mooring to the open sea, something always escaped the notice of Oscar, the niece, and, yes, even Isabella.

When the ship hit the first rocking swell, a loud clattering would be heard in the second-level kitchen—typically followed by Oscar's testy grumble.

The niece and her two cats had learned to stay clear of the galley during the first half hour after the ship's departure.

Oscar stood in the middle of the kitchen, holding an iron skillet and muttering. He couldn't remember where they'd stuck it during the outbound trip.

But his grumpiness was more than the usual presail consternation.

He'd discovered another portion of food missing that morning.

After the feast the crew had enjoyed upon their late-night return to the ship, there was no chance any of them had grown hungry before dawn. Most had still been too stuffed to eat at breakfast.

The stowaway was still on the loose. Despite his best efforts, he'd been unable to find her hiding place.

He feared the Knitting Needle Ninja would take another victim before they reached San Blas.

• • •

THE BARON STROLLED efficiently down the second-level hallway, heading for the stairwell leading up to the main deck.

As he passed the kitchen's open doorway, he caught a glimpse of the chef, standing in the narrow workspace, holding a skillet. The old man gripped the iron handle as if he were about to whap the attached metal surface over someone's head.

It had been a stressful journey, the Baron thought as he continued down the corridor. Whatever the issue, he hoped it wouldn't affect the chef's cooking. The food had been one of the highlights of the trip—that and, of course, the discovery of the San Francisco Bay.

Despite all the hassles—not to mention the ship's near-abandonment—the voyage had been well worth the Baron's time. He had gathered invaluable recon that would give him an advantage over his business competitors. As soon as he touched ground at San Blas, he would arrange to send a team north to start a permanent settlement.

As the Baron neared the stairwell leading to the top deck, he could hear the by-now-familiar sounds of creaking ropes and the snapping of canvas sails.

He'd never had much interest in sailing, but he'd taken a liking to it during this adventure. He might have to hire a mariner to give him some lessons when he returned home.

Just then, the Baron heard Father Carmichael's voice emerging from the chapel at the other end of the hall. He quickened his pace, leaping toward the stairs. He abhorred the priest almost as much as the phantom figure who had murdered the two crew members.

Next time he traveled this route, he would take a different ship.

• • •

CAPTAIN AYALA COLLAPSED into his top-deck chair and propped up his left foot, leaving Humphretto to supervise the crew.

The harried lieutenant took his duties seriously—even if the crew didn't fully cooperate in the handover. Simply put, Humphretto lacked the captain's gravitas. It was a struggle for him to convince the men to obey his commands.

This did not in any way dissuade the little man from trying. He trotted up and down the deck, shouting instructions left and right.

Then he stopped, put his hand on his hip, and shook his head.

Cupping his hands around his mouth, he called up toward the crow's nest. He knew his shout would have no effect on the intended recipient, a tall absentminded deckhand who was climbing toward the roost.

"Watch yourself, Vancouver! You're about to fall!"

First Day of the America's Cup Regatta

Modern-Day San Francisco

Chapter 63

SIDELINED

THE NIECE LOOKED up from her desk as Monty and Van rolled a television set through the reception area's front door.

She was deep into the reference book on the discovery of the San Francisco Bay that her uncle had sent her several months back. Despite the remoteness of the time frame discussed and the difficulty of construing the text's early nineteenth-century English, she'd grown intrigued with the project. She'd even started to decipher some of her uncle's handwriting in the margins. She just needed a few more hours of peace and quiet to study the manuscript . . .

"What are you doing?" she asked, frowning at the disturbance. "Why are you bringing that television in here?"

Monty plugged the power cord into the wall. "We're going to watch the race," he announced, as if there were nothing unusual about this activity. The niece leaned over the desk, trying to see his face, but it was hidden behind the roll-around cart carrying the set.

"I thought you were boycotting the regatta?"

Monty stepped from behind the cart and looked sheepishly at the niece. "I can't help myself. I have to watch."

"We're using your computer for the Internet feed," Van
added, holding up a cable.

"You can do that?" The niece scooted her chair back as
the intern crawled beneath her desk to access the main
console.

His muffled reply drifted up from the floor. "Do it all the
time at my parents' house."

Monty pulled an extra chair into the reception area from
his office. He positioned it close to the set and plopped down
on its seat cushion.

"Who's got popcorn?"

The niece glanced up at the clock. It was almost lunch-
time.

"How about soup?" she asked, heading for the door.

Rupert smacked his lips.

"Even better," Monty replied.

From underneath the desk, Van called out, "Make mine
minestrone!"

. . .

WHILE THE NIECE was rounding up the soup, Van and
Monty continued to work on the television hookup.

It turned out the setup wasn't exactly like the one Van
pirated at his parents' house. The first several attempts failed
to send the live video stream to the television.

From his prone position beneath the desk, Van called out
instructions to Monty.

"Stick the thingamajig in the receiver hole."

"The who in the what?" Monty replied. He leaned over
the back of the television. "Oh, you mean the whatsit in the
spigot screw."

"Yeah, yeah. That's what I said."

At the resulting static, Van suggested a different strategy.

"Hmm. Try switching it to the hootenanny plug."

From her observation post on the filing cabinet, Isabella's pixie face crinkled in confusion.

There was a pause as Monty attempted to complete the revised connection.

"It won't go in there. Wrong shape."

"How about the donut hole?"

Rupert, on the other hand, had no trouble interpreting the jargon. He especially enjoyed the donut reference, which immediately inspired images of his new favorite delicacy, fried chicken donuts.

The static was suddenly replaced by the whir of helicopter blades. The screen flickered to a sweeping shot of the bay and the adjacent city.

"Ah. Now we're cooking with gas."

Van crawled out from under the desk, no small feat given his extreme height. He looked up at the filing cabinet, ever hopeful that he might gain favor with the dominant feline.

"Excellent, dude."

Isabella stared back at him with disapproval.

Van tried another tact. "Er, um, dudette."

The cat was unimpressed.

"Ma'am."

Isabella finally relented.

"Mrao."

BOTH THE HUMANS and cats in the reception area were soon fixated on the America's Cup television coverage. It was a perspective of their city unlike any they had ever seen.

The cameras panned across the San Francisco shoreline, skimming over familiar hillsides and landmarks—as well as a few hundred curious citizens. Along the Marina Green, the Embarcadero, and inside the designated pavilion, pedestrians peered out at the bay, trying to catch a glimpse of the action.

Helicopters hovered over the water, the whirring flap of their propellers a dull background roar. Cameramen dangled from the aircraft's side doors, tethered to the framing by a series of straps and belts. After aiming their lenses at the shoreline, they focused their efforts on the boats below.

It was a daunting scene to capture on film, but the result was a live feed that enthralled viewers on television screens across the country—and inside the mayor's office suite.

Isabella scooted forward on her filing cabinet perch. Monty and Van shifted to the edges of their chairs. Even Rupert gazed in wonder at the images on the screen.

The sailboats approached the starting line, each angling for position. Both teams wanted to hit the designated spot at top speed, but neither could cross the mark before the official start time. The sailors scrambled from one side of the boat to the other, cranking the masts up and down, all the while dashing under swinging booms.

It was a clean start, announced breathlessly by the television commentator. The boats charged across the bay toward the Golden Gate Bridge, channeling the wind to hit speeds of up to fifty miles per hour—until they reached the first buoy.

The audiences on-screen and in the reception area gasped as both boats flipped around the turn at the far corner of the racecourse, teetering on their tiny hulls. Rudders lifted out of the water, scraping the surface like fingertips gripping a window ledge.

The camera zoomed in on the nearest boat as it performed the precarious maneuver, framing a tight shot of a muscled sailor in his chain mail wet suit.

"I wore one of those outfits," Monty said wistfully, forgetting that his short sailing expedition had ended in a disastrous dunking.

Van cringed at the close-up picture. "Dude, it looks uncomfortable."

"Oh, it wasn't so bad," Monty assured him. Then he added a wink. "And it makes you look like a warrior."

From the filing cabinet, Isabella issued a correction.

"Mrao."

THE REGATTA FOOTAGE only increased Monty's frustration. As the race continued, he jumped up from his chair and began to pace around the room.

Each time Monty passed in front of the television screen, Van, Rupert, and Isabella all weaved from side to side to see around him.

The interim mayor failed to notice the inconvenience he was causing the others. He threw his hands in the air, wildly gesticulating.

"We've got to figure out a way to get me back in this thing."

Chapter 64

A CHANGE IN PATTERN

THE NIECE SIGHED when she saw the daily soup line snaking around the foot of the central staircase, at least thirty customers deep. She had mistimed her soup procurement run. She'd been so caught up in Oscar's history book, she'd missed the short window early in the lunch hour for getting through the soup selection process without a lengthy wait.

The race would be half-over by the time she returned to the mayor's office suite.

Resignedly, she took up her spot at the end of the queue.

Even though she knew the vendor, soup acquisition followed a strict first-come, first-serve protocol. It was a necessary regulation, preventing the riot of hungry soup-eaters that would otherwise ensue.

No one was allowed to cut in line.

Not even the chef's niece.

• • •

MABEL WAS MAKING her regular rounds through City Hall when the niece emerged from the mayor's office suite.

While maintaining a discreet distance—and not deviating from her usual routine—Mabel tracked the niece to the rotunda's first floor.

The woman was picking up soup for herself and several others, Mabel surmised, just like she did every day. Although, Mabel reflected, on this particular occasion, the niece was a bit late in attending to her soup duties.

It was only a slight aberration in the pattern, but for the pattern-obsessed, a development of keen interest.

Mabel crossed to the ceremonial rotunda, keeping her thinly veiled focus trained on the niece.

It was an easy surveillance to maintain. Due to the nature of her disguise, Mabel could stand by the Harvey Milk bust, staring out over City Hall's vast interior, without having to provide any rationale or excuse for her presence.

As the niece slowly moved through the line, Mabel reached into her purse. Her fingers threaded through a skein of yarn until they found a pair of knitting needles. Her hand wrapped around one of the curved metal rods—a twitching, itching response to the visual display on the marble floor below.

Mabel felt herself nearing another off-kilter moment. She needed to change the pattern, create an erratic stitch.

Her eyes narrowed as the niece approached the soup vendor's cart and made her selections. The old man nodded and dutifully filled several paper cartons with the indicated soup formulations.

Mabel gripped the needle even tighter.

She was ready to make her next kill.

And this time, her victim wouldn't be an intern.

• • •

THE NIECE GATHERED her soup containers and carefully stacked them into a paper bag. Loaded with enough soup to feed an army of hungry mayors, interns, and cats, she started up the central marble staircase.

Midway up the steps, she stopped, startled by a feathered

shadow flitting past the stained glass windows that framed the rotunda's upper half.

She squinted up at the image of the *San Carlos* and then turned a slow pivot, her eyes scanning her periphery.

The regular collection of tourists cluttered the building. A few wedding parties were grouped near the licensing office in the south wing. And, of course, several City Hall employees had lined up for soup.

If Mabel was hiding amidst this crowd, she had done an excellent job of masking her identity.

The niece detected nothing out of the ordinary—nothing except for a faint trace of lemony-sweet perfume.

Chapter 65

A DELICATE COURTSHIP

THE BARON STOOD on his megayacht, watching the regatta's first race unfold from the ship's top deck.

So far, his team had performed admirably. With just a few more legs to go, the US boat was neck and neck with the challengers from New Zealand.

He expected his men to pull ahead at the next turn.

He glanced down at his watch and nodded with approval. Everything was running according to plan.

The only item on the day's agenda left to be achieved was a win for the first race.

BEING A TECH guru, the Baron had employed every possible tool to monitor his team's progress.

A pair of binoculars hung from his neck, ready for quick consultation. His headset was tuned to the official race radio, and a portable television hooked up on the yacht's deck played the live video feed.

Despite the multiple information inputs, there was little he could do, at this point, to affect the outcome.

Waiting was a frustrating activity.

Patience had never been one of his virtues.

SEEKING A DISTRACTION, the Baron thought back to the prerace festivities. This had been one aspect of the day's events that he could control. Every detail had been choreographed down to the letter.

The welcoming ceremony at the racing pavilion had been headlined by a talented stunt pilot who would be appearing throughout the regatta. His shiny red plane had performed a series of stomach-churning maneuvers in the sky above the venue.

A military band had played the national anthems of both the home and challenger countries. Following this fanfare, the crew members for each team had been introduced.

The only wild card of the morning had failed to show up.

The Baron had been relieved to see no sign of Montgomery Carmichael. He had taken every precaution to ensure that would be the case. An elite security team patrolled the pavilion perimeter. They were specifically tasked with keeping an eye out for the mayor and preventing any attempted incursions.

And, of course, if the guards caught sight of an evil-looking granny with a bag full of knife-modified knitting needles, they were to detain her and immediately call the police.

Truth be known, the Baron's fear of the former far surpassed that of the latter. He firmly believed that if he kept Monty out of the event arena, he would have no problems with Mabel.

"Nothing but bad luck, that priest."

The Baron frowned, shook his head, and corrected himself.

"I mean politician."

ABSENT THE TWO uninvited guests, the first-day crowds were a bit less than the Baron had hoped for—okay, a lot less.

But he took comfort in the numbers that had turned out. He could build on the local interest in the race. He was developing a support base from the ground up. Over the long course of his business career, he had done more with less.

The Baron knew his hometown, every finicky corner and curve. San Francisco was a city that must be wooed.

This would be a delicate courtship.

A mosaic of diverse, demanding individuals, the citizenry insisted on the best in food, wine, and entertainment. The city's grocery stores offered the finest produce in the nation; her dining establishments routinely received superior star ratings.

San Francisco would expect no less than excellence from this new sporting enterprise that had taken over her waterfront, and he intended to give it to her.

He cupped his hand over his brow and scanned the shoreline. All along the Embarcadero, pedestrians peered inquisitively at the spectacle unfolding on the water, the spectator watercraft jockeying for observation positions along the racecourse, the helicopters hovering overhead, and, of course, the unmistakably grand racing boats whose sky-high masts could be picked out from any vantage point.

The people were flirting coyly around the edges of the race, waiting to see what was on offer. They wanted to be lured in and seduced by the action.

He had no doubt that San Francisco would soon fall in love with sailing.

After all, he thought proudly, it was her birthright, her heritage. It was in her blood.

He just had to provide the right enticement.

The Baron jammed the binoculars against his face, muttering unheard orders to his crew members.

It would help immensely if the home team finished this first race with a win.

IT WAS A close contest for much of the route, but the challenger team from New Zealand took the lead on the last turn, gaining the advantage of a favorable wind. The Kiwis won the race by several boat lengths.

The Baron winced at the visible disappointment that rippled through the crowds, but he refused to accept defeat. Given the regatta's best-of-seventeen format, there were still plenty of races to go, including the day's second race, which would start within the hour.

His crew would quickly rack up the nine points needed for the championship, he assured himself.

Even if he had to hop on the boat and captain it himself.

Day Five of the America's Cup

Modern-Day San Francisco

Chapter 66

LOSERS

THE FIRST RACING loss was followed by another—and another—and the next six after that.

In surprisingly short order, the home team found itself down an impossible, seemingly irrecoverable zero points to eight. It was an unprecedented losing streak in the history of the regatta.

New Zealand needed only one more win to take home the America's Cup trophy and to top off their complete and utter humiliation of the US team.

The citizens of San Francisco were not impressed.

With each devastating loss, the Baron became more irritable and frustrated. He was unaccustomed to dealing with such gut-wrenching failure.

He held meetings to motivate his crew members.

He held meetings to denigrate them.

He threatened to fire the captain.

Nothing seemed to work or have any effect. Some of the races were close. Others were total blowouts. Either way, the end result was the same.

The Baron couldn't believe he had backed a team of losers.

WITH THE COMPETITION appearing to be all but over, the Kiwis became a bit cheeky.

While the New Zealand crew members tried to maintain a sense of sportsmanlike decorum, their supporters openly mocked the Baron, who they saw as having outspent their team with his lavish payroll and development budget.

Midnight following their fourth successful day of racing, a trio of Kiwis dressed in skintight hooded suits plastered his Russian Hill residence with New Zealand flags. The symbols were promptly removed, but not before a shaky cell phone video had been taken. By morning, the gleeful Kiwi display had been widely distributed across both San Francisco and the sailing world.

The Baron woke on day five testy and tense. They now faced a must-win situation for today's two races and, if they miraculously managed to make it past that hurdle, for six more straight races in the days after that.

It was an insurmountable hurdle.

There was no chance of success.

Resigned to the inevitable, he set off for the racing pavilion to meet with his team one last time before the ninth and what looked to be final race.

• • •

THE BARON SHOULD have drawn inspiration from his surroundings. If ever a place offered hope for the doomed and down-and-out, it was San Francisco.

It turned out all his team needed was a change in luck.

It would come from the most unlikely of sources.

Chapter 67

THE WINDS OF CHANGE

ON THE FIFTH official day of the America's Cup regatta, the television screen in the mayor's office suite sprang to life with the by-now-familiar video of racing sailboats scooting around the San Francisco Bay.

The scenic panorama was accompanied by a grim pre-race commentary. The home team was in a terrible position, having lost the first eight races in a best-of-seventeen racing series. The event that had started out with circuslike fanfare was now met with the solemnity of a funeral dirge.

Certainly, the atmosphere inside the reception area was much more subdued.

After making an early soup run, the niece sat at her desk, trying to tune out the television while she studied the reference text on the 1775 voyage of the *San Carlos*.

Van sat on the floor in front of the television, sleepily slurping the last bits of his minestrone. Rupert had retired to the cat bed for a postsoup nap. Even Isabella yawned from her filing cabinet perch.

Monty lay in a heap beneath the America's Cup poster, occasionally emitting a plaintive moan.

"How can I not be involved in this race?"

This had been the gist of Monty's ongoing commentary for the past four days—and yet, the meaning seemed not to have reached the conscious portion of Van's brain until just that moment.

"You know, I have a friend . . ." the intern said thoughtfully.

The niece cringed, anticipating Van was about to launch into yet another discussion about the book he was writing on his bicycle ride across California. In her estimation, each completed sentence generally equated to at least twenty minutes' worth of uncompleted fragments—if not more.

Isabella shared the niece's intuition. The cat shoved her head into her chest and wrapped her paws over her ears.

Van tossed his empty soup container into the trash can by the niece's desk. "My friend, he's got a boat."

This unexpected announcement received an immediate response.

"That's it!" Monty exclaimed, leaping up from the floor. "I'll borrow a boat and join the race on my own!"

He closed in on Van, who looked surprised at the sudden rush of attention. "Your friend, how much does he charge to rent out his boat?"

Van stroked his chin, considering the question, and then shrugged. "Don't know."

"Is it available this afternoon?"

There was another pondering pause. "Don't know."

"Would he let us take it out on the racecourse?"

This time, the silence stretched out almost a minute. "Don't know."

Monty opened and closed his mouth, temporarily stymied.

The niece sighed patiently. Much as she hated to intervene, this could go on for hours. "Can you ask your friend about the boat?"

"Okay. Yeah, sure," Van replied, as if that course of action hadn't occurred to him. Then he leaned his back against the front surface of the niece's desk and returned his attention to the television screen.

The niece peered over the top of her desk and cleared her throat. "Perhaps now would be a good time."

Another flash of realization spread across Van's face. "Oh."

Then he got up, slid on his jacket, and left the room.

"Where's he going?" Monty asked.

The niece hurried to the main door, cracked it open, and watched the tall intern step into the elevator.

"Hmm."

On a hunch, she trotted across the reception area and cut through the mayor's office to the windows overlooking the front balcony.

Monty caught up to her as she watched the pedestrians on the street below. A few minutes later, she spied Van's head, slowly meandering out of the building and lumbering in the direction of the nearest BART station.

The niece shook her head. She had little faith that this boat idea would pan out or even that such a boat actually existed.

They probably wouldn't hear from Van until the following day at the soonest. Given his penchant for wandering, she wouldn't be surprised if he disappeared until the following week.

She stepped away from the window and returned to the reception area, leaving Monty to gape at the disappearing intern.

"I guess he's gone to ask about the boat."

Chapter 68

THE LOANER BOAT

THE REGATTA'S FATEFUL ninth race was scheduled for a one thirty P.M. start, but Mother Nature refused to cooperate. Strange as it may seem for a sailing competition, there were strict regulations on both the upper and lower wind speeds that were deemed suitable for racing.

High wind conditions forced the race organizers to delay the ninth competition and reorganize the rest of the day's schedule. Likely only one race would get off that afternoon, and it wouldn't start for at least another hour, assuming the actual weather conformed to the forecast.

For the Baron and his demoralized sailing team, the postponement only extended their torture.

While outwardly, they proclaimed their intent to fight to the finish, inwardly, they had all but given up.

BACK AT CITY Hall, a lull had settled over the mayor's office suite.

The reception area was sealed off from the gusting

wind that had disrupted the day's sailing. In fact, the room had grown quite warm. The stuffy temperature combined with satiated stomachs to create a den of peaceful slumbering.

The television had mercifully been put on mute. Human and feline snoring filled the void.

Rupert sprawled across the cat bed, Isabella lay flopped across the top of the filing cabinet, and Monty had stretched his long frame over two office chairs.

Only the niece remained awake, and she was struggling to keep her eyelids open.

When the phone rang, she picked it up and said sleepily, "Mayor Carmichael's office."

"I got the boat."

"Van?"

"Well, yeah," he responded, somewhat incredulous.

The niece's comment instantly brought Monty back to life. He nearly fell to the floor in his scramble to reach the niece's desk.

"Did he get the boat?"

The niece nodded warily. "He got the boat."

At Monty's wild hand waving, she spoke into the receiver. "We're on our way."

TWENTY MINUTES LATER, the mayor's black town car stopped at a curb near the city's baseball park. There weren't any available parking spots, so this was the closest the driver could get them to the address Van had given them.

Monty jumped out and began lifting the cat stroller through the car's side door as the niece consulted a map.

"Van said to meet him at the Mission Bay boat launch . . ." She squinted at a walkway that ran beside the stadium, leading toward a dock beyond. While it was sunny directly overhead, a thick wall of fog had begun to roll in through the Golden Gate. "Um, I'm not so sure about this . . ."

Monty was already guiding the cat-filled carriage down

the sidewalk. "Come on! The race could be starting any minute now. There's no time to waste!"

VAN MET HIS City Hall colleagues behind the stadium and motioned for them to follow him down the walkway toward the pier.

"What kind of boat is this, exactly?" the niece called out, realizing she should have posed this question at the outset.

Van appeared not to hear her.

She soon had her answer.

When she caught up to Van and Monty, they were standing beside an inflatable raft. Van held an electric pump in his hand, which had presumably been used to inflate the tubing.

The niece stared at the raft, puzzling. "Wait, isn't that— the Batman boat?"

During every home baseball game, local fans took to the water outside the stadium in the hopes of catching fly balls or home runs that sailed over the wall and landed in the bay.

This being San Francisco, it wouldn't do to simply float about in black monochrome wet suits or unadorned canoes— such activity must be performed while wearing elaborate costumes and gear.

One of the most popular participants in this bonanza was a pair of sports enthusiasts who dressed up like Batman and Robin and drove through the stray ball zone on a hand-crafted Batman-themed boat.

The duo—and their distinctive inflatable raft—were regularly featured in cutaway shots from the televised game.

The niece looked up at Van. "Your friend is the Bat-man guy?"

Van cleared his throat. "Technically, I'm Batman. He's Robin." He shrugged. "Because I'm taller. But since it's his boat, he calls himself Batman, even though he wears the Robin outfit."

Monty murmured to himself, trying to follow the convoluted logic.

The niece shook her head, unable to imagine her intern as the masked figure she'd seen on television news clips.

"I never would have recognized you."

"Well, we wear costumes." Van opened a locker next to the dock. "The water's cold. You'll need to put on a wet suit."

Isabella poked her nose against the stroller's zipped cover, sniffing at the inflatable raft. Her eyes focused on the rubber tubing, inspecting its seaworthiness.

Monty reached for one of the decorated wet suits.

"I have to be Batman," he said emphatically. "I'm the mayor. I can't be Robin."

Van shrugged his shoulders. "I can't be Robin. I won't fit in the costume."

Monty and Van turned toward the niece.

"No," she said adamantly. "No way."

An overriding feline voice called out from the stroller. *"Mrao."*

MINUTES LATER, VAN waved as the raft pulled away from the dock, powered by an outboard motor attached to the rear of the inflated tubing. The motor had been rigged so that its power and direction could be controlled from a front-mounted steering wheel and drive shaft.

Monty stood behind the front console wearing the Batman wet suit, which included a long rubber cape and a pointed mask that covered the top half of his face.

The niece occupied the copilot position beside the mayor. Under protest, she had donned the red, green, and gold Robin outfit.

The cats, of course, couldn't ride along without some form of accoutrement.

Van had improvised their costumes from a stuffed animal that was typically mounted to the boat during the baseball sessions.

It took some convincing, but Isabella eventually allowed

herself to be fitted with a black waterproof vest. Rupert had agreed to wear the cat-sized cape.

With all of its passengers suitably attired, the raft, which was thankfully far sturdier than it appeared at first glance, sped off into the foggy bay.

"Which way to the racecourse?" Monty hollered over the motor's loud hum.

The niece was unable to point directions. She was too busy holding on to the front railing with one hand and Rupert with the other.

Isabella assumed responsibility for navigational instructions.

"Mrao."

Chapter 69

I'M BATMAN

RUPERT HUDDLED IN his person's arms, trying to avoid the spray coming off the water as the raft motored toward the buoys marking the eastern edge of the regatta racecourse.

Being a cat, he had only a vague notion of the famous superhero who had inspired the boat's elaborate décor. He hadn't read any of the comic books that featured the fictional character's Gotham City exploits. Nor had he seen any of the movies dedicated to the Batman franchise.

Rupert's only frame of reference was based on the humans he'd seen dressed up like the famous masked crusader. He gathered the costume gave the wearers a sense of empowerment—that it conveyed unique skills and made possible otherwise unachievable feats.

He was a little unclear as to why a bat-human hybrid would inspire such beliefs, but he could support the underlying theme.

Moreover, Rupert knew this about the caped crusader: Batman had opposable thumbs—thumbs that could be used to rifle through a phone book or to access online databases to search for the secret location of a kitchen with the capability of making both fried chicken and donuts—or, more important, fried chicken baked inside donuts.

Yes, a superhero could do that.

And he, Rupert, now wore a superhero cape.

Bravely, Rupert lifted his head, letting the breeze catch the tiny cape tethered to his neck.

He flexed his front paws, imagining the extra digits sprouting from his wrists.

I'm Batman.

Chapter 70

HELLO, SAN FRANCISCO!

THE LATE-SUMMER FOG filled the bay, a dense wall of liquid air that swallowed everything in its path.

The peaks of the Golden Gate Bridge rose above the mist, the red pillars floating as if suspended in midair. The city itself lay cloaked in a feathery gray boa that had been slung across peaks, valleys, and street shoulders in elegant adornment.

Despite the inclement weather, the niece had never seen so many watercraft squeezed into such a limited space. The area surrounding the racecourse was a literal traffic jam of boats.

Alcatraz was under siege, surrounded by an armada of yachts, motorboats, and local ferries, the last of which had been co-opted to provide special racing tours. The ferries still making their regular routes maneuvered with difficulty through the bottleneck of boats.

And there in the middle of it all was the Batman and Robin raft—which in addition to its regular cast of super-heroes today included two orange and white cats.

MUCH TO THE niece's chagrin, Monty had found a bull-horn in one of the raft's front storage compartments.

With delight, he steered toward a high-end yacht. After waving up at the yacht's regatta spectators, he hollered into the horn's mouthpiece, "Hello, people of San Francisco!"

Given the Batboat's popularity in the Bay Area, a few of the passengers raised their wineglasses and beer bottles in toast. Some even clapped and cheered—a sure indication that they hadn't recognized the mayor in the Batman costume.

Monty cleared up that misconception with his next announcement.

"It is I, Mayor Carmichael!"

Hisses and boos were hurled over the water. One man looked as if he was going to throw an empty bottle at the raft, but an environmentally conscientious colleague held him back.

Other observers were more interested in the raft's feline passengers.

"I didn't know Batman had cats . . ."

WHILE MONTY CONTINUED to blast the yacht specta-tors with his bullhorn, Isabella focused on driving. Perched on the front console next to the steering wheel, she was able to control the raft's direction—so long as Monty was suit-ably distracted.

The pedal that regulated the motor's speed, however, was beyond the reach of her back legs, a source of constant frus-tration. She glared down at the lever, cursing the raft's poor design.

"Mrao."

"Aren't we supposed to be staying outside of these buoys?" the niece asked, worried they were veering too close to the racecourse.

The question was answered by an earsplitting blast from

a Coast Guard cutter, whose horn volume far surpassed that of Monty's.

Monty waved cordially as Isabella steered the raft out of the zone.

IN THE DISTANCE, at the far west edge of the course, the two racing boats picked up speed, heading toward the starting line.

Shifting Rupert in her arms, the niece fiddled with a shortwave radio mounted onto the raft's console and dialed to the frequency broadcasting the race announcer.

"They're off! It's a clean break across the line!"

Monty revved the engine. Dropping the bullhorn, he wrapped his hands around the steering wheel, gripping it on either side of Isabella's paws.

"Let's go!"

UNDER ISABELLA'S EXPERT steering, the raft dodged in and out of the much larger boats that had been prepositioned along the edge of the course. Soon, the Batman crew neared the center of the race action.

The competing sailboats moved at breathtaking speed toward the buoy marking the first corner. Gasps were heard across the bay—and from the radio announcer—as both teams threw their craft into a whipping reverse.

The Kiwis tilted almost forty-five degrees. Sailors clung precariously to the hulls and cross-netting as the boat hung in the air and then landed, with a crushing *whomp*, back on the bay.

With nothing left to lose, the Americans were just as gutsy in their approach—and were rewarded with a far smoother landing. Steely expressions were visible beneath their plastic helmets and water-splashed visors. Despite the long odds, they were giving it their all.

It was no small endeavor to keep up with the racing

sailboats, but Isabella was the cat for the job. She hunched over the steering wheel, urging Monty to give the motor more gas. The raft bounced around the outer edge of the course, once more weaving in and out of the stationary ships lining the perimeter.

Helicopters hovered above the action. The cameramen, by now accustomed to filming while hanging out the aircraft's side doors, trained their equipment on the fast-moving race—and on the cat-driven Batboat.

The resilient Americans were neck and neck with the upstart Kiwis, but the race announcers were torn between providing play-by-play of the race and reporting on the superhero felines among the spectator boats.

"I've never seen anything like it. One of those cats is actually driving the boat!"

Monty nudged Isabella's shoulder. "A little to the right, Captain."

Her furry expression reflected annoyance, but she grudgingly complied.

"Mrao."

Seconds later, the Batboat zoomed past the Baron's yacht. Monty pulled out the bullhorn and aimed it at the fancy ship's top deck.

"Hey, Baron! How do you like me now?"

THE BARON WOULD have been furious at Mayor Carmichael for invading the regatta—except that his team had just won the race.

The Kiwis had been momentarily distracted by a Batman boat carrying two costumed cats the crew had seen circumnavigating the racecourse.

On Board the *San Carlos*

San Francisco Bay, August 1775

Chapter 71

FAREWELL, MY FRIEND

AFTER A SHORT but adventurous stay in the San Francisco Bay, the *San Carlos* raised its anchor and set course for the Golden Gate. The crew scurried about as the ship sailed away from its temporary berth at Angel Island, while the passengers stood on deck, taking in the departing view.

They would carry memories of this pristine place with them for the rest of their lives. Vivid descriptions of the vast protected harbor would be related to friends, family, and all who would listen.

But at least one of their number would not be making the return trip to San Blas.

This individual had decided to become a permanent—and the first Spanish—resident of the Bay Area.

Petey had given the idea a great deal of thought. It was no small matter for a domesticated parrot to part ways with a doting owner, not to mention the comfort of a warm bed and the assurance of three square meals a day.

As good as he'd had it living on board the ship, he couldn't ignore the call of the wild. He was determined to make his new home atop a steep rise on the bay's south shore, a prominent landmark that would later be named Telegraph Hill.

Petey circled the ship one last time, flying through its billowing masts.

Isabella paid her formal respects, nodding regally up at the bird.

Rupert gave his feathered friend a more enthusiastic send-off, romping after Petey as he fluttered above the deck.

Ayala's brow furrowed as the parrot landed on his shoulder. The captain reached up to stroke the red-feathered head as Petey gave him a gentle nuzzle.

A moment later, he was gone, disappearing into the perfect blue sky.

Ayala gripped the ship's steering wheel, trying to ignore the moistness that had crept into the corners of his eyes. For once, his heart ached more than his injured foot.

With a heavy sigh, he tried to focus on the narrow mouth at the far end of the bay.

This was no time to fall complacent.

The most dangerous segment of the ship's journey was about to begin.

Chapter 72

THE EXORCISM

AS THE *SAN Carlos* swept across the bay toward the Golden Gate, a crew member hoisted himself to the top of the main mast and climbed into the crow's nest.

Easily the tallest man on the ship, Vancouver was ill fitted for duty inside the barrel-shaped roost. It was a struggle to fold his long legs into the cramped quarters.

But what the post lacked in space, it made up for in solitude—that and Captain Ayala and his lieutenant often forgot about him when he was up in the sky. To the adage, "Out of sight, out of mind," Van often added "off the work duty list."

While others complained about the post's blistering wind, Van reveled in the constant blast.

"What a remarkable embodiment of nature," he'd reply to anyone who complained about the perch's stiff breeze.

The crow's nest assignment also gave Van plenty of time to think. He spent hours staring out at the ocean, pondering the book he was writing—or was going to write . . . eventually—about his many ocean travels.

After all, he reasoned, there was no need to hurry.

WITH A YAWN, Van pulled out a spyglass, extended the lens, and looked down at the ship's main deck. He spied Humphretto, hurrying about as always, yipping orders to the crew. The captain, still nursing his sore foot, manned the ship's wheel.

There was Father Monty, walking along the railing. And at the far end of the stern, the chef's niece with her two cats . . .

"Wait! What's that?" Van pulled back from the spyglass, rubbed his eyes, and then returned his attention to the viewfinder.

"Aunt Wanda??!!"

• • •

FATHER MONTY PARADED across the upper deck of the *San Carlos*, looking for the niece and her two cats. There were still several days left on the journey back to San Blas, and he hadn't given up hope that the woman would agree to a confessional session.

He found the niece staring out across the bay, watching the serene landscape as the boat neared the gaping mouth of the Pacific.

The niece held a sleepy Rupert in her arms. Isabella had propped her front legs up on the ship's bottom railing, giving herself enough elevation to peer out between the middle slats.

They were not alone.

Creeping across the deck, any warning of her approach drowned out by the wind and waves, was a crumpled old hag.

The stowaway.

The *murderous* stowaway.

Father Monty shuddered at the sight. Despite all of the rumors and speculation, the actual embodiment of the ghoul was far more fearsome than anything he had imagined.

The hag had scraggly dark hair, marked at either temple with a wide gray streak. She was filthy, covered from head to toe in dirt and grime.

He squinted at her face, which bore the focused expression of a skilled artisan in the midst of a delicate task.

And then he saw the object, glinting in the stowaway's clawed hand: a curved knitting needle whose tip had been modified with a sharp blade.

The niece wrinkled her nose at a surge of lemony-sweet perfume. She turned from the railing, and exclaimed in surprise.

The hag was mere feet away, advancing on her target, knife at the ready.

The niece looked over the woman's bent shoulders and locked eyes with Father Monty.

For once, he thought with a smile, she looked relieved to see him.

The stowaway followed the niece's gaze and surveyed Father Monty without concern. Wielding her weapon, she resumed her pursuit of the niece.

Monty reached into his robes and pulled out the crucifix he'd been carrying in his pocket for just this occasion.

"Stop!" he hollered, waving the cross in the air.

Once more, the woman looked back. Her chapped lips parted into a demonic leer that revealed swollen gums and a few whittled teeth.

Undeterred by the crucifix, she crept closer to the niece.

Pinned against the pointed rear of the ship, the niece had few options for escape. Rupert hid his face in his person's chest as she lunged to the left, but the hag was quicker than her age and decrepit appearance implied. She penned the niece in, all the while closing down the space between them.

Isabella hissed fiercely, jumping in front of her person, but this, too, had no deterring effect.

Leering, the stowaway raised the knifed knitting needle and prepared to strike.

"Father Monty?" the niece called out in panic. "A little help here!"

He stared at the cross he held in his hand, perplexed. "Hmm. It doesn't seem to be working."

The hag edged closer to her target.

"Maybe you're not using it right!" the niece called out, shuffling the opposite direction, but still unable to safely maneuver around the other woman.

Monty stared up at the sky, trying to remember the phrasing from the ancient text he'd used a few days earlier. "What was the ceremonial term? Ah yes. I remember now."

He adjusted his hold on the crucifix and stretched his arm out toward the stern of the boat. *"Expellorum!"*

The hag didn't flinch.

Monty shook his head. He frowned at the crucifix as if examining a defective mechanical device.

"I don't know what's wrong with it . . ."

"Monty!"

Hissss! Isabella bared her fangs as the niece tried to shield Rupert from the old woman's jabbing thrusts.

Suddenly jolted into action, Monty gripped the length of the cross, reared back his arm, and threw the wooden object across the deck.

The blunt end of the crucifix beaned the hag across the side of the head.

The knifed needle clattered to the deck as the old woman reeled sideways. A confused "Eh?" was all she could spit out.

Monty scooted across the deck and picked up the fallen crucifix. He waved it once more at the hag.

This time, the action garnered a far more wary response.

The hag climbed up on the nearest railing. With her back to the bay, she stared curiously down at the priest, the niece, and the two cats.

The ship heaved from a rolling wave, raising the side of the ship.

Releasing her grip from the railing, the old woman waved at the awestruck observers, flexed her legs, and jumped clear of the railing. Her ragged clothes flapped about her body as she dropped toward the water, landed with a splash, and then sank into the swirling depths.

Monty and the niece rushed to look down over the side.

A trail of bubbles floated up, but nothing more.

The priest slapped his hands together.

"And that, my friend, is how you perform an exorcism."

Isabella looked up at the priest with her most disapproving glare.

"Mrao."

Last Day of the America's Cup

Modern-Day San Francisco

Chapter 73

WHAT A DRAG

AFTER THE BAT-CAT-FACILITATED win on the regatta's critical ninth race, the home team went on to take the next seven races. The astonishing turnaround represented one of the most fantastic come-from-behind stories in the history of all modern sport.

The current eight-to-eight tie meant that today's race, number seventeen in the summer's long contest, would decide the championship.

The Americans were brimming with confidence, the Kiwis were utterly flummoxed, and the city was abuzz.

All of San Francisco spilled out across the shoreline, fascinated by the drama unfolding on the water. What began as a lukewarm curiosity in the regatta was now a full-fledged sailing fever.

Crowds thronged in the free admission area at the America's Cup pavilion. The members-only seating also filled in, with wealthy representatives from the city's booming Internet businesses, stock brokerages, law firms, and biotech companies showing up to flash their clout. Local politicians and their associated entourages mingled with both groups.

Along with the commoners and the elite, the event, of course, also drew a generous sampling of the eclectic.

There were mimes clad in silver jumpsuits and nudists clad in nothing at all. Body artists put their wares on display, showcasing their tattoos, piercings, and Mohawks. A number of people showed up wearing funny hats and face paint, but that's hardly worth mentioning.

And of course, there were those in costume: cartoon characters, a couple of forest animals, and most notably, a tall, slender Marilyn Monroe.

Somewhere within this grand mix lurked a murderer.

• • •

MARILYN SMILED AT the security personnel as she approached the pavilion's Embarcadero entrance. She recognized a donut-munching guard on loan from City Hall and approached his station to have her handbag searched.

With a goofy grin, he swallowed a bite of his pastry.

"Afternoon, Marilyn," he said bashfully, giving the bag only a cursory perusal. He was always far more distracted by the wedding coordinator's costume than any accessories—or knitting needles—she might be carrying in her purse.

Returning the bag, he took in a deep breath, sucking in the scent of the wedding planner's lemony-sweet perfume. It reminded him of jelly-stuffed donuts.

Such a lovely lady, he thought as he reached for another pastry.

MARILYN STROLLED ALONG the pavilion's main walkway, pretending to gaze out at the megayachts docked along the outer edge.

In truth, she was focused on an elderly gentleman with short, rounded shoulders who hobbled about twenty feet ahead. Marilyn had tracked the old man down the Embar-cadero from the Ferry Building.

It had been a long slow pursuit. The geezer walked with the assistance of a wooden cane and didn't seem to be in any hurry.

Even in the sturdy women's loafers, Marilyn's feet had worked up several blisters.

Her part would soon be over, she told herself with a wince. This was her last appearance as the famous movie star. With the payment for today's services, she would have enough money to buy the new mountain bike she'd been craving for the last six months. She'd pack up her gear and trek off into the woods. She'd find a nice tree to camp under and finally start to work on her book.

With relief, she watched her target veer toward the crowded area near the stage.

Making no attempt to disguise the natural—masculine—nature of his voice, he pulled a cell phone from his purse and punched the button for a preprogrammed number.

"All right, Aunt Wanda. The soup guy is circling toward the Jumbotron. I'm about to head out. If you'll just pass me my check, I'll be on my way . . ."

Chapter 74

REVEALED

MAYOR MONTGOMERY CARMICHAEL beamed with pleasure as the Baron called out his name and began a glowing introduction.

After acknowledging Monty's tireless efforts to promote the race and touting the mayor's fine leadership and invaluable contributions, the Baron added impishly, "The team is counting on your presence here today to give them the extra luck they need to bring home another victory!"

Monty waved to the cheering crowd as he approached the podium in the middle of the stage, squeaking with every step.

The mayor wore the rubber wet suit Batman costume—as he had for the last eight races. Lifting the mask off his face, he began a lengthy oration. This would be his last session in the America's Cup spotlight, and he was going to make the most of every second.

With the audience quickly losing interest, the Baron cut in, but it took the concerted efforts of the entrepreneur and three ushers to push Monty back toward his designated place at the rear of the stage.

Resuming control of the microphone, the Baron prepared to make his final remarks. His face took on a thoughtful expression. If his team lost the last race, the next installment of the regatta would take place in New Zealand. This might be his last chance to address the racing crowd, the last chance to reflect on San Francisco's unique history with the sailing world.

And so he began relating the story of the *San Carlos*, the first sailing vessel to pass through the Golden Gate.

The audience fell to a hush, listening to the story, and the cameramen filming the event began to pan the crowd.

• • •

OSCAR LEANED ON his cane as he watched the Jumbotron feed of the ceremony taking place about a hundred yards away.

He grumbled with relief as Mayor Carmichael was shuffled to the rear of the stage. With the Baron launching into his remarks about the history of the *San Carlos*, the camera's focus drifted into the audience.

Oscar picked out the niece and, sitting in the woman's arms, Isabella. A gust of wind tossed the niece's hair as the frame passed over the orange and white cat.

He sucked in his breath, startled by the feline's expression.

Isabella had detected an ominous presence in the crowd.

It could only be the Ninja.

OSCAR LEANED TOWARD the Jumbotron screen as the camera skimmed over the spectators. He studied each face that popped into the frame, dismissing several racing fans from New Zealand and the Marilyn Monroe wedding planner from City Hall.

The video switched back to the stage, where Monty was trying to push his way back to the podium. Apparently, the mayor had remembered an important item that was left out

324 Rebecca M. Hale

of his previous remarks. After a quick shot of the subsequent scrum of the Baron's security team tackling the mayor, the cameraman swung his lens back to the crowd.

Oscar muttered under his breath.

"No, not Hoxton Finn. No, not the first mate." He shook his head, trying to clear his thoughts. "I mean, Humphrey."

The screen captured an image of the president of the board of supervisors, standing with his entourage.

Keep moving, Oscar urged the cameraman.

Then he saw her, and a chill ran down his spine.

Mabel.

Something in the way the sunlight hit her face revealed the impersonation. She'd been there all along, right in front of him. How could he have missed it?

Oscar feared for the fate of the real Wanda Williams. Surely, the woman had met a grim end—as another of the Ninja's victims.

Leaning heavily on the cane, Oscar spun away from the Jumbotron. His eyes searched the crowd, looking not for Wanda Williams, but the woman who had taken her place.

He had to catch her now. If the Ninja slipped out of the event pavilion, there was no telling what disguise she might take up next.

This was his last chance to right the wrong, or to at least mitigate his poor judgment in selling Mabel the antique knitting needles—and to retrieve the deadly weapons before they caused any more harm.

Chapter 75

BEHEADED

VAN WANDERED THROUGH the crowd surrounding the stage, searching for his aunt Wanda—or rather, searching for the woman he thought was his aunt Wanda.

He was starting to sweat inside the Marilyn Monroe costume, and his feet were absolutely killing him.

Just then a loud *squawk* echoed across the shoreline. A feathered green arrow swooped down from Telegraph Hill and dove toward the pavilion.

• • •

INSIDE THE CAT stroller, Rupert lay curled up, snuggled in his blankets. He smacked his lips as visions of fried chicken donuts danced in his head.

But at the squawking sound, a fleeting image interrupted the dream. Rupert saw himself cuddled up with a redheaded green parrot. From beneath the blankets, the cat called out a sleepy welcome to his feathered friend.

"Wrao-woo!"

The niece glanced down at the stroller.

"What's gotten into you?"

•   •   •

VAN FILTERED THROUGH the crowd, still looking for his aunt Wanda.

He noted the startled expressions of several surrounding spectators, but it took him a moment to realize that their stares were for something more than the Marilyn costume. It was a bystander comment, accompanied by a pointed finger, that did the trick.

"There's a parrot on your head!"

Van raised his hands, trying to knock the bird off, but the wig was rather tall and the bird easily evaded his reach.

More onlookers gathered as he spun in a circle, swatting the air.

Suddenly, Van had a far greater problem. The parrot dug his clawed feet into the wig. Flapping his wings, he tried to lift the bouffant hair from the intern's head. The bobby pins securing the wig in place began to fall to the ground.

Pling. Pling. Pling.

One man stood with his jaw dropped open, gaping at the scene. Another bystander hopped up and down, attempting to scare off the determined parrot.

Petey paid them no heed. His red head bobbed as he flapped his wings. His shoulders pulled upward, straining against the last constraining pin.

Pling.

The wig launched into space, soaring like a blond balloon up into the sky.

Van screeched in alarm, covered his head with his hands, and sprinted out of the stage area and down the pavilion's long walkway.

THE NIECE SQUINTED at Van's fleeing figure, wondering what her intern was doing in such a ridiculous costume.

Isabella was far more concerned that the Knitting Needle Ninja had just disappeared from the crowd.

The cat's voice warbled tensely.

"Mrao."

Chapter 76

THE NINJA TAKES ANOTHER?

WANDA WILLIAMS—OR rather, the woman who had been impersonating her for the past six months—shifted through the crowd, moving with precision and ease toward the hangar displaying the sailboat prototypes at the far end of the event pavilion.

Thanks to Van's phone call, she'd spotted the old man standing in front of the Jumbotron.

This moment had been a long time coming. Ever since she'd learned of Oscar and his dratted painting, the one that had outed her as a serial killer, she'd been looking for the right opportunity to lure him into a trap.

When she saw the stunned expression on his face, that look of awed realization, she knew her cover had once more been blown—and that this was the time to strike.

At the hangar entrance, she glanced over her shoulder, pausing to confirm that Oscar had taken the bait. Seeing his lumbering figure cross the pavilion, she slipped inside the hangar, conducted a cursory review of the interior, and chose her hiding spot.

Her hand wrapped around the knitting needle she'd brought with her just for the occasion.

All she had left to do was wait.

CROUCHED IN THE shadows at the corner of the hangar, Mabel reflected with pride on her latest secretarial incarnation. She'd known Wanda Williams for years during their joint tenure at City Hall, so she was familiar with the woman's facial expressions, her speech patterns, her ticks.

The toughest part had been modifying her appearance. She'd posted a photo of Wanda on her full-length mirror at the Theater District apartment, taking care each day to match her costume and makeup against the (deceased) original.

Wanda's nephew had been an added bonus to the charade. Van had been a useful—and completely unwitting—accomplice.

It had been an entertaining ruse, hiring the hapless fellow to parade around as Marilyn Monroe. A part-time job, she'd called it. He'd needed the money, and he had plenty of experience with costumes.

What a strange man, she thought, shaking her head.

Things got even better after she inserted him as the mayoral intern, supplementing her existing surveillance on the mayor's office suite. Van had dutifully overlooked the spy-cam equipment and scent disperser that were hidden in the ceiling vents, assuring the niece he saw nothing out of the ordinary when she asked him to climb up and inspect the area around the sprinklers.

The rubber tip of Oscar's cane thumped against the concrete, and Mabel focused her attention on the hangar entrance.

She was closing in on her final kill—one that would top all others.

This murder was not for interest or curiosity.

This was for revenge.

MABEL WATCHED OSCAR limp into the hangar, tracking him as he glanced over the sailboat models on display.

She read his expression—wary but on the verge of concluding that the hangar was empty. Oscar hobbled to the nearest watercraft and peered down one of the side hulls.

Mabel approached, by now well practiced in the art of stealth, and silently drew her weapon.

But before she could reach around his midsection with her curved needle and generate that oh-so-satisfying spurt of blood, he crumpled to the floor.

A stabbing pain filled his chest—but it wasn't her doing. He had collapsed on his own accord.

Oscar was having a heart attack.

Mabel slid the cover back onto the needle, sheathing the blade. There was no point now in creating a mess. She'd waited too long to exact her revenge.

Her whole being sagged with disappointment. A present she'd been waiting to open had suddenly been jerked away.

MABEL TRUDGED OUT the hangar's exit and then hovered, indecisive. She knew she should leave and let nature run its course, but she couldn't quite shake the sense of emptiness, her sudden lack of purpose.

The audio of the Baron's speech echoed dimly in the background.

"San Francisco is a young city."

Turning toward the crowd that surrounded the stage, she spied a substitute for her obsession, a potential victim almost as good as the old man himself.

His niece.

Mabel had the strange feeling that she'd tried to kill the woman before.

She pulled out her cell phone and dialed the mobile number for the mayor's administrative assistant.

"This is Wanda Williams," she whispered tensely. "Your uncle—the soup vendor? I think he's having a heart attack."

Chapter 77

DÉJÀ VU

THE NIECE DIDN'T stop to wonder how Wanda Williams knew the soup vendor from City Hall was her uncle.

She didn't pause to ask herself why the adversarial secretary had called the niece instead of 911.

All she could think was that her Uncle Oscar was in trouble and that, given his frail health, this might be the end—not a fake death or a subterfuge to escape the attention of the authorities, but a real and final termination of his life.

The niece rushed across the pavilion and into the hangar, pushing the stroller at breakneck speed, bumping its wheels over the rough seams in the concrete.

Isabella poked her head and shoulders out of the passenger compartment, while Rupert hunkered down just below the sightline for safety. There hadn't been time to rezip the cover.

When the niece saw the crumpled heap on the floor, she knew she was too late.

Panting, she knelt beside her uncle's body and rolled

him onto his back. A gray lifeless color had taken over his face. His blue eyes were fixed with death's final gaze. Rupert nudged Oscar's arm, but there was no response, no pulse.

Isabella murmured her sincere condolences.

"Mer-mrao."

The niece held her uncle's hand, crying at the cold texture of his skin.

He had warned her that this day would come.

No one lives forever, my dear.

She had always hoped that maybe, for Oscar, there might be an exception.

AS THE TRIO mourned their beloved friend, they were joined by a fourth being, this one not the least bit sympathetic to their loss.

Tearstained, the niece looked up to see Wanda Williams silently walking across the hangar.

But was it Wanda? There was something different in her demeanor.

Isabella let out a vicious hiss. Arching her back, she stepped protectively in front of her person.

The niece glanced down at her uncle's lifeless face. His death might have been from natural causes, but his presence in this empty hangar was the calculated result of an evil, demented force.

Leering at the niece, the secretary held up a curved knitting needle and pulled the cap off its knifed end.

This wasn't Wanda Williams, the niece realized with horror.

It was Mabel.

"Issy, we've got to get out of here," the niece said, scooping up Rupert.

But Mabel had already cut off the exit. The niece was pinned against the side of the boat.

Cackling with glee, Mabel jabbed the air between them.

Then, in the doorway, the niece spotted a familiar wet suited figure with a long Batman-style cape.

An odd feeling of déjà vu swept over the niece as she called out, "Monty! Help!"

Chapter 78

EXORCIZED

"WANDA? WHAT ARE you doing in here? Is that a knitting needle? What happened to Oscar? Wait a minute . . . You're not Wanda . . ."

It took Monty several seconds to process the scene. He stroked his chin, pondering the implications. "How long has Mabel been masquerading as Wanda?"

Meanwhile, the niece was busy fending off Mabel and her advancing needle-knife. The niece had scooted to the far end of the boat and was nearing a corner where she would be trapped against the hangar walls.

"Monty!"

Startled, the Batman-clad mayor swept into action. He sprinted across the hangar—but stopped short a few feet away from Mabel, held back by her glancing blade.

From the ground at her person's feet, Isabella stopped hissing long enough to issue a sharp *"Mrao."*

The niece provided the interpretation. "Monty, the cane!"

As Monty lunged for the wooden rod that lay on the floor

beside Oscar's lifeless body, Mabel directed her blade at the mayor.

For a split second, the niece thought back to the moment in the mayor's office suite when she'd wondered what she might do in a situation such as this . . .

Then she shrugged off the notion as ridiculous. Dumping Rupert to the ground, she moved in to try to disarm Mabel.

"Monty, watch out! She's coming after you!"

Monty looked over his shoulder just in time to see the needle's blade coming down. He whipped his costume cape in front of his body.

The blade sliced through the wet suit fabric with ease, missing its target by inches.

"What are you using to sharpen that thing?" Monty asked in amazement as he stared at the shredded tear.

Mabel extracted the knife from the cape and adjusted her grip, preparing to make another stab.

Isabella had had enough. She crept along the rounded top of the boat's plastic hull, sizing up the jumping distance to the crazed attacker.

As Mabel flexed her arm for another thrust, an orange and white blur leapt through the air and landed square across her shoulders.

"Eh?" was all Mabel got out before four sets of claws dug into her skin.

The subsequent screech could be heard across the pavilion.

"Oh my," Monty said, flinching at the sight.

"Isabella!" the niece cried, rushing forward this time without regard for Mabel's knife.

Mabel flailed about, trying without success to remove the snarling beast who had attacked her.

Screaming in pain, she ran out the hangar entrance.

The niece chased after them, sprinting out onto the walkway that lined the pavilion—as a loud splash hit the water.

Isabella stood at the edge of the walkway, gazing proudly down at the trail of bubbles.

"*Mrao.*"

To herself, the cat thought, *Now,* that's *how you do an exorcism.*

On Board the *San Carlos*

Just Outside the Golden Gate

August 1775

Chapter 79

HOW TO CATCH A CAT

THE MOON GAZED down from the daytime sky, watching the *San Carlos* sail out the Golden Gate. As the ship began its return trip along the California coast, the moon knew the world would never be the same.

Her precious bay had been discovered. She could no longer keep it to herself.

In future years, a settlement would sprout on the protected shore. Over time, San Francisco would be invaded by gold miners, overrun by hippies, and taken over by technophiles. Earthquakes and fires would raze the city, but each time, it would rebuild and reinvent itself anew.

And one day, these gracious waters would host a famous sailboat regatta, a competition that would thrill spectators and break record books with a fabulous come-from-behind win by the home team.

In the meantime, the moon would enjoy the few quiet days that remained.

• • •

DOWNSTAIRS IN THE ship's kitchen, the chef stood at his counter, pondering the menu for that evening's meal. Expertly shifting his weight with the rocking of the ship, Oscar surveyed the remaining provisions. He'd run out of sausage. He would have to improvise for tomorrow's breakfast. He had biscuit dough and plenty of leftover fried chicken.

"Hmm . . ."

The niece sat on a stool nearby, reading a book—until her ears picked up on a conversation in the ship's center hallway.

"Rupert, I think it's important, now that Petey's gone, for you to maintain some form of exercise."

Getting up from her stool, the niece walked to the kitchen doorway and stared out at Father Monty, who crouched on the floor next to her cat.

"I think you should find something else to chase," the priest said, strumming his fingers against his knee.

Isabella sauntered past, her tail sticking up in the air, the orange tip kinked to one side.

Monty pumped his eyebrows and wrapped an arm over Rupert's furry shoulders. "I've seen your technique. You could use a few pointers. Let me give you a couple of tips on how to catch a cat."

Isabella stopped and looked back at the priest with disdain. To her brother, she gave a don't-you-dare look.

"Mrao."

From *New York Times* bestselling author
REBECCA M. HALE

HOW TO PAINT A CAT

A Cats and Curios Mystery

Aided by my two cats, Rupert and Isabella, I try to follow Uncle Oscar's painted clues on a trail that leads
across San Francisco—all while hoping my uncle's
sudden disappearance is unrelated to the murdered intern at City Hall.

Just when it seems our search has hit a wall, we receive some surprising help from beyond. But will it be
enough to save us from our own brushes with death?
Here's hoping we don't paint ourselves into a corner…

**"Warning: Like cat treats,
this series may prove addictive!"**
—*Fresh Fiction*

travelingwithbooks.com
facebook.com/Rebecca.M.Hale.author
facebook.com/TheCrimeSceneBooks
penguin.com

M1529T0714

When is a white alligator a red herring?

From *New York Times* Bestselling Author

REBECCA M. HALE

HOW TO TAIL A CAT

A Cats and Curios Mystery

An albino alligator on the loose in San Francisco is pretty darn exciting, but my cats and I are investigating the mysterious Steinhart brothers, the 1900s-era benefactors who provided the original funding for Clive the alligator's aquarium.

In the media circus surrounding Clive, one clown—our own aspiring mayor, Montgomery Carmichael—gets a little too close to the renegade alligator. We'd hate to see Monty meet an undignified end, but we're on a hunt of our own—for Uncle Oscar's latest treasure. Assuming, of course, that the whole thing isn't a crock…

PRAISE FOR
THE CATS AND CURIOS MYSTERIES

"Will delight mystery readers and elicit a purr from those who obey cats."

—Carolyn Hart, author of *Ghost Gone Wild*

"This exciting road trip goes from danger to humor and back." —*Genre Go Round Reviews*

howtowashacat.com
facebook.com/Rebecca.M.Hale.author
facebook.com/TheCrimeSceneBooks
penguin.com

M1386T0913

THE *NEW YORK TIMES* BESTSELLING SERIES FROM

· Rebecca M. Hale ·

HOW TO MOON A CAT

A Cats and Curios Mystery

When Rupert the cat sniffs out a dusty green vase
with a toy bear inside, his owner has no doubt this is
another of her Uncle Oscar's infamous clues to one of
his valuable hidden treasures. Eager to put together
the pieces of the puzzle, she's soon heading to Ne-
vada City with her two cats, having no idea that this
road trip will put her life in danger.

facebook.com/TheCrimeSceneBooks
penguin.com
howtowashacat.com

FROM *NEW YORK TIMES* BESTSELLING AUTHOR

Rebecca M. Hale

Aground on St. Thomas

A Mystery in the Islands

The tropical paradise of St. Thomas is shut down as the FBI seizes control of the island to apprehend government officials on bribery charges. Tourists and locals are stranded until FBI agent Gabe "Friday" Stein can cut through the corruption and find the missing governor and two senators who have eluded capture.

Also available in the series:

Adrift on St. John

Afoot on St. Croix

mysteryintheislands.com
facebook.com/Rebecca.M.Hale.author
facebook.com/TheCrimeSceneBooks
penguin.com

M1582T1014